ETHERWORLD

Also by Claudia Gabel and Cheryl Klam

Elusion

ETHERWORLD

CLAUDIA GABEL & CHERYL KLAM

KATHERINE TEGEN BOOKS
An Imprint of HarperCollins Publishers

Katherine Tegen Books is an imprint of HarperCollins Publishers.

Etherworld
Copyright © 2015 by Claudia Gabel and Cheryl Klam
All rights reserved. Printed in the United States of America.
No part of this book may be used or reproduced in any manner whatsoever without written permission except in the case of brief quotations embodied in critical
articles and reviews. For information address HarperCollins Children's Books, a
division of HarperCollins Publishers, 195 Broadway, New York, NY 10007.
www.epicreads.com

Library of Congress Cataloging-in-Publication Data
Gabel, Claudia.
Etherworld / Claudia Gabel & Cheryl Klam. — First edition.
pages cm
Summary: "Teens go deep within Elusion, the dangerous virtual reality program,
to try and stop the company who made it before it is too late"— Provided by pub-
lisher.
ISBN 978-0-06-212244-5 (hardback)
[1. Virtual reality—Fiction. 2. Science fiction.] I. Klam, Cheryl. II. Title.
PZ7.G113Et 2015   2014026694
[Fic]—dc23   CIP
                                                                                                       AC

Typography by Erin Fitzsimmons
15 16 17 18 19   PC/RRDH   10 9 8 7 6 5 4 3 2 1
❖
First Edition

To Sadie and Lily, the best daughters and fans ever

ETHERWORLD

Contact: Leslie Hartwick
Tab: 313-555-8001
InstaComm: lhartwick@orexis/NET

FOR IMMEDIATE RELEASE

HOTTEST APP IN AMERICA APPROVED BY CENTER FOR INTERFACE TECHNOLOGIES

Elusion Slated for National Release by the End of April

Tech giant Orexis announced today that its most popular product to date, Elusion, has received the Center for Interface Technologies seal of approval, granting the company permission to sell the app on the US open market.

Invented by the late programming specialist David Welch, then refined by his young protégé, Patrick Simmons, Elusion transports users to a virtual reality where they can enjoy a variety of Utopian-type

1

landscapes, all within the comfort and privacy of their own minds. The app is administrated through three combined components, known as the Equip; a visor, earbuds, and wristband work in tandem to redirect brainwaves through trypnosis, allowing the user to Escape to hundreds of destinations.

As of today, Orexis has sold 4.2 million units in three test cities—Detroit, Los Angeles, and Miami—and first-week sales projections post–national release are close to 9 million. Elusion has been named "the most anticipated virtual reality app of the year" by fifteen top-rated journals and magazines, including the *MIT Review*.

"Now more than ever, people need a respite from the polluted environment and Standard 7 work schedules," said CEO Cathryn Simmons at a recent press conference. "With Elusion, it's never been easier to get away! The app truly is a must-have for people who crave both relaxation and a little bit of adventure."

Orexis is a Fortune 500 company specializing in the development of cutting-edge technology that strives to change the face of modern society. Orexis continues to lead the industry with award-winning devices, including the Florapetro refinery tool "XPet" and the "Zimmel" laser pen. Orexis also recently announced a military contract with the US Department of Defense.

###

If you would like more information, or to schedule an interview with Leslie Hartwick, contact James Donovan at 313-555-8025 or InstaComm James at <u>jdonovan@ orexis/NET</u>.

The Los Angeles Record
Breaking News Alerts

New Lead in Missing Teens Case
by Rosanna Rodriguez

Local police are working on a solid lead in the case of three teens missing since mid-March: Claire Wilberstein, 19, a freshman at UCLA; Piper Lewis, 15, of Wilshire; and Wyatt Krissoff, 17, of Inglewood.

A witness, who does not wish to be named, has come forth identifying all three kids as part of a secret "E-fiend" society that frequently met inside an abandoned warehouse in Gardena, allegedly to hack into their Equips and interfere with Elusion's safety settings so they could stay inside the virtual world for longer time intervals.

"They were addicted," said the witness, a shipping and receiving clerk at a nearby business, who watched the kids as they frequently entered and left the site. "Every time I saw them, they looked sicker and sicker. Like they hadn't eaten or slept in days."

This is not the first report of teen users reengineering their Equips in order to increase their doses of trypnosis. Photos of IV bags, pills, mattresses, and Equip parts taken in a Detroit warehouse were made public soon after Anthony Caldwell, the seventeen-year-old son of a suburban high school principal, was found in a coma, allegedly from an unconfirmed Elusion overdose. Caldwell recently died. The attributed cause was a form of brain damage that has doctors baffled.

Police turned up items that belong to the teens in the Gardena warehouse. Evidence of the same nature has been discovered at a similar location in Detroit.

"It's too early to say what this all adds up to, but if anyone has additional information on these kids, we ask that they call our hotline," Captain Victor Grassi said.

Cecily Wilberstein, one victim's mother, expressed hope that her daughter will be found unharmed. "I just want my Claire back home, where she belongs."

Patrick Simmons, president and chief product designer at Orexis, the manufacturer of Elusion, could not be reached for comment.

However, Avery Leavenworth, host of the popular vlog *AveryTruStory*, spoke on the record: "Elusion is a menace to society. It's only a matter of time before the truth comes out. I just hope nobody else dies before it does," she said.

Her statement comes despite a court injunction against her site, issued on behalf of Orexis.

ONE

"THERE IT IS, REGAN," MY FATHER SAYS, pointing to a mountain range made out of great heaps of soot. "The way out of Elusion is hidden in those hills."

The wind blows a funnel of dust in front of us. Patches of fog linger in the air, creating shapes that appear and vanish like ghosts. The sky here is forever dark and cloudless, with hints of light coming from a moon that never seems to appear. Still, I can see a glow of determination in my dad's pale eyes as he examines the area around us, like he's about to lead a charge across a battlefield.

And he is, in a sense. There are fifteen people trapped inside this dismal, virtual world, trying to get back home. But right now it's just the two of us, and when I look at him, I'm grateful he's alive. For months, I thought he had burned to death in a HyperSoar crash over the Florapetro-clogged skies of Detroit, but all this time his mind has been locked inside the program he created, his body hidden in the corporate offices of its manufacturer.

"It's weird," I say, looking at the steep mounds of ash that seem to move back and forth with the blink of an eye. "Sometimes the hills look like they're right in front of us, other times far away."

"Yes. It's hard to trust what you see," my dad says. He stares at the rocky path, which looks like jagged granite. The desolate, charred landscape of Etherworld is so different from the beauty of Elusion, which my dad designed so people could escape our polluted, overcrowded world and experience nature. With just an app, earbuds, a visor, and a wristband, Elusion provided an escape from the drudgery of everyday life. "I just want to get everyone home before anyone gets seriously hurt," he says.

I think back to the first time he took me to Elusion. How we jumped off a cliff and soared through the fresh, clean air on hang gliders, the sun sparkling above the river below us. He told me that nothing could ever harm me inside Elusion, but he was wrong. Elusion can cause addiction, hallucinations, and maybe even death. But I can't bring myself to tell him about the worst of it yet. A part of me doesn't want to spoil the feeling of relief I've felt since I found out he was alive.

So instead I say, "I know."

My dad wants us all to be safe, and we are, at least temporarily. Etherworld, a virtual dimension located behind the firewalls of my father's Elusion domain, offers such low stimuli that our minds are preserved in a suspended state with zero brain activity. That's why colors look so faded here. Although I can still see a hint of brown in my dad's hair, his eyes are translucent, void of any pigment.

Another gust of wind whips around us, and I shield my eyes from the silver particles floating on the breeze like radioactive snow.

"Maybe we should've stayed at camp and given you a chance to get acclimated," he says.

"I'm fine," I say, a little embarrassed. Ever since I arrived I've been overcome with body aches, chills, and fatigue. "It feels like I've been sleeping for days. How long have I been here?"

"I wish I knew," he says, gazing up at the dark sky. "There's no way to keep track of the time. I guess I should've designed a sun. . . ."

"Or moon," I say.

He flashes a tired smile, and hesitates as if there's something else he wants to say. After a moment, he turns back toward the path and says, "Are you sure you're feeling up to this?"

"Yes, I want to help," I say. Everyone else is out working at some place my father calls "the mines," preparing to carry out an escape plan that he hasn't told me much about. While we've had some nice moments together as he's nursed me back to health, he hasn't really explained what his strategy is, probably because he doesn't want to overwhelm me.

But I can be here for him, if he'll just let me.

"You're still recovering from those delta-wave episodes," he says. "I don't want to push you."

"I'm okay. Promise. You don't have to worry."

"It's my job," he says. "I started worrying the day you were born."

"I can take care of myself. I managed to figure out all those signs of yours and find you here, didn't I?"

My dad gives me a look, like this is the last thing he wants to talk about. "I've never doubted how strong you are," he says softly.

I grin at him.

"The mines are just across that bridge," he says, motioning toward a wooden plank in the distance. From here it looks at least a hundred feet long.

We walk another fifty yards or so, and the bridge is there, in front of us. "Be careful crossing," my dad warns.

When he sees me sigh, he says, "I have a right to worry. There are deep cracks in the surface."

He's right. The bridge isn't very wide and doesn't have any railings. It sways with the wind, as if it might break free from the side of the hill. At least the fog makes it impossible to see how far we'd fall.

I hold my breath as my dad makes his way across, his arms stretched on either side of him for balance, like he's walking a trapeze wire. Only when he's safe on the other side do I step onto the bridge, my arms stretched out beside me. The bridge shifts under my weight and I freeze, staying motionless until it stills. I take one step and then another, and before I know it, I've made it to the other side. I step off the bridge and my feet sink into clumps of soil.

When a deep moaning sound echoes through the cold, dim sky, I recognize it right away. It's the cry of the slug-like monster that roams just outside the firewall.

The survivors I've met in Etherworld—the youngest looks about thirteen, the oldest twenty or so—have been living in fear of this disgusting creature for weeks, maybe more. But the survivor who matters most to me is the one who came here with me: Josh Heywood. Military-school tech geek. Loyal friend.

Or boyfriend, if you count all the kissing.

The wailing gets louder, and even though my dad has told me the giant worm can't reach us, I feel a shot of fear run through me. I can still picture its jagged teeth and yellow drool; I can still smell its rancid breath. The beast attacked shortly after Josh and I arrived here, and if Josh hadn't been there to distract it, who knows what would have happened?

We continue on, the wretched sound echoing above the howling wind. My father's pace is even quicker than before.

"Why is that creature in here anyway?" I ask, trying to keep up.

He pauses, like he's trying to think of an answer. "It was an accident. I never had a chance to finish this place. Like these," he says, gesturing at the leafless trees that frame the path.

At first, I don't see anything strange about them, but then I notice something odd. They all have the same bare branches, the same shape.

"They're identical," I say.

"That's right," he says. "I didn't have time to complete their design. And the same goes for almost everything on this side of the firewall. I guess any minor blip could have led to the creation of that . . . thing."

"That's one hell of an accident."

I feel a little bad when my dad winces at my curse. I never used to swear, at least not in front of my parents. It's just one of the things that have changed since he's been gone.

"When did you start building this place?" I ask.

"After I found out that Elusion could cause nanopsychosis," he says, referring to the addiction disorder caused by the app. "It's a prototype, though. I never intended for anyone to actually live here."

"And Cathryn and Bryce can't get in?"

It makes me sick to even say their names. Cathryn Simmons and Bryce Williams, my dad's former boss and colleague, falsified the research for Elusion so it would receive approval from the CIT. When they found out my dad had set off a destruction system, they kidnapped him and forced him into Elusion so they could trick his subconscious into revealing how to stop it. Then they faked his death so no one would know what they had done.

But my dad outsmarted them.

And later, so did I.

"Not yet," my dad says, not offering any more information.

He's been acting like this since we left the makeshift base for all the survivors—answering my questions after long pauses, as if he's holding something back and deciding what to say.

Like he's still trying to protect me.

But I want to know more, so I'm going to keep asking him questions, even though it's obviously making him uncomfortable.

"So did you have the plan for Etherworld in your back pocket from the beginning, in case the sodium pentothal didn't work?"

"Sort of," he says. "I knew we needed to solve the problem. I never liked the idea of inserting a drug into the wristbands. Besides, I knew from your mom's work at the hospital that people can develop—"

"A resistance to the meds?" I say.

He nods. "I just wish . . ." His voice cracks, and he chokes the words back. "I wish I'd pulled Elusion out of trials right then. I was still hoping I could fix it. I didn't want to give up."

"You didn't realize how dangerous it was," I say. "And it's not like Cathryn would have listened to you anyway."

"The day I found out she and Bryce went behind my back and altered the data, I knew they couldn't be trusted. So I created a passcode to Etherworld, put *Walden* in a lockbox, and . . ." He trails off, like he's not sure if he remembers what happened next.

Or if he should keep his thoughts to himself.

"Anyway, you know the rest," he says, marching ahead.

I follow right behind him, undeterred. "But why did they think trapping you in Elusion was going to stop the destruction protocol?"

"It's very . . . technical."

"Seriously, Dad? I think I can handle it."

"That's not the problem," he mutters.

"Then what?"

"In Elusion, theta brain waves are manipulated, so they used trypnosis to force my subconscious to reveal how I planned to take the program down," he says. "But when I escaped to Etherworld, where the brain goes into delta sleep, they couldn't influence me at all."

My hands clench at my sides, and a chill runs through me. How could Cathryn imprison him inside Elusion like this?

"She underestimated you," I say.

"She underestimated both of us," he adds.

The path ends at the edge of a precipice. Down below us, a steep, rocky slope runs between one mound of ash to the next. A group of people are gathered around the opening of what looks like a cave tucked under the ash hill. The entryway to the cave is framed by pieces of thick wood and branches and lit by torches that have been dug into the sandy soil. People are walking in and out, carrying loads of round objects and adding them to several pyramid-shaped structures.

"What are they doing?" I ask.

"I'll show you," he says, leading me down the slope and toward the mine.

Halfway into our descent, I catch sight of Josh standing next to his sister Nora. He risked his life to get here, just like I did. Nora is pointing at one of the structures like she's giving him instructions. The hiking shirt and pants he's wearing are covered in dust, but he still looks great, the sleeves of his shirt rolled up and his forearms flexing as he folds his arms across his chest. If we were in the real world, my reaction would be enough to make me blush, but considering that I'm standing next to my dad, I'm hoping that's not the case. I smile at him and wave.

"The bombs are ready!" Josh calls out, shifting his gaze toward my father.

"Good!" my dad yells back as my smile fades away.

What did he say is ready? The bombs?

My father's "way out" is a massive stockpile of explosives?

"I don't understand. Why do we need *bombs*?"

When I first came to Etherworld and my father recounted the reasons he'd been trapped in Elusion, he told me that the digital paradise he'd built would eventually self-destruct, thanks to the malware he'd unleashed on the program right before his abduction. But if that's the case, why are these mines stuffed with explosives?

"The malicious scripts I wrote aren't enough to destroy Elusion," he says. "All they did was arm the triggers in the Escapes. We're going to have to do the detonation work ourselves."

Josh jogs back to Nora and helps her place an object near the base of the pyramid. Seeing them reunited like this should make me happy, but all I can think about is the fact that they're handling bombs. And there's something else. If you want to see someone in Elusion, you have to program in their invite codes. How are *any* of us reuniting with one another exactly?

I'm surprised I didn't think of this before. I was so excited to be with my dad again; maybe questioning how it happened just wasn't important to me.

"I didn't program in their codes," I say. "I've never even met them before."

"What's that?" my father says.

"The survivors," I continue. "How can we all be here together without having each other's codes?"

My dad's face blanches, like I've caught him completely off guard, but then he clears his throat and gestures to the group working at the mines.

"It was a giant hack job," he explains. "One of the kids used an advanced algorithm to get into the Orexis cloud, and got hold of the access code to my Elusion domain, which is connected to the entire system. He shared the info with his friends, and they all went to my domain, cracked the firewall's passcode, and got access to Etherworld."

At first I find it hard to believe that anyone could break through Orexis's sophisticated security grid and get that information, but then I remember hearing how the company outsourced its security measures to another organization so they could keep costs down. The satisfaction I get from his response only lasts a minute, though. More niggling thoughts bubble to the surface, like the motives of the kids who tried to enter my father's domain. And how did Josh and I make it to Etherworld without that algorithm?

I'm about to prod my dad some more, but he cuts me off before I get a chance.

"You've always been inquisitive, and I know there's a lot that I haven't explained," he says. "But what's most important right now is completing this mission. It's the only way to get home."

"So we're going to blast our way out of here?"

"We don't have a choice," he says. "Everyone has been exposed to heavy doses of trypnosis. Our best chance of survival is to disable Elusion from inside the program. We have to destroy every Escape in my domain."

The way he's talking makes me wonder if he already knows about Anthony and the others. I look at him, and his brow furrows with concern. Obviously it's killing him that he can't rescue me from all this.

"So what's going to happen to us all when we attack Elusion?" I ask. "Will we be okay?"

"We're about to find out," he says, and starts down the hill in silence.

TWO

THE MINUTE WE FINISH MAKING OUR WAY
down, my dad is surrounded by a mob of kids throwing out all
sorts of questions.

The dusty air fills with words like "detonation," "targets,"
and "survival." I back away from the crowd and stand aside,
listening to my dad hand out orders I don't quite understand. I
guess my shock about the bombs is wearing off, and I just want
to know what's going on.

A cool hand takes hold of my wrist, turning me around.

"Glad you made it," Josh says, grinning.

The calm tone of his voice melts away the rest of my anxiety. "Me too," I say.

There's an ashy grime on his face, but I don't think I've
ever seen him look this cute. Although he's undeniably good-
looking, it's his imperfections I love the most—the slight gap

between his teeth, and how his ears stick out a little bit due to his buzz cut. I look into his eyes, and though they're colorless like everyone else's here, they're still brimming with intensity.

"I was beginning to worry," he says, his fingers entwining with mine.

"About what?"

"That you realized you're too good for hard labor."

"Very funny," I say with a laugh.

"You feeling better?"

"I am now."

Forgetting that we're in the middle of a crisis, I lean toward him, hoping to give him a discreet kiss. But when my dad breaks away from the crowd and heads in our direction, my heels slam back to the ground. Josh lets go of my hand, straightening his posture like he's about to salute a superior officer.

"Sir," he says, giving my dad a polite but distinctive nod.

My dad raises an eyebrow in my direction, then tells Josh, "This isn't the academy. You don't need to call me sir."

I cringe a little, wondering exactly how much Josh shared with him while I was recovering. Does my dad know about Josh's criminal record and that he was sent to military school as punishment?

"We've almost recovered them all," Josh says.

"Really? That was fast," my dad says, astonished.

"Recovered what?" I ask.

"The adaptive bombs," my dad replies. "They have to be mined by hand. It's a delicate procedure, to say the least. Josh figured out the best way to extract them."

"He just got his tech-master certification," I blurt out, and Josh gives me this strained look, like I'm embarrassing him. But I don't care. After Nora contracted nanopsychosis and dropped out of college, vanishing without a trace, Josh did everything he could to find her. I want my dad to know how smart and brave and selfless he is.

"Good, we could use another master in the group." Dad claps his hands and rubs them together, like he used to do back at home when he had an idea. "We have Zared and Malik, but they're not as talented as Patrick, I'm afraid."

The corners of Josh's lips turn down at the comparison to my best friend, Patrick. But I know my dad's not doing it to be cruel. Patrick was more than just my father's protégé at Orexis; he was like part of our family. But even still, I was quick to blame him for the problems with Elusion, convinced that he'd known about them all along. I even blamed Patrick for locking Josh and me inside a disintegrating Escape.

But I was wrong. Patrick wasn't responsible for a lot of things I thought he'd done and the guilt has been weighing on me since I realized my mistake. Still, he worked in my dad's old office. He had access to my dad's old computer. He could've helped me figure out what happened to my dad, but he didn't. For some reason, that only makes me feel worse. Patrick is my closest friend, and I miss him.

"I know I'm not in Patrick's league," Josh says, holding my father's gaze. "At least not when it comes to programming."

"As long as it works," my dad says, keeping an eye on the kids as they rush out of the mines, their arms filled with bombs. Josh reaches into his pocket and pulls out a glass sphere the size of my fist.

"It doesn't look like a bomb," I say.

"They're not dangerous until they come into contact with the triggers," he says. "Kind of like Elusion."

I understand the analogy. For most people, Elusion isn't harmful. But if the user is a "high responder"—someone under twenty-one who happens to be particularly sensitive to Elusion's stimuli—there's a good chance it could alter their brain activity, inducing nanopsychosis. At that point, a high responder will experience obsessive behavior that could drive them to do things they know they shouldn't, like breaking through Elusion's firewall.

Which is what happened to all of us.

"Where are the triggers?" I ask, leaning forward to get a closer look at the sphere.

"They're bits of code located inside each Escape," my dad says, rejoining the conversation. "I didn't have enough time to get the destruction protocol ready, so I had to put the bombs in a safe place, as far away from Elusion as possible because—"

"They took time to develop, since they have a similar code to Elusion," Josh says, finishing my father's thought.

I smile at his brilliance, but thanks to a loud crashing sound, my dad barely notices.

"Sorry, sweetheart. I have to go deal with . . . whatever

that was. Josh can take it from here."

Josh pulls me close. "You okay?"

"Sure," I say. "I just didn't think, after everything, he'd still be this . . ."

"Busy?"

"Yeah, I guess."

"He doesn't mean anything by it. He's just trying to get us out of here," Josh says, his lips grazing the roots of my hair.

"He seems like he's becoming . . . closed off all of a sudden," I say. "I don't know, maybe he's just frustrated with me."

"No," Josh says, giving me a little squeeze. "You mean everything to him. He's just under a lot of pressure."

I look up in time to see him grin at me.

"We're all going to get through this. Trust me," he says.

"I think you've turned my brother into an optimist," chirps a voice that makes Josh roll his eyes.

Josh's sister smiles and walks toward us, her jeans and T-shirt covered in ash and soot. Even with Etherworld's dull colors, the family resemblance is obvious. They both have big eyes, defined cheekbones, and the same cute gap in their teeth.

"That's a compliment, right?" I say.

"Definitely." Nora looks at Josh and her smile disappears, a shadow of sadness forming in her eyes. "After everything I've put him through, I'm surprised he has a shred of hope left."

"Stop it, Nor," Josh says.

"I can't," she replies. "If it weren't for me, you wouldn't be stuck here."

I step away from Josh a little, wanting to give him and his sister some space, since it's obvious she's feeling pretty guilty. But Josh won't let me go far, clinging to one of my belt loops with his thumb.

"Regan, how's Avery doing?" Nora asks.

"I said she was fine," Josh interjects before I can answer.

Under normal circumstances, Nora's girlfriend is not someone I would ever describe as "fine." Opinionated, yes. Stubborn, yes. Antagonizing, yes. What else would you expect from a young social activist hell-bent on exposing Elusion's dark side?

"And that's all you'd tell me," Nora complains. "I walked out on her, Josh. And then I went missing. She's probably scared out of her mind."

"She's handling it okay. She just misses you," I say, hoping to comfort her a little.

"I miss her too," she says. It's obvious Nora is a lot more composed than the erratic, troubled mess of a girl Patrick painted her as back in the real world. Even so, I can see her lower lip trembling.

"Hey, why don't we do something useful and help out with these?" Josh says, trying to distract Nora. He holds up the ball and the glass glimmers a little, reflecting the pale yellow color of the torch flames.

"What are we doing with them exactly?" I ask.

"Your dad wasn't sure how to get them into Elusion without Bryce and Cathryn finding us," Nora explains. "So Josh told us about this tactic he learned in military school—search and destroy."

"That sounds . . . ominous," I say.

"In a dangerous situation like this, not everyone goes on an attack mission at once," Josh states.

"Or else they'd spot us," Nora adds, leading me toward the mine.

A few feet inside the entrance a girl with a pierced nose and a milky-brown braid that drops down to her waist uses her hands to pry a bomb out of the wall. Working next to her is a skinny boy who couldn't be more than thirteen, while another boy with curly hair and a big chin stands at attention, overseeing everyone and offering advice.

"So what do these bombs do?" I ask Nora.

"When you attach them to the triggers, all the programming files associated with that Escape will be deleted."

"How do we connect the bombs and the triggers?" I ask, confused.

"We have to carry them through the tunnels and into the Escapes," Josh answers.

"Can we go from Escape to Escape?" I ask.

"No," Nora says. "The ping tunnels connect Etherworld to David's domain, but that's it."

"Your dad told us that once the bomb is detonated, we need to find the portal back into the firewall," Josh says.

"Getting back to Etherworld through the tunnels won't be easy either," Nora says. "The worm on our side of the firewall isn't very friendly."

I choke out a laugh. "That's the understatement of the century."

"Hey, Nora!" the curly-haired guy calls out to her. "Stop slacking off with your new friends and get back to work!"

Nora levels him with a stony glare that rivals Avery's signature look. The boy stands there, staring, but when Nora doesn't move, he just shakes his head and starts talking to someone else. Josh smiles. I guess he's familiar with her defiant streak.

"Who's that?" I ask.

"Zared," Nora says, still sneering. "He and I go to college together."

"Is he in charge or something?"

"*He* thinks he is," she says. "Zared founded the Stealth subgroup about your dad, which is where we all met, so he has one severe superiority complex."

"Stealth? What's that?"

"It's this underground forum network where techies share information," Josh explains. "Like how to bypass security systems and reengineer hardware like Equips."

"Zared builds chips that can crack almost any algorithm," Nora says.

"So he's the one who hacked into Orexis and got the access codes to my dad's domain?"

"Yep," Nora says. "Your father is his inspiration. Same with Malik. Actually, he started a whole subgroup of David Welch followers."

"Who would want to start a group to talk about my father?"

"People who didn't believe he was dead," says Nora.

"What?"

"There was this whole legion of Elusion fanatics who thought everything about David's accident was suspicious," Nora continues. "Rumor had it that your dad went into hiding because his project was being stolen. It really lit a fire under the group and made them want to infiltrate the program's firewall more than they already did. They were pretty protective of him."

I can't believe what I'm hearing. I spent months mourning my dad's death, and the entire time, there was a secret group of people who thought it was a hoax? Not only that: from what Nora was saying, they were as fiercely dedicated to my dad's legacy as I was—and am.

"So everyone here was part of all this?" Josh asks. "Even you?"

"Yes, we were," Nora answers, her voice softening. "Zared founded the subgroup a week after David's accident and ran it from our dorm at U of M." She points to a girl with a light-colored ponytail who's working deeper in the cave. "Claire joined the forum from LA a few days after that." She gestures back to the girl in the front with the braid and young boy by her side. "Ayesha's from Miami. She got roped in a month or two ago, after Malik, the kid next to her, cracked the passcode for the firewall and posted it."

"I don't know about you guys, but I'm about ready to kick Zared's ass," says the girl with the light hair, wiping her grimy hands on her shorts as she exits the mine. "I don't know what makes him think he's the boss."

Now that she's up close, I can't help but notice her lean arm muscles and broad shoulders. She looks like she could bench-press Josh.

"Regan, this is Claire."

"It's nice to meet you." I extend my hand and Claire gives it a firm shake.

"Any kid of David's is a friend of mine," she says.

I've been a little worried that Nora and her crew might blame my dad for what Elusion has done to them, but it's the exact opposite. They seem as loyal to him as ever.

"I've heard a lot about you," Claire goes on. "Your dad is always 'Regan this' and 'Regan that.' It's kind of cute."

The past four months have been the worst time in my life. But I can't imagine how my dad must've felt, trapped in here and separated from his family.

"So what's going on out there in the real world? Does anyone know that Elusion is addictive?" Claire asks Josh and me. Zared turns back toward us as Ayesha, Malik, and several others stop work, waiting for my response.

"Word is starting to spread that the app can hurt people," I say, suddenly feeling uncomfortable about being questioned in front of everyone.

"Do you know how long we've been here?" asks Malik, his high-pitched voice and small frame confirming what I suspected. He looks like the youngest one in this group.

"It feels like weeks. Maybe even months," Ayesha says, her brow creasing with worry.

I reach for Josh's hand as more people swarm around us. The facts aren't pretty—all of them have been in Elusion way longer than the recommended time, and there's no saying how much damage it's causing their bodies. But before I can reply to Malik, there are more questions.

"Are we still missing?"

"Has anyone found us yet?"

"Is Josh's search-and-destroy plan going to work?"

Zared lets out a whistle and everyone quiets down, waiting for him to send them all back into the mine. Instead he closes in on me, his gray eyes locking with mine.

"A few people left Etherworld and snuck back into Elusion, against your father's instructions," Zared says. "Do you know what happened to them?"

I know that some kids were recently found in comas, all said to have been avid users of Elusion.

"Wait, why would they leave?" Josh asks. "Especially when David said not to?"

Zared crosses his arms tightly in front of his chest. "I don't know."

"What are their names?" I ask. "The people who left."

"Anthony, Maureen, and Kelly were all from Detroit," Claire says. "Ayesha, what were the names of the other two from Miami?"

"Cole and Anderson, right?"

"Yep," Claire says. "That's it."

Josh and I exchange a tense look. Some of those names are

27

familiar. The day we arrived here, Anthony had been found unconscious with visor marks on his forehead and died not too long after. Kelly is the name of the girl who was discovered comatose. Maureen must be the girl who Josh and I found at the dilapidated house we searched in the Quartz Sector, when we were looking for his sister. Barely conscious, she had Nora's tab and the number 5020 scrawled on her arm—which I thought was a coded message from my father, but according to my dad, it's actually the room number of the lab where Cathryn and Bryce are keeping his body.

No one here knows what happened to their friends, or to themselves. None of them realize how dangerous it is for them to return to the real world. I'm kind of wishing I told my dad the truth when I had a chance, but then again, he didn't specifically ask about the other kids, and he knows the danger of staying in Elusion too long. In fact, he hasn't inquired about anything besides my health and my mom's. He's never even once asked how much time has gone by since he entered Etherworld.

Strange.

My dad returns to the clearing outside the mine shaft with a short, stocky kid I hear him call Wyatt. My dad's forehead is wet with perspiration, which is odd because the temperature in Etherworld can't be more than sixty-five degrees.

I can't help but wonder if my dad is okay. He's been living in this virtual reality longer than anyone else. That has to have taken a toll on him.

"What's the count, Zared?" my father asks, bounding over to us.

Zared takes a moment to look at the stacks of bombs and do a quick mental tally. "Five hundred eighty-two," he says.

"Great, then we're ready to move them to the entrances of the ping tunnels," my dad says.

"We have a bunch of carts. They're lined up in the valley," Wyatt says, gesturing over his shoulder.

"All right, let's get this party started!" Claire yelps.

She's the only one who appears excited, though. My father must see the weary, concerned faces in the crowd as clearly as Josh and I can. Wyatt starts to lead the group to the carts when my dad grabs him by the arm and stops him.

"Before we begin loading, I want to talk to you all about something," he says, running his hand through his hair.

The group stands still, their eyes fixed on him.

"Some of you know I'm hooked up to an autotimer that will pull me back into Etherworld at the first sign of overexposure to stimuli. But since you all hacked into the program and dismantled the safety settings, the minute you reenter Elusion, your wristbands will automatically reboot. Which means if the brain experiences too much stimulus—"

"The wristband will register it and the safety settings will kick into gear," Zared says, filling in the blanks.

"But then the program will just send us back to reality," Malik says cheerfully. "That's a good thing, right?"

"Hey, maybe that's why Caldwell and the others bailed and

went back to Elusion," adds another boy.

Josh is holding one of the bombs in his hands, his head bowed like he doesn't want to look at anyone, especially Nora. Maybe he fears that his sister will be able to see the truth in his gray eyes—that returning to reality from Etherworld at this point could be a death sentence.

But we have to tell her, don't we? Don't we have to tell all of them?

"I'm not sure what will happen. That's why I designed the autotimer to begin with. I just wish it was something I could connect everyone to from the inside of the program, but I can't," my dad says, his voice wavering. "So please remember what I've said. Purposely leaving Elusion is dangerous, especially since we've been here much longer than the allotted hour. The level of trypnosis we're under is deep, and high responders like you will have trouble when you're disconnected from your Equip. Once the app is terminated, though, you should be able to regain consciousness."

"So you're saying our worst enemy is our minds?" Claire asks.

"Exactly," he says, folding his hands. "Which is why you have to do everything you can to control your thoughts. When we enter Elusion, you have to believe that we're going to succeed, 'believe' being the key word. And remember, the destruction you're witnessing is not real. You're playing a game that you know you will win. And we *will* win. We will beat Elusion."

This is the uplifting speech I was hoping for earlier, but I can't take comfort in what he's saying. I guess I know too much.

"And if we can't?" Wyatt asks, gazing at my dad with the same pleading eyes I used to use as a kid.

My dad pats him on the back and forces a confident smile. Exactly like he did with me.

"Just do your best," he says. "That's all any of us can do."

Josh finally lifts up his head and we share a look, each knowing what the other is thinking.

Our best might not be good enough to save us.

THREE

WHEN WE'RE THROUGH, WE ALL RETREAT
back to base camp, which consists of a huge, open-air common area, nicknamed the Great Space, surrounded by an
eight-floor, honeycomb-shaped cavern. A crude motel of sorts,
it's constructed from a mix of wood and stone. It has arched
doorways and an outdoor staircase. Platforms lead to small
cave-like rooms that act as sleeping quarters.

We load and distribute the bombs among the ping tunnels leading toward the Escapes for what seems like hours. It's
exhausting work and the one bright spot is that my dad, Zared,
and Josh are able to find a way to temporarily anesthetize the
slug-like creature, using some kind of special code in one of
the tunnels. My dad says it'll appear again, but he can't predict
when or where.

Josh is stationed eight floors above me. I wonder if the setup is intentional and physical separation is another one of my dad's attempts to protect me. But if so, he underestimated our determination. As everyone heads into the common area, we manage to slip away unnoticed.

Alone with Josh, I walk around his circular room, tracing the rough edges of the wall with my fingers. I feel bad about not telling the others, or even my dad, about the fate of their friends. But before we inform everyone that there's a decent chance none of us will make it back home, we really need to discuss it.

"I don't know," Josh says. "It's just . . . what's the point of telling them?" He's sitting cross-legged on the floor, leaning back on his hands and watching me. "It will kill morale. And that will jeopardize the mission, because psychologically everyone will be a mess. Which could kill them for real. And they might even boycott the mission altogether, and then what would we do?"

I understand the military perspective: morale is more important than weapons! But don't they deserve to know? How can I continue to keep this secret from my dad?

"You're really quiet," Josh says.

"I'm thinking," I say.

"Well, think out loud or something. I want to know what's on your mind."

I stop midpace and look at him, not wanting to admit that deep down I completely disagree. We definitely don't need any tension between us.

"It's okay," he says, coaxing me with a warm smile.

"I feel we need to tell them the truth," I say. "If I were in their shoes, I would want to know."

Josh stands and brushes the ash off his pants. Then he walks over and steps in front of me, blocking my path. He slowly runs the back of his hand down my cheek, and the tension in my body begins to release.

"People have kept things from you, including me," he says softly. "But sometimes you need to have secrets. They're not always bad. Sometimes they serve a noble purpose, like when you're trying to protect someone."

I think about when I was questioning my dad earlier about Elusion—and how he cut me off—and wonder if Josh is right. Maybe there are things my father's not telling me so that he can keep me safe.

"I don't believe in that kind of protection. The person who benefits always seems to be the one with something to hide."

Josh sighs, but it's not out of frustration—it's because he knows I'm right.

"But we don't actually know how Anthony died," he counters. "He could have contracted pneumonia from being out on the streets. And for all we know the others could have already recovered, so there's no—"

Josh stops talking the moment we hear noise coming from the narrow passage that leads to his room.

"Did you hear that?" he asks me, his voice low.

I nod and he walks quietly toward the door, me trailing behind. Someone has been listening to us.

We step in front of the archway just in time to lock eyes with a girl wearing a filthy sundress, tears streaming down her face. It's Piper, one of Claire's friends. I want to invite her in and explain, but before we can say anything, she bolts away.

Josh and I chase after her, but she must be some kind of track star in the real world, because by the time we're halfway down the passage, she's gone. Josh sprints ahead of me, hoping to catch up to her.

"Hurry, Regan!" he shouts, barreling to the end. He stops and leans over the railing that overlooks the Great Space. In the distance, we can see the rest of the group gathered by the bonfire.

"Where did she go?" I whisper when I reach him, a little out of breath.

"There!" he says, as we see a flash of Piper's faded copper hair.

She's headed toward the Great Space. She's going to tell them everything.

My calves burn as Josh and I tear down the ramp, my arms swinging hard. I can't see Piper, so I don't know how far ahead of us she is. How the hell is she running so fast?

We're four levels from the bottom when Josh's foot gets caught in a crevice and he stumbles. He falls face-first, but braces himself with his hands and tumbles over into a forward roll that would be really impressive and sexy under any other circumstances. I reach out my hand and help him up. "Are you okay?"

"Fine," he says, and then we're off again.

We sprint to the end of the ramp and burst into the center of the Great Space. Everyone looks like they're in a state of shock. Piper stands in front of them, her mouth moving a mile a minute as the flames from the bonfire flicker beside her. Ayesha is comforting Malik, clutching him in her arms. Zared's head is hanging low, his face buried in his hands. Wyatt and Claire sit near each other, completely stone-faced. Others are just quiet, retreating inside themselves, exactly like I did when I thought my dad was dead.

But there he is, seemingly very much alive as he shivers near the fire, the flames casting a bit of white light on his face. He's staring off into space, his jaw clenched. Why didn't I confide in him earlier?

Josh and I need to do some damage control.

I walk over to the spot where Piper was just standing, and when I look at the group, I feel like I'm about to give a eulogy. They appear so shaken, and I want to say something to ease their pain. But I know from experience just how impossible that is.

"I'm not sure what Piper has told you," I begin. "But I wanted to say how sorry—"

"Sorry isn't going to bring Anthony back," says an angry voice in the crowd. "It's not going to wake Maureen or Kelly up either."

"I know, but . . . we're not sure what happened. Anthony was found in Miami, on the street, unconscious, and—"

"It doesn't matter," says Piper. "You weren't going to tell us at all. We asked you point-blank and everything."

"This could happen to us," Zared mutters. "We could die if we're sent back before we have a chance to destroy Elusion."

My father gazes at me with empty, emotionless eyes. I'm not sure I can go on, but when I feel Josh's arm settle around my shoulders, I'm able to take in a big breath and continue.

"Please, just hear me out," I say.

"Why should we?" says another voice.

Claire stands up now. "Just let her talk, okay?"

"Yeah, give her a chance." Nora appears by Claire's side, planting her hands on her hips, just like I've seen Avery do. "You guys are acting like what happened to Anthony is Regan's fault, and it isn't."

"No, it's mine," says my dad, walking through the crowd and stepping in front of me.

Protecting me from all the scrutiny, accepting blame when he shouldn't—I can't let him do this.

"Dad, don't. You know that's not—"

My dad spins back around and faces the rest of the crowd. "None of you are going to risk your lives out there. I started this mess and I'll get us out of it."

"But Dad—" I plead.

"I mean it, Regan. I'll do this alone," he says, and then stalks off. I try to follow him, but Josh holds me back and we watch my father vanish into the darkness.

The group breaks off into small cliques, whispering among themselves, while Josh and I linger on the outskirts until the flames of the bonfire are nothing but smoke, the only light cast by the dim glow of Etherworld's invisible moon. I look up at the charcoal sky and make out the outline of the closest ash hill, which has a peak that's shaped like a lowercase *R*.

"So what do we do now?" Josh murmurs.

I have no clue. Not only that, but I feel like Josh was right. In this case, finding out the truth wasn't in everyone's best interest, especially my dad's—he seems to be in a full-fledged guilt spiral. It's weird: I almost feel like Patrick might have been sincere when he said he was trying to protect me, now that I'm seeing things from a different perspective. And once again, I'm hit with a wave of guilt.

"Regan? Are you okay?"

Nora is walking toward us, her hands shoved in her pockets, just like her brother likes to do—except I feel like Josh hides his hands to make himself less intimidating.

"How's everyone doing?" Josh asks her.

Nora shrugs. "Most of us are holding our own, but some people are really scared. Especially the ones who were close with Anthony."

"That's understandable," Josh says. "Are you okay, though? About your friend?"

It seems like Josh may have already told his sister about our failed hunt for her in the Quartz Sector and how we found that girl we now know is Maureen.

"Claire suggested that the tribes take a vote, to see who still wants in on this mission," Nora says, ignoring his question and avoiding his eyes.

"Tribes?" I ask.

"That's what your dad started calling us, since we're from different cities," she says.

"So what's the verdict?" Josh asks.

"The majority want to keep going. Even though your dad's protected by the autotimer, they don't feel like he can do this mission all by himself. Time is running out for all of us in the real world," she explains. "But a few want to stay back, like Piper and Zared."

Josh looks relieved for a moment, but then his face fills with doubt. "But how can we help if David won't let us?"

"Let me talk to him," I say.

Josh nods reassuringly. "If there's anyone he'll listen to, it's you," he says.

When I enter my dad's dimly lit room, I almost expect him to be huddled over a computer or staring intently at his tab, just like he'd always be at our house on Hollow Street. Instead he's standing at a workbench made out of slabs of rock, hunched over one of the glass bombs, rolling it back and forth on the uneven surface like a marble.

There's a cot in the corner, barely big enough to fit him. The pillowcase has a water mark on it, and for some reason I think back to my mother's stories of working in the ER during flu season and having to change the bedding every hour because of how much the patients were perspiring. I only snap out of my wandering thoughts when I hear my father sigh, meaning he can sense my presence. He's always had a way of knowing I was near. When I was little, I would try to sneak up behind him and give him a scare, but it never worked.

"I don't want to talk right now," he says without turning around to look at me.

"I know you're upset," I say. "I'm sorry. Josh and I should've told you earlier about Anthony. . . . We were just trying to figure out what to do."

"You have nothing to apologize for." My dad lets the bomb roll until it nearly slips off the workbench and onto the floor, but he catches it before it does. "I'm the one who killed Anthony. I created this product. I knew it had problems. He lost his life because I failed him. I failed them all."

"No." I walk toward him, but he turns his back to me. "You were doing everything you could to figure out what was wrong with Elusion. If Cathryn and Bryce hadn't gone behind your back, none of this would have happened. *They're* the ones to blame. They're the reason we're all here."

"Waiting to die," he mutters, his shoulders slouching forward. "Even if I could get to all the triggers myself, I can't be sure everything will operate the way it should." He motions toward the workbench. "The signals inside that adaptive bomb are firing erratically, and I have no idea why."

"It's one bomb, Dad. From the looks of those pyramids, there's a lot more—"

"My point is that there are an infinite number of variables

here," he says, interrupting me. "Many of which I can't even begin to predict."

"So what are you trying to say? That we should just quit?"

"I don't know what I'm saying." He finally turns and makes eye contact with me, his forehead glistening with perspiration again. "Now that I know just how harmful Elusion can be, I'm second-guessing every decision I make. I regret reaching out to you. I wish I'd never seen you on that beach and asked you to find me."

"Well, I'll never regret coming after you."

I wander over to his cot and sit down, patting the thin, worn mattress. He takes a seat next to me, staring off into the distance.

"Do you know why I kept those copies of *Walden* under lock and key?" he asks.

I shake my head. In the past week, I found two copies of *Walden*: one my dad kept in a lockbox at the repository, the other in his office keepsakes.

"Before the meeting with Cathryn and Bryce, I stashed a few things away, hoping that if something went wrong, you'd find them and eventually figure everything out, including the anagram." He gives me a little smile. "We were so good at those puzzles, weren't we?"

"We *are* so good at those puzzles," I correct him.

It's like a part of him believes we're already dead and gone. How can he be losing faith, when we've come so far? I'm here with him, against all odds—shouldn't that convince him that anything's possible when you stand up and fight?

Thankfully, I see a small glimmer of acknowledgment in his eyes.

"Right," he says. "And I knew if you ever found my pass-card, you'd realize things didn't quite add up."

"And those messages, like numbers written on walls and strangers telling me things only you and I could have known."

"I was trying to contact you."

"But why did you run away from Josh and me in the ice cave?"

Remembering the moment I saw him in the Mount Arvon Escape gives me the chills. I would have chased my dad to the ends of the earth to be with him again.

He shakes his head and his eyes turn hard. "Don't you see? I was trying to lead you *away* from all this. I never intended for you to come after me *inside* Elusion. I wanted you to search in the real world, so you wouldn't be putting yourself at risk. Instead, I led you here. And now my mistake might cost you your life."

"You're not responsible for me or anyone else who's stuck here," I say, my voice firm. "So you have to stop punishing yourself. You're a scientist. You know there's no way to prevent a negative outcome. You eventually get the results you want through trying again and again until you get it right."

My dad loops his arm around my shoulders. "You sound just like your mom."

"Really?"

"Ever since college, she's been able to talk me off the ledge."

I imagine what the two of them were like back then—students at the University of Michigan, young and full of promise.

"If she were here, she'd want you to keep fighting," I say. "You know that, right?"

"Yes," he says.

"She'd also want to be by your side," I say.

"Regan," he says, after a pause. "I can't let you go on this mission. Especially not now."

"Why not?"

"What father would allow his daughter to put herself in the line of fire? That would be crazy," he says.

I stand up, suddenly irritated. "Wait, are you saying . . . you're going to leave me behind?"

My dad uses his sleeve to wipe the moisture off his brow. "You're safer here at the base."

"But I could help you," I say.

"She's right," says a strong, deep voice.

My eyes dart toward the doorway, where Josh is standing with a subtle grin.

"I know you're worried about Regan," he says, strolling inside. "But she can help you. We all can. You just have to give us an opportunity to prove it."

"I appreciate your opinion. But right now, the best course of action is to decrease the risk as much as possible," my dad replies. "I have the autotimer on my side, and all of you are practically defenseless."

"But how will going out there alone decrease the risk?" Josh counters, his tone measured and respectful.

"It's the law of probability," I say. "If you're the only one out there looking for the triggers, the odds are it'll take much longer to find them."

"Search and destroy," Josh reminds him. "Like I said before, a small group working in tandem will allow us to save time—and ourselves."

"You don't understand; there's more to it than connecting the bombs to the triggers," my dad says. "The nucleus of Elusion—the original four Escapes in my domain—needs to be destroyed in order for the program to be terminated. But those Escapes were created before the firewall, so it doesn't reach them. At least, not yet. We'd have to tunnel our way toward them, attacking Escapes as we go; then hopefully the firewall would adapt accordingly, reconfiguring itself around the core."

"But what about Thai Beach and Mount Arvon? Those were already destroying themselves when I saw you there," I say.

His gaze lingers on the glass sphere on the workbench, and it takes a moment for him to reply. "None of that was real. I was in your Escape, remember? You must have had raised cortisol levels, which caused a hallucination."

"So everything that happened there was all a dream?"

"Everything but me," he replies.

"Sir, I've assembled the first team," Josh says. "We're ready to see your plan through, wherever it leads."

I cross the room and wrap him in a hug. We hold on to each other for a moment, and then I pull away, suddenly shy with my father standing there. Josh and I look at him, and he gives us a small nod. "Okay," my dad says. "We'll give it a try."

"I'll tell the others," Josh replies, a hopeful grin forming on his lips.

When Josh leaves, I glance toward my dad and say, "Thank you."

"You can thank me later," he says. "Once we're home."

"That's a deal."

"We just have to make some adjustments to the plan before we go back into Elusion," he adds.

"Like what?" I ask.

"If anyone from Miami or LA is kicked out of the program after we enter the Escapes, they have to tell someone as soon as they wake up," he explains. "They have to go to the press and explain what they experienced here. Maybe that will trigger a bigger investigation of Elusion."

"Okay, but what about us? The people from Detroit?"

My dad hesitates and then gives me a quick smile. "You have the tougher job."

"Which is?"

"Proving I'm alive," he says. "If one of you can get into Orexis and then inside that lab, you'll find hard evidence that I was never killed in that crash—that someone abducted me and faked the whole thing. The police will have to get involved; they might force the company to halt production temporarily until they sort it all out."

I've broken into Orexis before, so I know it can be done. But my excitement fades when I think of the other kids. How the hell will they get past security at company headquarters? It's looking like I'm the only one who can reveal the truth, and from the concern clouding my father's gray eyes, it seems he realizes the same thing.

"I'll do whatever it takes," I say.

"I know you will," he says. "But you shouldn't disconnect me or anyone else from their Equip if we can't be revived with the emergency button on our wristbands. We'll need to stay hooked up until Elusion is destroyed."

"Because of the trypnosis exposure?"

"Yes," my dad replies. "The levels of cortisol in the brain will be too high, especially in the people who've been under trypnosis the longest. The cortisol levels will decrease once the program is disabled, but pulling off the Equip while the mind is still engaged could send the user into shock."

I squeeze his hand lightly, wondering if I should say what I'm about to, given how hard everyone took the news about Anthony. But I find myself going ahead anyway. "Everyone has been asking us about what's happening in the real world. They wanted to know if they were still missing and how long they'd been gone. But not you." I swallow and ask, "Why?"

"Because . . ." Another one of his long, thoughtful pauses takes the air out of the room. And then he shrugs and says, "It's out of my control."

FOUR

MY DAD LEADS OUR SMALL POSSE THROUGH
an acrylic tunnel laced with little blue and green lights, all of
us bathed in a turquoise glow. I know we're getting close to the
opening, because the curved walls that surround us are getting
bigger and we no longer need to crawl. Still, it seems like we've
been winding our way through this narrow tube much longer
than it took Josh and me to arrive in Etherworld.

"How do we know we're not walking in circles?" Nora asks.

"My dad designed this," I say, a little more sharply than I
intended. "If anyone knows where we're going, he does."

"Relax. I think your dad is capable of answering questions
himself," Claire says.

Nora casts her eyes down toward her feet. Oh God, I think
I've hurt her feelings. The last thing I need right now is a rift
with my boyfriend's sister, but after seeing how upset my dad

is about everything, I'm feeling protective of him.

I don't want him to think we don't trust him.

My dad halts suddenly, looking at the side panels of the tunnel. He presses some of the electric-blue squares and a door appears, revealing a steep set of steps leading to the floor below. We follow him down into what feels like a large closet with the same acrylic walls and lights as the tunnel. I recognize it as the entrance to the portal, the room that welcomed Josh and me when we broke through the firewall. We shuffle inside, crouching shoulder to shoulder.

"If any of you are having second thoughts," my dad says, "it's not too late to turn back."

We gaze at one another through the eerie turquoise light, but we all keep silent, waiting for my dad's next instruction.

"Remember, this is the White-Water Rapids Escape. The trigger was a rock near the firewall, three miles directly north of where we are entering."

"Was?" I ask.

"In order to keep them hidden from the programmers, I created triggers that would adapt to their environment. So even though I designed this one as a rock, it's mutated into the Escape by now. It will remain distinctive in some form, but it might be difficult to detect."

"Let's do this!" Claire says, pumping her fist.

I laugh under my breath, thinking how this girl I know at school—Zoe Morgan—probably would have said the same thing if she were here. From what I know of her, she and Claire are a lot alike. Fearless and bold.

"You're so weird, Claire," Wyatt says, shaking his head.

She nudges him and smiles. "If by 'weird' you mean 'awesome,' then I agree."

"Once the trigger is detonated, head for the firewall, and an emergency portal will open," my dad says, his urgent tone cutting through Claire and Wyatt's banter. "And don't forget, the minute you step into the Escape, your brain activity will be monitored through your wristbands."

"I hope so," he says.

"What if we miss? Or what if we throw the bomb at the wrong target?" Claire asks.

"The second the bomb makes contact with something inside the Escape, even if it's not the trigger, Orexis will be able to determine your exact location," he replies. "So be very careful."

I force a grin and nod, trying not to show my nervousness. My dad turns back toward the wall and begins pressing the squares of light, alternating blue and white, as if tapping a sequential code.

Josh grabs my hand, reminding me that he's right next to me.

There's a sudden brightness, and the sweet smell of pine trees fills the air. I hear something that sounds like white noise, so loud that I want to cover my ears. I squint into the light and realize that my dad's shadow is blocking the portal of the tunnel. But I know one thing. It's not white noise that I'm hearing.

It's the sound of rushing water.

My dad exits the portal, dropping down into the other world. I leap after him, following him into the bright light and landing on my back in a pile of soft, moist grass. But instead of pulling myself up, I begin to tumble, my stomach filled with a giggly energy as I roll down a gentle hillside that's covered in Elusion's signature fairy dust. I stop at the bottom and lie still, my eyes closed. All the problems and desperation that just minutes earlier were so overwhelming now seem inconsequential.

Why am I here?

I open my fist and admire the small translucent ball. I hold it up to the indigo sun, the colors spinning like a kaleidoscope. I know the beauty is deceptive and that this object has some kind of purpose, but I can't remember what it is.

I stretch out and run my legs and arms over the soft purple grass as if I'm making an angel in the snow. It feels so good to be back in Elusion.

It's only when I hear voices—the sound of my own tribe—that I'm motivated to pick up my head and look around. I'm feet away from a river, which is pulsating with a raucous stream of tangerine water. A row of single-seat kayaks is lined up alongside the bank.

"Awesome!" Claire says, running over to one of them. Her blond hair is flowing around her shoulders; the blueberry-colored sun is radiating above her head. Her skin is illuminated with a light tan, and her ratty Etherworld clothes have been replaced with a yellow life vest and bikini bottoms.

And her eyes? I finally get to see that they're a beautiful shade of green.

She waves me over. "Grab a kayak!"

I think I've been to this Escape, with Patrick, before my dad's so-called accident. My memory is still fuzzy, but I remember him wanting to do a heart-pounding, death-defying kayak ride down the rapids, while I was more into hiking.

But now all I can think about is getting into the rough water and seeing where the current takes me. A surge of adrenaline pumps through me, and I feel capable of anything. I check my wristband to see if it has to do with my ExSet level, but the keypad doesn't respond to my touch.

I'm not bothered by the broken keypad though. Maybe this burst of energy is exactly what I need.

"Regan!" my father shouts. He appears around the side of a hill, slowly walking toward me with Josh, Nora, and Wyatt by his side. He looks healthy again, his skin practically glowing. In fact, the entire team is like a human rainbow, all of us bronzed and wearing different-colored T-shirts and bathing suits. The sight triggers a recollection—that we're supposed to be a band of soldiers here, that there's a mission that needs to be accomplished and our lives might depend on it.

That the ball in my hand is our saving grace.

"Wait for us!"

It's Josh, bounding toward me, his handsome face lit up with a grin.

I'm possessed by an urge to kiss him, even though his sister and my dad are following close behind him. But for some reason, the lure of the river is much too great.

I need to get to it before anyone else does.

"Regan, hold on!" my dad calls out.

I ignore him, grabbing on to a kayak with my free hand and launching myself into the river. Claire is right behind me, cheering me on and following my lead. As I careen down the rapids, with the mysterious crystal sphere between my bare feet, I'm paddling as if I've been white-water rafting my whole life. I go faster and faster as foam sprays in my face, my heart beating in anticipation as Claire catches up to me.

She smiles as she points her paddle ahead of us. "Rapids!" she screams.

These are not the rapids I've seen on the Net. Here it looks like the river just stops, as if we're about to fall off the edge of the earth.

If Claire feels any fear or doubt, though, she doesn't show it, hooting and hollering as she dips her paddle into the water, steering directly toward the edge.

She quickly loses control of her kayak, the boat changing direction by ninety degrees and teetering at the edge of the rapids. Claire's hair is whipping in the wind as she shoves the paddle under the hull and then grabs onto the sides of the kayak for support.

Then her kayak flips over, cascading down the rapids.

As much as I long to follow her, a faint voice of reason urges caution.

I twist around to look for the others, but no one else is there. Either the river has split or Claire and I have gone too far ahead of the rest of the group to see them. My kayak is getting closer to the edge of the abyss. The churning current crashes against the rocks, ricocheting into the kayak, making it heavy with water. I know I'm about to achieve something really spectacular or fail in a big way.

And suddenly I'm there, hovering above the edge. The wind whips through my soaked clothes. This is not the pretty and foamy waterfall I've seen in books, but a giant, swirling vortex of white that heads straight down into oblivion. I can't even see the bottom, and I can't see Claire, either.

Did she make it?

I shove my paddle in between my legs and my kayak tips. It dangles over the side, and for a second I think that I have somehow willed it to safety. Just like that, I'm gone, holding on for dear life, screaming at the top of my lungs, my eyes wide open as the kayak plummets.

I crash into the freezing-cold water and plunge underneath. Totally submerged and still stuck inside the boat, I battle toward the surface, my arms stretching out in a breaststroke, my toes gripping the ball tucked under my feet. The kayak jerks and then soars above the water like a dolphin coming up for air. I blink the water out as I breathe in deeply, my lungs slowly reviving.

I made it.

I hear a hearty laugh and see Claire in front of me, her arms in the air.

"Finally!" she yells. I grin, relieved to see her.

We're in a valley surrounded by deep cliffs on either side shading the sun. No one else is here. I slowly paddle away from the falls, trailing Claire down the river toward calmer water.

"That was wicked!" Claire says as soon as we're far enough away from the roar of the falls to be able to hear each other speak.

"Definitely," I say.

"When we get back home, I want you on my team," she says. "Really. You should think about national league—"

She stops in midsentence, her eyes growing wide. "Look!" she says, motioning toward the valley wall. An unusual-looking red rock is sticking up out of the cliff on our right. And it comes back to me, the reason why I'm here.

The sphere between my feet is a bomb.

We have to find the triggers in order to detonate it.

We have to destroy Elusion.

"Is that the target?" Claire asks.

Is it? I don't know. My dad said it would be near the firewall, three miles north of the entrance. I glance up at the sun. I'm pretty sure we've been traveling north, but it doesn't seem like we've gone three miles. Then again, we have been moving fast.

Maybe it *is* the target.

Claire pulls out her adaptive bomb from underneath the hull of the kayak. She studies it a beat, and then throws it as hard as she can. The ball speeds through the sky, missing the rock and landing on a grassy knoll before blasting into a million pieces of brightly colored glass confetti.

I brace myself, as if expecting an explosion. But nothing happens, and our boats continue on the current. Claire looks at me, concern in her big green eyes. The girl who was not afraid to go inside Elusion knowing it could mean death, the girl who just dropped off a cliff in a kayak without an ounce of hesitation, is afraid. And then I remember.

We threw the bomb. Even though we missed, it made contact. And that means Orexis now knows we're here. They can send us back. And that might just be a death sentence.

We need to destroy this Escape and return to Etherworld as quickly as possible.

"Throw your bomb!" Claire shouts. "Do it, Regan!"

The orange water is splashing around my ears and up onto my face. I clear it away as Claire's kayak speeds past me, rocking back and forth against the current. But this time she's not enjoying the ride. She's no longer paddling; instead her hands are gripping the sides of the kayak, barely hanging on.

Twisting around in my seat, I hold on to the kayak with one hand and use the other to pull the glass ball out from between my feet. I've never had great aim, and the chance of me hitting my mark under the best of circumstances is slim. And now we're much farther away than when Claire attempted her throw—but I don't think I've ever felt so determined. I hurl the bomb as hard as I can, watching as it smashes against the jagged rock.

I did it.

I hit the target.

My kayak continues to speed down the river, bringing me closer to Claire, who is clapping for me. I give her a little bow, then turn around, looking for Josh and my dad, wanting to share this exciting moment. I smile as I spot three kayaks in the distance, getting closer. In a few minutes, we will all be celebrating.

But what if that wasn't the detonator? What if we just wasted two perfectly good bombs? What if all we've done is alert Orexis?

A wave rushes my kayak, nearly tipping it over, and I'm jerked to my knees as water blasts over the top of the boat. I right it again, but now there's water in the hull. Weird. The river was freezing cold just seconds earlier, but this water is warm. Really warm. I steady the kayak and dip my hand in the current. I'm not imagining things. The water has become almost hot. And it's not just a rambunctious current any-more—there are actual waves.

But unlike normal waves that crash toward the shore, these begin on opposite riverbanks and crest in the middle, where they rise and swell, crashing into one another as they split open. And it's not just the conditions on the water that are starting to deteriorate. Thunder erupts as black clouds fill the sky.

I've seen this before. The Escape is disintegrating.

"We need to get out of here!" I yell to Claire. She nods and turns toward the shore.

The water is suddenly bubbling and boiling, with steam

rising off the surface. I look behind me and am relieved to see that Josh, my dad, and the others have already made their way down the waterfall and are battling across the current toward us.

I hear an alarming scream, and turn back to see Claire clutching her arm by her elbow, looking terrified. "My hand! It feels like it's on fire!"

Her hand is glowing, not with flames but as if it were lit from within.

"Hold on!" I shout. Another wave crashes into me, coming at me from the side, as if trying to keep me from Claire.

She screams again, leaning forward as her body shudders with pain. Her entire arm has disappeared. Her body is a bright yellow, and I'm close enough to see the tears in her eyes. "Help me," she calls out. "Help!"

With a huge bang, Claire's boat explodes, knocking me back against my kayak.

When I lift my head, Claire is gone, and so is her boat. Nothing remains.

"Everyone to the shoreline!" yells my dad.

I know I should use my paddle, but I can't seem to find it anywhere. My kayak is speeding down the river, away from the others. What just happened to Claire? Was she sent back to the real world? Is she still alive?

I can see the firewall now, looming in the distance. Its gray wall disappears into the sky, casting the world beneath it in a dark shadow. I'm heading directly toward it, gripping tightly onto the sides of the kayak.

I jolt to a stop as Josh wedges his kayak in front of mine, redirecting me toward the sandy bank. "Take this!" Josh says, sticking out his oar.

I grab it and begin to paddle. Beyond the rocky shoreline is a thick patch of woods. Clouds of smoke steam out of the trees, as if the disaster that has hit the water has also affected its surroundings. Wyatt reaches land first, his kayak slamming into the shore. He jumps out and heads back into the water, his arms bulging with effort as he grabs Nora's kayak, yanking it to safety.

My kayak comes to a stop behind Josh, breaching onto shore as the earth begins to tremble. I heave myself out and turn back toward the churning river. My dad's still in the water, battling the current. I head in after him, the water so hot it's burning my feet. Fiery liquid is beginning to fly off the river, spewing straight up and back into the atmosphere like drops of lava. A funnel begins to form behind my dad. It's just like the one that snatched him away from me in the Thai Beach Escape.

"Run, Regan!" my dad yells. "Get to the firewall—"

Before he can finish, the funnel hits my dad's kayak and I lose sight of him as it explodes in a whirlwind of debris.

I scream his name, but he's already gone, pieces of his boat floating like confetti in the choppy waves.

"Hurry," Josh says, grabbing my arm and leading me toward the woods. Pockets of fire are encroaching the shoreline, narrowing our path. I give Josh a nod and turn back toward the wall. I have to do what my dad said, and even though I'm stunned by his violent departure, I have to believe he's okay, that the autotimer sent him to safety.

The smoke grows thick as we head into the trees, coughing as we inhale the acrid air. It clears enough for us to spot the firewall, soaring into the sky. The fire slows us down, the blazes around us jumping and flickering, fire meeting fire, ravaging the forest around us. We're constantly rerouting, trying to avoid the flames.

By the time we arrive at the wall, the forest behind us has turned into a roaring inferno. There's no time to waste. We've all broken through this force field before, and we know we have to find the letters etched inside the brick. The portal will only appear once we've found ones that spell Thoreau and Walden. We fan out, each one of us staring at the aged-looking bricks. We brush away the moss as we desperately make our way down the wall, crackling embers lapping at our heels.

"T," Wyatt calls out, tracing the letter with his finger until it glows a bright yellow.

"N," I yell, the letter glowing underneath my fingers.

"Regan!" Josh yells in warning. I instinctively crouch down, barely avoiding a ball of flame as it shoots toward the wall in front of me.

I jump up and brush myself off as I give him an apprecia-tive look, turning my attention back to the wall. The heat is unbearable, the bricks sizzling as if they were in an oven.

"We're not going to make it!" Nora yells.

I want to give her some words of encouragement, but I'm worried that she's right. Even with all of us searching for let-ters, this is taking too long. The fire is all around us, pinning us against the wall. I scan the bricks, looking for more letters, but the smoky fog has made it nearly impossible to see.

However, I notice something etched in the brick in front of me and push away the moss. It's another letter.

But I don't have time to touch it.

The wall seems to groan and then shudder as loose pieces of concrete fall from above. The bricks shimmer and shift, sliding around and changing position, forming a small opening, just as they did the first time Josh and I discovered the passcode. The letters fade away and we can see the eerie blue light peering out from the cracks of the portal.

It's opening, but how? We didn't even come close to spelling Thoreau and Walden. The blue light is becoming brighter, until the passageway is exposed.

And then I hear something too good to be true.

"Everyone, hurry!" I hear from inside the portal.

My dad's not only okay. He came back for us.

I land hard and lean over, my forearms resting on my knees. It's cramped in here with all of us, but the close proximity of the team isn't the cause of the tightness in my chest. It feels like my lungs are on fire and my muscles are being ripped to shreds. I steady myself while Josh, Nora, Wyatt, and my dad huddle around me in similar states of physical distress. We're still too winded to talk. I drop to the floor, exhausted. My hands begin to tremble uncontrollably as my vision grows hazy.

My dad sits next to me and wraps his arms around me.

"You okay?"

I nod. "I wasn't sure you were, though."

"I know. It was kind of a rough toss over the wall," my dad says. "I think because I fought it so much. I did not want to leave you guys out there alone."

"We were almost consumed by fire," Nora says, hysteria in her voice. "If you hadn't opened the portal—"

"But he did," Josh gently interrupts.

"What happened out there?" Wyatt asks my dad, his tone accusatory.

A long silence follows, punctuated by Nora's labored breathing.

"I . . . I wish I knew for sure."

My hands become steadier, and I push myself away from my dad as I start to feel normal again. "Is Claire okay?" I whisper.

"I don't know," my dad says.

"Do you think her wristband reset?" Now Josh is questioning my dad, his voice raspy, like he swallowed a scrap of sandpaper. "Is that why her boat blew up like that?"

Josh's jaw is clenched tight. I know he's as frightened as I am, but he's trying not to show it.

"Possibly," my dad replies. "If Claire's brain exhibited any kind of heightened activity, whether it was fear or exhilaration, there's a chance the safety settings rebooted on her wristband and her time in Elusion expired."

I swallow as the blue lights in the ping tunnel flicker in a frantic pattern that hurts my eyes. It must signal something important to my dad, because he lifts me to my feet without asking me if I'm all right.

The fear that he's keeping something from me is stronger than before. Maybe I'm still paranoid because of everything that's happened and all the lies I've been told. But I can't help it—there is so much that he seems unable, or unwilling, to explain: too many variables for someone who is supposed to know everything about Elusion.

"*Safety?* No one is safe out there," Nora says, her hand latched on to Josh's arm.

Avery said almost the same thing when she stood up at Patrick's press conference and claimed that Elusion was addictive. And even though we all know Avery was right, I still feel like I should defend my dad.

"He said he couldn't guarantee anyone would be safe, remember?" I reply.

"But nobody said anything about *suffering*." Nora wipes at her eyes and pulls away from Josh. "Claire was in agony."

I'm about to respond when my dad steps in between us. "I know what Claire went through was terrible, but what happened to her in the real world might not be nearly as bad," he says, as if he's trying to convince himself.

Wyatt crosses his arms in front of his chest and sneers. "Tell that to Anthony Caldwell."

"Or Maureen Baker," Nora chimes in.

Josh walks over to Wyatt, squaring off against him. "I told you before, we don't really know why Anthony died."

"I wouldn't say that," Nora counters suspiciously, as she gestures at my dad. "We don't know how Anthony died, but I think we can all agree we have a pretty good idea *why*."

My dad stands very still, waiting for something—another flash of lights in the tunnel, perhaps? I can tell from the creases in his brow that he's desperately trying to undo the horrors that haunt this place.

Wyatt starts to pace, his nerves obviously getting to him. "All I want to know is if there's really a chance for us. Are we going to have lives when we get home?"

"I hope so," my dad mumbles, his eyes still scanning the panels in the tunnel, searching.

"That's all we have left? *Hope?*" Nora says, her tone sharper now.

"Cut it out, Nor. You're just making things worse," Josh says curtly. "We're all freaked, okay? But getting upset isn't going to change anything."

"Josh is right," I say. "If we don't stick together, destroying Elusion will be impossible."

I look to my dad to support me here, but he's quiet and lost in thought. Nora is staring at him, her face full of doubt. I'm worried about what's going to happen when we return to base camp. Will anyone listen to or trust him after this? If not, how can we possibly destroy Elusion?

"Wyatt, are you still with us?" I ask.

He sighs and says, "Yeah."

I turn to Josh. "What about you? Do you still want to go on?"

He doesn't even hesitate. "Definitely."

Nora says nothing and turns her back to us, like she'd rather think this through without all of us watching and waiting for her. I step forward, wanting to push her for an answer, but Josh puts his hand on my shoulder, stopping me. Maybe he just wants to talk to her himself.

But before he can explain, another patch of flickering lights floods the tunnel; it's followed by a blast outside the entrance. The ground beneath us rumbles, knocking us off our feet.

"What the hell was that?" Wyatt yells.

"We need to get out of here!" my dad shouts.

I take Josh's hand and sprint down the tunnel.

As we turn a corner, I glance back over my shoulder and see my dad struggling to keep up. Josh and I slow down, but my dad motions for us to continue.

There's no way I'm leaving him behind. I turn back toward him as another monstrous blast ricochets through the tunnel. I let go of Josh's hand, grabbing onto the wall as I fight to regain my balance. The ground splits open, dividing the group. Nora, Josh, and I are on one side of the crevice; my dad and Wyatt are on the other. The gulf is too wide to jump over.

"Dad!" I shout, moving as close as I can to the ledge and reaching out to him.

"It's going to be okay," he says. "I know another way out!"

"Come on; we have to keep moving," Josh says.

"*No!* Not without my dad," I say.

"We'll meet you back at the base!" my dad yells. "Go!"

Josh pulls me away from the ledge against my will and forces me to run with Nora in the other direction.

FIVE

"HAVE YOU SEEN MY DAD?"

I'm standing in the Great Space beside Josh and Nora. We've just interrupted Zared and Ayesha, who are engulfed in some kind of emotional conversation. Given the strained looks on their faces and the fact that they're holding hands, I can tell that they're more than just friends. But after what just happened in the tunnel, I could care less about their private moment.

"Not yet," Ayesha replies. "You guys are the first ones here."

"Are you sure?" Josh cases the area with his eyes, but it's deserted except for us.

"We've been keeping watch since you left. There's no way we could have missed them," Zared says.

Behind her, Piper dashes out of the cavern, heading toward us.

"Why?" Ayesha asks. "What happened? Is everyone all right?"

"We destroyed the Escape," Josh says, giving my hand a supportive squeeze. "But we got separated."

"Where's Claire?" Piper asks.

Nora steps out from behind Josh and me, her eyes fierce. "Claire's gone," she says, her voice completely hollow.

I wish she hadn't just blurted that out. I don't want the news about Claire's disappearance to send panic through the ranks—not when we need the whole group to carry out my dad's plan.

"What do you mean, 'gone'?" Piper asks, wringing her hands. "Did she get lost or something?"

"During the mission, she just . . . vanished," I say.

"David said Orexis may have locked on to her," Josh adds.

"Because of the excessive brain-wave activity, right?" Zared says.

"Probably," I say.

Nora turns toward me with an unwavering glare. "Why aren't you telling them the truth?"

It's so strange hearing her say this to me, mostly because this has been my line for the last week. But I'm not going to let Nora characterize me as a liar. Not when there's so much at stake.

"I am," I reply.

"Oh yeah?" she says. "Then why leave out the grisly details? They deserve to know exactly what happened to Claire."

"What happened to her?" Piper asks, on the verge of tears.

"If we're putting ourselves at risk, we need to know what to expect out there," Ayesha says.

I give Ayesha a reassuring look. "Of course, but—"

"Claire didn't vanish; she *disintegrated*," Nora interrupts. "One minute we're rafting through these rapids, and the next her boat explodes. There was nothing we could do but sit there and watch her die."

Piper's hands fly up to her mouth, and Zared swallows hard before casting his eyes to the ground. I wince too, remembering how Claire called out to us for help, the terror in her screams. My thoughts drift to Wyatt and my dad, how maybe their late return is a sign that they suffered the exact same fate she did, and I feel sick.

"It's my fault," Piper says, her shoulders slumping forward. "I should've gone with her. I should've been there—"

"Don't blame yourself," Nora says gently, like she realizes she may have overstepped. "Trust me, I know it's hard not to," she says. "But to be honest, we're all victims here."

None of her words are a comfort to Piper, whose eyes are filling with tears. She turns back toward the cavern with her head bowed.

"Nora!" Josh takes her by the arm and leads her a few steps away. "We're all upset about Claire. But there's a lot we don't know yet, so assuming she died doesn't make a whole lot of sense."

"That's the point. There's way too much we don't know," Nora says. "Sometimes it seems like David's just making everything up as he goes along. So why can't we try to come up with some other solution?"

"Preferably one that doesn't involve us getting blown up or killed," Zared says wryly.

"Wait a second," I say. "My dad may not be able to predict everything here, but he knows what he's talking about. We were able to destroy the Escape, just like he said. Isn't that enough proof that he can handle this situation?"

"I'm not so sure," Ayesha says meekly. "There has to be another way out. Something safer."

I can tell she's frightened—and I don't blame her for feeling that way. But if Nora keeps creating more skepticism within the group, there's a good chance she might splinter off and form another crew that decides to leave Etherworld in search of an alternate way home.

Josh has lost his sister once already—would he ever let her go again?

It's sort of a selfish worry, but without my dad, Josh is really all I've got.

"Exactly. Six of us went on this mission, and only three of us came back," Nora says.

"Those are some shitty odds," Zared mumbles.

"Wyatt and my dad will be here any minute," I say, looking at Josh for some reassurance, but something has changed. The confidence I always see in his eyes—even now that they're gray—is beginning to dim.

"Maybe it wouldn't hurt to have another strategy. Kind of like a fallback," he says.

I can't believe this. Josh is second-guessing my dad too?

"So who's going to come up with that strategy?" I ask, my hands trembling a little. "Who knows Elusion as well as my dad does?"

"Actually, we all do," Zared says, with an obnoxious level of certainty. "Everyone here was obsessed with Elusion from the beginning. That's why we went Stealth. That's how we connected with each other."

"And got to David's Escape, and past the firewall," Ayesha adds.

"Right." Nora smiles. "And that's how we'll get home."

I wait for Josh to interject, to tell Nora not to disrupt my dad's plans, but he stays silent. I want to remain perfectly composed right now, but it's difficult to ignore the bitterness rising inside me.

"I have some ideas on where we could start," Zared says. "Malik probably does too."

"I don't know. He worships Regan's dad. I doubt he'd try anything that David didn't approve of," Ayesha says.

Zared shrugs his shoulders. "That may not be a problem. David isn't here, and who knows if he'll ever be back," he says, in this cold, matter-of-fact way that's somehow also void of maliciousness.

"Jesus, Zared. Don't be such an asshole," Josh says, reaching out to me when he sees my reaction. What I need most right now is some time alone to think—and keep myself together, which is getting more and more difficult every second my dad isn't here.

"I'll be right back," I say, and start walking toward the underbrush and rotted tree limbs that line the pathway to the cavern.

"Regan!" Josh calls out. "Wait."

Even though I'm momentarily comforted by the sound of his voice, I don't stop. "I just need a minute, okay?"

He catches up to me and gently grabs my arm, pulling me toward him. I can see he's upset. "I'm sorry. Nora can be a handful sometimes."

"It's fine, whatever."

"You're definitely not fine." Josh lets go of me and steps away.

"None of us are, now that everyone's doubting my dad," I say.

"Don't you think other people deserve a say about this?" Josh asks, not backing down. "You saw what happened to Claire. Your dad said himself he didn't realize how painful the return could be. Even he doesn't know what happened to her in the real world."

"So what's your solution? You want to stay in here forever? How long do you think our bodies will survive? We have no idea if we're getting any food. We don't know how any of us are holding up."

"No one is arguing that. But people have a right to offer other ideas about getting out. Especially when their lives are at stake."

In another place and situation, I might agree with him. But not here.

Not now.

"Then I'll find him myself. He and I can probably pull off the protocol together. No one else has to risk anything."

He shakes his head. "No, your dad told us to stay at the base."

I throw my hands up in frustration. "Come on, Josh. Didn't they tell you in military school to never leave a man behind?"

"Yeah, but I also learned that you can't make good decisions when you're scared."

He's right. I am scared. I'm terrified by the thought of losing my dad again, and by the threat Elusion poses to users. I haven't felt this helpless since my mother and I first heard about my father's death. I watched her spiral into a misery so deep she didn't leave the house for months. There was nothing I could do to help her. When I began to suspect that my dad was alive, I was determined to do everything in my power to bring him back to her.

But the helplessness I'm feeling now is amplified by new suspicions, suspicions that are directed *at* my father. As much as I'd like to keep these thoughts to myself, I can't contain them any longer.

"Is there a chance that what happened in the tunnel wasn't an accident?" I say.

Josh narrows his eyes at me. "What do you mean? Like he rigged it to blow up or something?"

"No, but maybe my dad wanted to get separated from us on purpose," I say, crossing my arms in front of my chest.

"Why would he do that?"

"He didn't want me to go back to Elusion. He didn't want any of us to, and now he's gone." I swallow hard. "My father told me he ran away from the firewall in the Mount Arvon Escape to keep me out of danger, so maybe he's doing that again."

"I hardly know him, but I don't think he'd abandon you like that," Josh disagrees.

"That's the thing: I *do* know him," I say, my voice strained. "And I don't think he's telling us everything. It's little things, but they add up. Like on our way to the mines, he seemed reluctant to talk to me about Etherworld, and when things didn't make sense, it was like he just wanted to distract me."

"What wasn't making sense?"

"How you and I got here, for one," I say. "We were able to enter Etherworld through the firewall of Patrick's Phase Two Escape, but Zared and the others couldn't—they needed to break an algorithm to get into my father's domain. How do you explain that?"

"Gimme a second." Josh paces a little. He's quiet for a moment, but then out of the blue he snaps his fingers. "What if the Phase Two Escape is connected to your dad's domain, just like the rest of the system? Your dad's domain was created first, so maybe it functions like a foundation for the Escapes that are being built. Maybe the Escapes aren't separated until they're completed."

Leave it to the tech master to come up with a rational response.

"Yeah, but it doesn't explain why my dad has been acting so cagey," I say. "I have to find him."

I pivot on my heel and walk in the direction of the bridge that leads to the ammunition piles, but Josh steps in front of me, blocking my path.

"No one knows that tunnel better than your dad. What if he comes out only to find that you've gone back in? How much time will that waste?" His voice is calm. Reasonable.

"I can't just sit here and wait. If someone you loved was out there, you wouldn't be able to stay either."

He hesitates, looking into the night sky. "You're right; I wouldn't," he says finally, turning back in the direction of the firewall. "Let's go."

"You're coming with me?" I say, touching his arm and stopping him.

"We're a team, remember?"

I grin appreciatively as I take his hand. I'm glad I'm not in this alone.

"Regan! Josh!"

The sound of a panicked voice pulls us out of our bubble. We turn back toward the Great Space. Wyatt is on the ground, covered in soot with torn clothes, gasping for air. Malik is on his knees, peering at him.

"I found him at the third entrance," Malik says. "He's been screaming for Zared, so Nora and Ayesha went to go get him."

"He was in the tunnel with my father." I squat down so that I can meet Wyatt's frantic gaze. His pupils seem really dilated.

"Where's my dad? What happened to him?"

"Zared, we need Zared," he mutters. He's in some kind of trance.

"Wyatt," I say, placing my hands on his cheeks and forcing him to look at me. "Where is David? Where is my dad?"

"What happened in there?" Malik asks, his voice cracking a little bit.

"The tunnel split, separating us from Wyatt and David," Josh informs him.

"So your dad is still stuck inside?" Malik asks me.

Before I can answer, Wyatt points over my shoulder, shouting, "Zared!"

I turn around and see Zared, Ayesha, and Nora running toward us. Wyatt tries to stand, but his legs buckle underneath him. "We need to go back, now!"

"Whoa," Zared says. "Where's David?"

"He got more ammunition and went back in," Wyatt says slowly, as if every word is painful. "He's going to try and destroy Elusion by himself."

I was right. In an effort to spare us, my dad's intentionally leaving us behind.

"We have to go back in. We have to get him," Wyatt says again, pleading with Zared.

"It's impossible," Ayesha says. "No one knows the code for the portals to the Escapes besides David."

"How did Anthony and the others get back into Elusion?" I ask.

"We're not sure," Malik says. "David swears he wasn't followed through the tunnels, but I don't know how else they would have gotten through the firewall."

Wyatt is still staring at Zared, who starts backing away from us. Like he has something to hide.

Like he knows something he's not supposed to.

I narrow my eyes at Zared. "Do you know how to open up the portals?"

He hesitates, glancing toward Ayesha.

"Answer her, Zared," Josh demands. "Do you?"

He nods.

"How?" Malik asks. "David wouldn't give those codes to anyone."

"That's confidential," Zared says through a nervous cough.

"Are you kidding me?" I say, outraged.

Zared sticks out his chin, totally defiant.

"You opened the tunnel for them?" Nora says. "When David specifically told us that we shouldn't leave?"

"They looked like they were getting sick, okay? They were sweating all the time; it was as if their bodies were coming down with some kind of fever," Zared says, pacing, probably to avoid our stares. Ayesha puts her hand on his back to comfort him, but he shrugs her off and turns away. "I warned them about returning, just like David warned us, but they were so sure they'd be okay."

Zared stops speaking, too choked up to continue. He feels guilty. But I'm guilty too. I saw how badly my father was sweating down at the mines and in his room, and I didn't even mention it.

"Wyatt, where did my dad go? Did he tell you?"

He takes a deep breath and says, "To the Red . . . Canyon."

"Zared, can you lead us through the tunnel and open the portal to that Escape?" Josh asks.

"I think so," he says.

"I'm coming too," Malik says, puffing his chest out. I smile gratefully.

"Count me in," Ayesha says.

"Oh, that's great," Zared snarls, and starts pacing again. "You and Malik on a suicide mission."

"He has a point, Regan." Nora walks over to me, her face practically wrinkling with worry. "Please, call this off. Before we lose anyone else."

Josh gently puts his hand on her shoulder. "We can't, Nor. This is the only way to get home. We should just stick to—"

"The 'search-and-destroy' plan? It's already failed; can't you see that?" Nora says, pleading with her brother. "There's no way I'm letting you go back in there after what happened to Claire."

Josh's eyes lock with mine. I'm not sure if Nora means to do this, but she is asking him to choose between her and me—a choice he shouldn't have to make. Although his main motive throughout this ordeal has been to save his sister, he's already sacrificed so much for me and my dad. The idea of telling him to listen to Nora—to let me go alone—is making my head pound, but I need to try.

"You should stay behind," I say. "Zared can teach you the code for the tunnels and portals. Just in case—"

"Regan . . . ," Josh begins.

"It's okay," I say. "I'll come back, and then we'll finish this together somehow, I swear."

"Let me be clear: there's no way in hell you're going in without me." He gives me a half grin and then turns back to Nora. "Sorry."

Nora crosses her arms over her chest. "Do you *ever* listen to reason?" she asks.

"Guess I take after my big sister," he says with a shrug.

Nora rolls her eyes, playfully elbowing Josh in the ribs.

"Ouch," Josh jokes. Nora barely touched him.

"You deserve a lot worse for being so pigheaded." Nora smiles.

As I watch them laugh off the tension, I can't help but think about how Patrick and I used to make each other stronger. How we never let anything or anyone come between us. I have Josh now, but I still miss the comfort that comes with having a best friend.

"If you won't stay here, then I'm going back with you. Even though I think it's crazy," Nora says, letting out a great big sigh.

"You don't have to do that," Josh reassures her.

"Yes, I do," she says. "Regan might be the reason you found me, but I'm the reason you came looking."

SIX

I LEAP THROUGH THE PORTAL OF THE RED
Canyon Escape and land on my feet. In front of me is a trail
framed by two towering walls of sedimentary rock. Everything
is a shade of red, tinged with Elusion's golden shimmer. There
are crimson pine trees and a narrow stream of water that looks
like a long ruby ribbon; even the bright, cloudless sky looks
like a canopy of rose petals.

I let out a deep, cleansing breath and feel buoyed by a sense
of hope. I stand up, noticing that Elusion has automatically
outfitted me with deep-treaded sneakers, spandex shorts, and
a pair of fingerless bike gloves. In my right hand is a sleek,
transparent ball that gives me purpose.

This time, I haven't forgotten why I'm here.

"Hello?" I call out.

I turn around, searching for the team that came with me through the tunnel that Zared secured for us—Josh, Ayesha, Nora, and Malik. But unlike in the previous Escape, there is no sign of the firewall, nor can I see anyone else. It's as though I've just arrived out of thin air.

"Josh?" I yell, cupping my hands around my mouth. My voice echoes through the canyons, fluttering along on a breeze and then returning to me like a boomerang. If he were in proximity, he would've responded. He and the rest of our crew were right behind me when the portal opened. How can I be the only one here?

"Dad!" I shout.

Nothing.

I'm alone, but I feel strangely comfortable, filled with a sense of déjà vu. I head toward a winding trail and follow it down and around the side of the cliff. I glance at the lush, red-hued ravine below. No wonder I feel like I've been here before. My dad showed me animated stills of this Escape when he was developing it. But it's even more beautiful than I could have imagined.

In fact, it's almost a shame we have to destroy it.

I pause to inhale the comforting smell of pine, and feel a sense of unbridled gratefulness that the Escape is still intact. My dad couldn't have found the trigger yet, or else I would have walked into a nightmare. I know he's around, somewhere.

There's so much ground to cover, and I don't have my bearings. I look at my wristband to see if it might help me figure out where I am, but the only thing on the screen of the key pad are two sets of blinking double zeros.

I stop as I see a row of black mountain bikes perched near a swath of blossoming shrubs. I hurry over to them, filled with a sense of relief. This is going to make life so much easier. As I get closer, I notice another bonus: there are pouches connected to the frames, which the bombs will fit in perfectly.

I pick out a bike—the one with the fattest tires—and place the bomb inside the pouch. I grip the handlebars and roll the bike backward. I'm about to hop on when I hear someone calling my name.

"Regan!" Josh is making his way toward me, running from around the bend. He's holding a glass sphere in his hands and is wearing a similar outfit to mine, the tight Lycra shorts showing off the muscles in his legs. He's smiling widely, as if he hasn't seen me in years.

The moment he's in kissing range, I put my free hand on the back of his neck, my body jolting with a subtle electricity as I gently pull him toward me.

I press my lips against his, closing my eyes, every thought evaporating. All I can think about is Josh and this moment. We're here, together. And I don't think I've ever felt this good.

Josh moves his mouth to my cheek and then to my ear, covering my face with soft kisses. I'm so distracted, I almost drop the bomb. I catch it in the nick of time and slowly wiggle away. As much as I want to lose myself in him, there are more important things we have to do.

"Check it out," I say, motioning toward the bikes. "We have wheels."

"Nice," Josh says, giving a thumbs-up.

"Where's your sister?" I ask. "And Ayesha and Malik?"

"They aren't with you?"

"No," I say. "When I jumped through the portal, I just materialized here all by myself."

"Same with me," Josh says, squinting like he's putting together the pieces of this mystery.

"Do you think something happened to the tunnel before we exited? Zared said that might happen if the Escape was unstable."

"I don't know. Look around, everything seems so . . ."

"Peaceful?" I ask.

He nods and then asks, "Should we wait for Malik and the girls?"

I check my wristband again, hoping some kind of coordinates might have miraculously appeared. But now it's showing two sets of blinking double fours. Are these random numbers a sign my time in this Escape is somehow being measured? But before I express my concern to Josh, it evaporates. I'm staring into Josh's amber eyes, inhaling the fresh, sweet air.

What were we talking about?

Malik. Malik and the girls and whether we should stay here and wait for them. "I don't know," I reply. "What if you're right and something happened to the tunnel? What if instead of entering the Escape at the top of the cliff they came in through the ravine?"

"Good point," Josh says.

"I think we should head down," I say.

Josh nods in agreement. We place the bombs in our respective pouches before climbing on the bikes.

"I'll lead the way," he says. "Be careful. The terrain looks rocky."

"Got it," I say cheerfully. In spite of the situation, I'm feeling pretty optimistic. "Let's go!"

Josh uses his legs to launch his bike forward, pedaling hard and hovering over the bike with his butt a few inches above the seat. A plume of red dust forms as his tires grind through the trail. When I ride through it, it feels like I'm drinking in pure oxygen.

As Josh dips down the hill toward the ravine, I pedal faster, trying to catch up. I lose control for a second, barreling down. I'm still upright, but the frame of the bike is vibrating with every bump in the ground, and I have to hold the handlebars so tightly my knuckles are turning white. Trees are whizzing by, creating a blurry red curtain.

I follow in Josh's path, dodging tree roots and ducking underneath ledges. Grit from the ground is kicking up all around us, covering my arms and face, and now I'm starting to feel . . . like a warrior.

Like I'm about to save the world.

"Watch out!" Josh shouts as a sharp turn in the trail sends him skidding to the right.

I brake lightly, which helps me navigate the turn more easily than he did. Josh recovers, managing to take the lead once more.

"We're getting close to the bottom," he says over his shoulder.

My feet don't need to pedal anymore. I'm just coasting, letting gravity take control. My eyes scan the canyon, searching for Nora, Malik, and Ayesha, hoping that they're around the bend, waiting for us with my father.

I risk a glance at my wristband. The numbers have changed again and are now two sets of double sixes. I feel a soft pressure on the tips of my fingers, moving slowly into my palms. It doesn't hurt but just tingles, like my hands have fallen asleep.

A strong gust of wind funnels through the ravine, almost knocking me off my bike. But thanks to Elusion's precise programming, I handle it like a pro, maintaining control.

Josh comes to a stop at the bottom of the canyon, smiling as he sees me approach. I ignore the strange feeling in my hands and clench the handlebar brakes, the bike skidding out before stopping in front of Josh.

"What took you so long?" he says, grinning.

Before I can answer him, a tall thicket of desert flower bushes begins to rustle. My dad, Nora, Ayesha, and Malik emerge, with no trace of weariness on their faces.

"Dad!" I call out, jumping off my bike. As I take a step toward him, the tingling spreads into my arms. It's so intense, it's almost painful. I clench my fists, trying to fight it off as I make my way toward my dad.

I'm not supposed to feel pain in Elusion.

"Regan," my dad says, meeting me halfway and giving me a hug. He doesn't appear angry that we've followed him to this Escape, and I'm no longer upset by the fact that he left us behind at the base. Due to the wonderful effects of trypnosis, all those negative thoughts are gone.

But the pain in my arms isn't. In fact, it's growing worse. I ignore it, smiling cheerfully at my dad.

If Orexis is trying to send me back, they're going to have to work a hell of a lot harder than this.

"David knows where the trigger is," Malik says.

"Where?" Josh asks.

"It's a stone submerged in a pool of water," my dad replies.

"A few hundred yards west," Nora adds.

"Come on; let's hurry," Ayesha says, tugging on my sleeve.

My legs are now beginning to ache as well, and by the time we've reached the water, I'm having a hard time keeping up. I think about Claire, remembering her agony as she disappeared. But I'm still here—and in nowhere near as much pain, so I keep pretending I'm fine.

"How far down does this . . . hole go?" Malik asks my dad.

"Maybe ten feet," says my father. "Possibly more."

"That's not too bad," Nora says.

Ayesha squats down and does a quick inspection. "So who's going to take the plunge?"

"I am," Josh says.

I'm not surprised that Josh is volunteering. But even though my emotions are numbed, I'm still worried.

"Are you sure?" I ask him.

"I have a mastery badge for this." Josh takes the bomb from

my dad, who is smiling appreciatively, and kneels down in front of the small circle of water. He grins at me and then says to my dad, "Hold on to my feet and pull me up when I tap your arm."

"You got it," he replies.

Josh sucks in a big breath and plunges in face-first, while my dad clamps his ankles, keeping him anchored to the surface. Nora nervously bites her nails, as if the power of Elusion is wearing off on her as well. We all stare at Josh's feet for what seems like forever, waiting for some kind of movement. Suddenly, his sneakers twitch. The sky rumbles, like there's a storm forming in the distance.

There's another crackle of thunder as the ground beneath us shakes with such force I'm knocked on my back. Pieces of rock begin to fall as the canyon starts to crumble, but I can't protect myself.

I'm numb all over, lying on the ground, unable to move.

Suddenly, I hear Josh coughing and gasping for air.

Thank God. He made it.

"We've got to get out of here," I hear my dad say.

A searing pain shoots through my wristband and up my arm. My eyes cast down at my right hand, and I see that now two nines are flashing on the screen. My hand begins to fade into a fluorescent yellow glow, feeling like it's being consumed by fire.

This is what happened to Claire, just before she dissolved into nothingness.

It's as if I can still hear her screaming, but it's actually Josh. He's soaking wet, leaning over me, and frantically calling to my dad for help. My dad crouches next to him, and even though he tries to soothe me by telling me that I'm going to be okay, I know I'm not.

I'm fading away, and no one can stop it. Not even my dad.

"Don't go," Josh whispers in my ear, his voice shaking.

I desperately want to say something. Anything but good-bye.

But no words ever come, because in a heartbeat, I'm gone.

My eyes burn so much I can barely make out where I am or the shape of the hazy figure who's looming above me. Even though I can't move, I can feel every internal bodily function with a significant amount of clarity—the blood shooting through my veins; the sharp, rhythmic pulse of my heart; the nervous spasms in my stomach. My bones even seem to be shifting and twisting, like they're trying to pull away from my muscles and push through my skin.

The figure leans closer; the fuzziness begins to fade from my vision. Fragments and pieces start to slowly drift together until I recognize the outline of a familiar face: an angular jaw, a narrow nose with a slight upward slant at the end. Then come the eyes, bright and blue and tormented all at the same time.

Patrick.

"Talk to me, Ree. Say something!"

I have enough strength to move my chin down, but my

throat feels swollen and raw, so the only thing that comes out is a raspy cough.

"Don't worry. You're going to be fine. Do you hear me?" Patrick sounds just as frightened and confused as I am. "The Aftershock will wear off any second now. Just try to relax."

Aftershock?

The phrase kindles a flame inside my mind, igniting flashes of memories that burst open and explode.

My father is alive in Etherworld.

I was helping him destroy Elusion.

And apparently, Orexis didn't eject me from the Red Canyon Escape. Patrick must have woken me up.

But that doesn't mean I'm going to survive, does it?

I don't have a lot of time to consider that question, because memories are bleeding into every corner of my thoughts; vivid images of Josh, Nora, and the rest of the crew pierce through me like some kind of mental shrapnel. Then, suddenly, I'm able to wiggle my toes and flex my fingers.

Maybe I'm going to be okay.

I slowly pick my head up and I realize that I'm in my bedroom. This is where I was when I put on my Equip and went to the Prairie Escape to confront Patrick—before the rolling meadow turned into rock and mud and everything went to hell. Even though I've been fighting to return home, it's sort of strange to be back here. Nothing has been disturbed since I left. The titanium Equip case is on top of my nightstand. My grandmother's quilt is in a heap on the floor. The sensor lights are on a low setting, and I can still hear the faucet leaking in my bathroom.

How long have I been gone?

Patrick places his hands around my wrists, tugging me toward him and into a sitting position. My head pops back a little, a clear sign I'm still struggling to regain control of myself, and he pulls me closer. My left cheek is resting against his chest, and his heart is thumping rapidly. The half-eaten microwave pocket sandwich I had for dinner is on the same square plate, right on the edge of the media console next to my InstaComm wall. My laundry is still in a neat pile on top of my dresser. My mother put it there right before she left for work.

Is it possible I was only in Etherworld for a few minutes?

My hazy thoughts begin to trip over one another. *No, that can't be. Patrick and I had a huge fight when we were in Elusion. It would have taken him at least a half hour to make it over here.* But why did he come to my house in the first place? He had no idea I was locked inside the Escape—I remember my dad telling me that Patrick wasn't at fault, as I'd thought—so he must have had another reason. Maybe he wanted to tell me he was sorry? Maybe he wanted to let me know that Elusion has been taken off the market? There are so many questions I want to ask him, but my throat still feels raw.

"Can you stand up?" Patrick asks.

"No," I barely manage to say.

"God, you scared the shit out of me. There was an error code flashing on your Equip. I pushed your emergency ejection button, and when you didn't wake up right away . . ." He trails off, as if he can't bring himself to say what he thought might have happened.

Emergency button. Patrick was able to revive me, even though I've been in Elusion longer than the allotted hour. That has to be a good sign, especially for Josh, since he and I were trapped in the program at the same time.

"Did you . . . do this because of me?" Patrick asks.

I try to focus on forming a coherent sentence, but this is all that comes out:

"D-do whaaa?"

"Mess with the safety settings on your Equip," he says, waiting for a response. I want to shake my head, but I can't just yet, so he rattles on. "Your mom called me. She said you told her about breaking into Orexis. She asked me not to press charges. I know I threatened, but do you really think I'd send you to jail?"

It slowly comes back to me, my last awkward conversation with my mom. I admitted hacking into Patrick's computer at Orexis. It had originally been my dad's, and Josh and I had hoped that the secrets locked inside could help us find out what was wrong with Elusion.

"I know you're angry at me. Is that why you did all this? To teach me a lesson?"

Patrick's mother, Cathryn, might have been the mastermind behind the crazy plot to fake my father's death and hold him hostage, but Patrick still hid things from me about

Elusion, and lied to my face when I challenged him. Some of his decisions made things worse. Of course I was angry.

But I find it interesting that Patrick seems to think that I did something to my Equip—that he doesn't seem to understand that our emergency buttons weren't working. It suggests he doesn't know anything about his mother's crimes or that his coworker Bryce has been conspiring with her. And the fact that he's here, caring for me like this, means that he's in the dark about the plot against my dad.

I regain control of my neck, lean back, and look up at him. When our eyes meet, all I can see is kindness. Any leftover hurt that he might have caused falls away, and when I think about telling him what kind of ugly deeds his mother is capable of, I want to show him some mercy. I don't want to hurt him, to tell him the truth about his mom. I need his help. I need to go to Orexis and find my dad, which will be so much easier to accomplish with Patrick by my side.

"I d-didn't . . . d-do anything," I finally answer.

"So it was Josh, right? This was all his idea?" He gently lays me back down as he walks to the other side of the room. He begins to pace and sets off the sensor-activated picture frames on my wall. Photos of my family in happier times flicker in front of us—birthday parties with my mom's lop-sided homemade cakes, Patrick making faces at me during my middle-school graduation, my father smiling proudly as I sit at his work desk on Take Your Child to Work Day. Looking at them almost causes me to lose track of what Patrick is saying.

"I know he's mad at me. And I'm sorry I fought with him," he continues. "But it's just . . . he has no right to get you mixed up in something that's way over both your heads."

I push myself up from my bed. "No, y-you don't under—"

"I felt awful after I left you behind, you know," he says, cutting me off. "As soon as I got back from Elusion, I tried calling and texting you. I wanted to apologize. But you weren't responding. Which is why I came over here. Can you imagine how freaked I was? Going into your room and seeing you still hooked up to your Equip, an hour later?"

An hour.

I was only inside Elusion for an extra *hour*.

"What time is it?"

"A little after eleven. If I hadn't come over here, you would've been . . . Ugh, I don't even want to think about it."

Patrick just confirmed what I already know: staying in Elusion longer than the recommended time is extremely dangerous. After an hour, I was so deep in a trance that even he had trouble waking me. No wonder my dad warned survivors not to leave Etherworld before the destruction protocol was complete, and that he warned me not to remove him or anyone else from their Equips if the emergency button didn't work. They've been under trypnosis too long. The only way for them to wake up is to destroy the entire system.

I think back to my dad's plan, the mission he explained. I need to find him and I don't have a minute to lose.

"Has Elusion been recalled yet?"

He stops pacing. "No. In fact, they've bumped up the release date. In two days it's going national."

"You need to listen to me, okay?" I swing my legs over the edge of the bed and rise to my feet, slow and steady. "I didn't mess with my Equip. Someone locked me inside Elusion. Josh too."

An image of Josh at his uncle's trailer, still hooked up to Elusion, flashes in my mind, and my idea of going straight to Orexis begins to fall apart. I have to get Josh out of Elusion before it's too late. But my dad should come first, shouldn't he? He's been inside that lab for months now.

Either way, I can't go anywhere without Patrick, which is why I have to tell him everything.

"That's impossible," he says. "I was able to get you back by just pressing your emergency button."

"I know. But Josh and I tried to leave the Prairie Escape right after you, and we couldn't. The emergency button didn't work on either of our wristbands. The sky lit up with the words 'administrator lockout.' We were trapped."

"Wait, an admin lockout? That doesn't make any sense." He begins to pace again, kneading his hands together nervously.

I walk toward him, each step a little less wobbly than the last. "It was Bryce."

Patrick comes to a dead stop. "What?"

"He's the one who tampered with the Escape. Remember how it began to destroy itself while we were there?"

He stares at me blankly. Why isn't he admitting to seeing the chaos?

"After Josh and I were both locked in, he pretty much tortured us so we wouldn't get past the firewall."

"Nobody but me has access to that Phase Two Escape. How could Bryce get in?"

"He must have figured out a way. All I know is that he didn't want me to find my father. He's alive, Pat. Bryce and your mom have known all along."

I know how terrible it feels to discover that your life has been built on a stack of lies. He closes his eyes and leans back on his heels, like he's been blown over by a mighty wind. He must be going into some kind of shock or something. Then he looks at me, his lower lip trembling a little.

"Maybe we should get you in the shower. The hot water will help clear your head, and make you less . . . confused," he says.

Oh God. He thinks I'm still reeling from Aftershock.

"I'm fine, okay? You have to listen to everything I say, and you have to believe me. Because if you don't, more people are going to die. Including my dad."

"But Ree . . . your dad is—"

"*Alive,*" I say. "I saw him in Etherworld."

Patrick squints at me, like I'm speaking another language and he's trying to understand me. "Etherworld? What the hell is that?"

"It's an alternate dimension inside my dad's Elusion domain. He built it when he found out about nanopsychosis. It has very low stimuli, so the brain is protected against the damage that can be done when it's exposed to trypnosis for too long, and—"

"Hey, you're talking way too fast." Patrick walks back over to me and takes one of my shaking hands in his.

I guess I'm not as stable as I thought.

"We need to hurry," I say.

"No, you need to explain to me what's going on. Slowly. Because I didn't follow anything you said."

"I'm trying, but it's so complicated."

Patrick squeezes my hand. "Why don't I ask you some questions and you can just answer them as best as you can?"

I nod my head in agreement.

"So how did you find this Etherworld place?"

"We went through a portal after we breached the firewall."

"And how'd you get past that?" Patrick asks.

"We cracked the passcode," I say. "Nora had written it on a piece of paper that Josh found at the warehouse."

"Wait, there's a *passcode*? How would Nora know that, and not me?"

"My father gave it to her." When Patrick doesn't come back with a follow-up question, I keep going. "He was sending messages to us through these ping tunnels that connect Elusion and Etherworld. That's why the number fifty-twenty kept popping up all over the place. He wanted us to find him."

For a moment, I can't read Patrick's expression. "And what does fifty-twenty mean?"

"It's the room number of a lab at Orexis," I say. "Your mom and Bryce have been holding him hostage there for months. He found out that they had sent Elusion to CIT for approval when they knew it had serious problems, and then they trapped him in his Elusion domain when they realized that he was going to destroy the program. Your mom wanted to force him to reveal how to stop its destruction, which is why he had to retreat to Etherworld. He's not the only one there, either. There are lots of kids who broke through the firewall, including Nora."

Patrick's fingers peel away from mine, but he doesn't say anything. His eyes are glazing over, as if it's all too much for him to comprehend. Even so, I push forward, telling him every bit of information that my father gave me, including more details about why Etherworld was constructed and the plan to attack Elusion. The truth spills out of me at such speed, I don't even think I'm breathing while I talk.

And when it's all over, Patrick silently recoils from me, burying his head in his hands, like I've torn his world apart. Which I have. After a few beats of disturbing quiet, he lifts his chin and says in a composed voice, "So what do we do now?"

It's not the response I was expecting, so I just stare at him for a second, waiting for him to flip out or something, but that second turns into a minute and nothing happens. He's staring at me too, and yet it's like he's not seeing me at all. It's almost as though he's looking right through me, because he can't bear to accept what I've told him, that his mother is at the root of all this chaos and deception.

But I know what we should do now. Even though I really want to go be with Josh, I made a promise to my father—a promise I have to keep, since millions of lives are depending on it.

"You have to take me to Orexis to find my dad," I say, grabbing my tab off my bed and searching for Avery's number. "Please. I really need your help. I need everyone to know he isn't dead."

Patrick doesn't protest like I expect him to. He just gestures to my bedroom door and says, "Okay. Let's go."

I still have one thing left to do. The moment Avery's number comes up in my list of contacts, I quickly send her a text, praying that she'll see it right away.

911. Josh is stuck in Elusion. Go 2 his trailer & press ejection button. I'll be there as soon as I can.

Then I look up at Patrick and say, "I'm ready."

SEVEN

PATRICK ENTERS THE PRIVATE ACCESS
tunnel, his fingers clenched so tightly around the wheel of
his cobalt-blue sports car, they're turning white. When traffic
slows, he begins driving on the shoulder to make better time.
He hasn't said a word since we left my house, keeping his eyes
focused on the road.

I can't say I blame him. When you find out that everything
about your reality is just an illusion, it's hard not to completely
shut down.

"Are you all right?"

Obviously, a stupid question, but despite everything that's
happened between us, I'm worried about him.

Patrick presses his foot down on the gas, picking up
speed. I glance out my window as the fluorescent lights from
the tunnel become a blur, flashing by. "Yeah, I'm okay," he

says, downshifting the car.

"Are you sure?"

"What? Don't you believe me?"

I shrug. "Well, it's not like you've been honest with me lately."

The car jerks to the left as Patrick swerves to avoid a slick patch of Florapetro residue that's collected on the roadway. I brace myself as the car skids, but he quickly regains control.

"Maybe you should slow down," I say. I guess my comment really got to him.

"I wish I could take it back," he says, his voice cracking with emotion. "I wish . . . I was a better person."

His confession of remorse takes me by surprise, and I turn away, willing myself not to come undone. Patrick has made mistakes, and he's far from perfect, but he's here now, trying to help make things right. In spite of all the accusations against his mom and the havoc I've caused, he's coming through for me, just like he used to, when we loved each other like family.

"Thank you," I murmur, my eyes drifting back toward him.

He downshifts again, and looks at me. "For what?"

"For not turning me in to the cops when you found out about the QuTap. For coming to find me tonight. For hearing me out, back at my house. I know none of that could have been easy. I had a hard time believing it myself. Your mom . . ." My voice trails off. I can't imagine how Patrick must feel. Even I can't accept that the woman I grew up trusting so completely was responsible for kidnapping my dad and staging his death. Under the circumstances, Patrick is handling the news pretty well. "I'm sorry," I say, but he doesn't respond.

In spite of my advice, we seem to be going faster. I peek at the speedometer and see that we're doing about ninety miles per hour. At this rate, we'll be at Orexis in a few short minutes.

I nervously glance at my phone. Avery hasn't texted me back. Why? Is she still at the hospital with Maureen? Did she go to the police? I send her another message, begging her to go over and check on Josh.

Patrick must sense the spike in my anxiety, because he clears his throat and starts a conversation.

"So, the other people you met in Etherworld. Who are they? People you know?"

"No, I hadn't met any of them before," I explain. "They're kids from the three cities where Elusion was released."

"So they're total strangers?" Patrick asks, his voice tinged with what sounds like worry.

"Yes. And they—"

The car exits the tunnel and we practically ram into a delivery truck stopped in front of us, thanks to the late-night traffic. As Patrick tries to maneuver his way through the blitz, I stop talking, focused on the high-rise buildings that surround us, the Traxx zooming above on elevated steel rails, and the oily Florapetro clouds floating over a crescent moon.

We've made it to the Inner Sector—Detroit's congested, noise-infested, corporate jungle. It's always been a mesmerizing yet overwhelming place, filled with nonstop energy and crammed with people. When the grand spire on top of Orexis headquarters comes into view, everything else drops away.

The sound of a horn blares as Patrick cuts off another car and pulls into a lane designated for emergency vehicles.

"Take it easy, Pat. You're going to get us in an accident."

He presses a button on the dash, activating the car's Auto-Comm. A monotone female voice seeps through the speakers.

"Please announce desired connection."

"Inner Sector Medical," he replies.

When the AutoComm politely says, "One moment, thank you for your patience," I glare at him and punch the off button with my fist.

"What the hell? You're taking me to the *hospital*?"

He swallows hard, apparently bracing himself for my wrath. "Ree, you're sick. You have all the symptoms of—"

"I'm. Not. Sick! I'm telling you the truth about Etherworld. You have to believe me."

"I know *you* believe everything you told me was real, but it's not."

"I don't have nanopsychosis, and I can prove it. Just take me to Orexis."

He rolls his eyes. "To room fifty-twenty. Where my mom and Bryce have your dad hooked up to Elusion."

I throw my hands up in the air. "Yes! Everything will make sense to you if—"

"I can't do this anymore," Patrick says. "I can't stand by and watch horrible things happen to people. It's going to stop, right here, right now. I'm taking you to the hospital. You need help."

"No! If you do that, you're putting even more people at risk!"

"Remember what Bryce's memo to your father said?" Patrick zooms through the emergency lane, his eyes barely on the road. "Nanopsychosis makes you hallucinate things. It makes you paranoid and obsessive. If you could listen to yourself, and really hear what you're saying, maybe you'd accept the fact that you need medical attention."

"Don't do this. I'm begging you."

The automatic wipers swish against the windshield, and for a moment that's the only sound in the car.

"I'm begging you, too. I'm begging you to hear me out. There's no such thing as Etherworld. And if there were, all the people you saw there would've needed to invite you into their Escape in order for you to make contact."

"No, this kid Zared used an algorithm to break into my dad's domain," I say, trying not to sound like a maniac.

"Look, you tried to tell me what was going on, but I didn't want to listen," he says. "When we were in the Prairie Escape, I saw it all coming apart too, just like you said. I felt this weird, overpowering rage. That's not supposed to happen. I know there's something wrong with Elusion, okay? And . . . you're sick because of it. I'm going to make this right."

"Good! That's what I want you to do. But you're not going to be able to make it right if you stick me in the hospital."

Instead of answering, he stares straight ahead. I know this

stonewalling move of his—he's trying not to lose his resolve. I think about what could happen to Josh, my father, and everyone else if Patrick is successful in having me admitted.

I have to get out of here. Now.

My hand creeps up to the door handle as I try to hatch an escape strategy. The car's moving too fast for me to open the door and jump out. I'd break my neck. But if I wait for Patrick to stop, there's no way I'll be able to make a run for it. He'll come after me.

I put my hand in my pocket, feeling the slick screen of my tab. I could call the police right now, tell them I'm being abducted and give them Patrick's plate number, but who would believe Patrick Simmons was capable of kidnapping? And they're certainly not going to believe me when I tell them that my dad is still alive.

I'm better off taking my chances with a broken neck. I eject my seat belt and pull the door handle as hard as I can, but it doesn't budge. The car is fully passcard operated, and there's no way for me to open the door without one.

"Let me out. I mean it, Pat."

No response. Nothing.

I scan the inside of the car for any weaknesses, and the gearshift comes into focus. Most hybrids have automatic transmissions that adjust on their own, but when it comes to his precious automobile collection, Patrick likes things "antique."

I lunge to my left and grab the gearshift. Patrick slams on the brakes and the car spins out of control, veering dangerously close to the guardrail before stopping.

Patrick grabs my hand, wrestling it off the gearshift. I'm out of my seat, clawing at his arm, trying to reach the lever again. He knocks me away and my head snaps backward, hitting the window of the door. I sit there limp and out of breath as Patrick runs a trembling hand through his hair.

"I'm sorry," he says quietly, as the car roars to life. "I know you might never forgive me for this, but I don't have any choice."

Within seconds, we're speeding past a sign that reads *Inner Sector Medical—1 Mile.*

"Shit," Patrick says under his breath as we pull up in front of the main medical pavilion, a pentagon-shaped structure that stretches up into the sky for what seems like miles.

The entrance is an atrium made out of tinted-glass panels, and surrounding it is a horde of reporters, all wearing their O2 shields. When Patrick stops the car, they swarm the vehicle.

"Assholes. They must have found a way to hack into my AutoComm." Patrick blares his horn to make them move, but only a few of them flinch.

I hated it when the reporters blockaded Orexis and Patrick's apartment, but this time I'm happy to see them. Maybe we won't be able to get out of the car, and Patrick will have to take me away from here.

He presses a button on the driver's console, and his window slides down just a crack. Flakes of Florapetro residue float into the car, causing us both to cough.

"Back up! I have a patient here who needs to get inside!" Patrick shouts.

But the reporters don't move, and instead begin to inundate him with questions. Dark red blotches begin to form on his neck, and his jaw becomes rigid with anger. I'm actually a little afraid he's going to step on the gas and plow through the mob, but before he does, we hear the high-pitched squeal of a siren. A hospital security cruiser pulls up behind us and a burly man and woman exit the vehicle, herding the reporters away from the car.

"I'm going to come around to your side and walk you in, okay?"

He reaches into a compartment in between our seats and grabs a pair of O2 shields. He waves his passcard in front of the lockpad and leaps out of the car. A few reporters try to corner him, but Patrick shoves them away as the hospital security staff holler into their tabs, probably calling for reinforcements.

Patrick opens my door, expecting me to get out, but I don't move. I just sit there, staring at the windshield and listening to him plead with me. This is one of the most childish things I've ever done, but it's the only option I have left. I can't be admitted to the hospital—I have to find my dad; I have to be with Josh.

Finally, Patrick grabs my arm and yanks me out of my seat. I don't fight him, but I make sure that I'm dead weight, forcing him to drag me toward the hospital atrium. The security guards do their best to keep the reporters at bay, but the sight of us has thrown them into a frenzy.

"Regan Welch! Do you have the E-fiend disease?" a reporter shouts through his O2 shield, jumping in front of us and shoving his tab in my face.

"Ms. Welch!" another reporter says, breaking through security. "What would your father think of the Elusion scandal? What would he think of his invention making his only daughter sick?"

"Leave her alone!" Patrick barks, elbowing them away from me.

"Step aside; they need to go in!" shouts a security guard, pushing them back.

Patrick grips me tighter, his fingers digging into my arm as he picks up his pace, practically carrying me toward the automatic doors. They slide open and I see my mom standing in front of the patient registration desk. Her eyes are red and swollen, as if she's been crying. Her brown hair is pulled back and she's wearing her nurse's uniform of blue scrubs and clogs. Standing next to her are two strong men wearing the same uniform, with an empty wheelchair in reach.

When Patrick sees her, he finally lets me go. "Your mom found a specialist in brain disorders. We're going to get you well, I swear."

I'm too furious to speak. He knows how emotionally fragile my mom is and how hard I've worked to take care of her and protect her since my dad's "death" was announced. And now Patrick has dragged her into this.

"Regan? Are you okay?" my mom says, walking toward me.

"The press just showed up out of nowhere."

"Hi, Mom," I say softly.

She gives me a little smile and wraps her arms around me, hugging me gently. Despite this insane situation, it feels so good to be with her, like I'm safe and no one can hurt me. But then her body starts to shake a little, like she's crying, and the comforting feeling disappears. The last few months my mom has barely been holding it together, ready to dissolve into tears any second. A few days ago she seemed better, but who knows how far this incident has set her back.

"I'm fine." I pull away and try to reassure her with a soft smile. It was only hours ago that she left me at home, peacefully asleep, after giving me a little medication to counter a sudden bout of insomnia—something my dad struggled with when he worked at Orexis. She must be so confused and upset, with the frenzy of reporters outside and people telling her that I'm sick.

"But Patrick said . . ." She hesitates, glancing toward him.

"Mom," I say, taking her trembling hands in mine. "There's nothing wrong with me. I promise."

The men who were standing next to her begin to walk toward me, the sensor-activated wheelchair rolling alongside them. Big and goony, they look more like bouncers than hospital employees. My throat tightens when I realize how close I am to being stuck here. I have no choice but to tell my mom the truth and hope that she'll believe me.

"Josh and I were trapped in Elusion," I say.

"She thinks she saw David," Patrick interjects.

"She told me that yesterday," my mom says to him. "Maybe I should have had her checked out then, but—"

"Stop talking about me like I'm not here," I snap. My mom flinches a little, her hands slipping away from mine, and I remind myself that I need to stay calm. I can't give either of them any more signs that I'm unstable, even though that's how I feel with these two goons standing next to my mother staring at me.

"I know this sounds crazy," I say. "But Dad really is alive. We need to go to Orexis. That's where he's being held prisoner."

She looks toward one of the goons, her lips tightening at the corners.

She doesn't believe me.

"Take me to Orexis," I plead. "Please. He doesn't have much time."

Her gaze shifts back to me, her features so heavy with doubt and guilt, I'm afraid I won't be able to get through to her.

"I just . . . I need you to believe me," I say firmly, with all the strength I can muster.

"I'm sorry, sweetie. I . . . I have to protect you," she says finally.

Out of the corner of my eye, I see Patrick wince, as if he can't bear to watch. I turn around and one of the goony staffers is suddenly holding a syringe. I run toward the atrium doors, but I'm not fast enough. A meaty hand grabs my shoulder and I feel a sharp prick above my elbow. I make it a couple more steps before my knees grow weak. As I lose control of my lower legs, the automated wheelchair swiftly moves behind me, catching me as I collapse. Restraints clamp over my forearms.

"We're going to get you help," my mom says.

"I'd like to stay until we talk to the doctor," Patrick says to my mom.

She turns back toward Patrick, her eyes watering again. "I think you've done enough." My mom doesn't raise her voice, but her words are sharp.

"I swear to God, I'll fix this," he says.

My mom presses a few buttons on the wheelchair and it begins to move, circling around Patrick and heading toward the elevator bank.

"Please, Mom," I say. "Dad needs us. We have to rescue him."

"Try and relax." My mom follows the wheelchair and waves off the men who just drugged me. "We have a doctor from California. She's an expert on delirium. She's been treating some of the other Elusion patients out west, trying to stabilize them." Her words may be upbeat, but the tremor in her voice is unmistakable.

The elevator dings and the doors slide open. The wheelchair carries me inside, and my mom presses the button for the 205th floor. The steel elevator darkens as the lights flash above us, a soothing, mechanical voice announcing the floors as we ascend. She leans forward and impatiently presses the elevator button again, as if that might speed things up.

"Patrick thinks Josh and I were stuck in Elusion because

we overrode the system," I say. "But it's not true. Do you really think I would do something that stupid?"

All I can hear is my mother's labored breathing behind me, but I keep going anyway. If I tell her every single thing I can think of, maybe she will come around.

"Dad left us those Thoreau books in case anything happened to him. He was hoping I could figure out the passcode."

"What?"

"The passcode to get into Etherworld, where Dad is hiding. It's an anagram, made up of the title and author. If you press *HATE OUR NEW LAND* into the firewall, you can get inside."

I'm trying to stay composed, but everything is tumbling out of my mouth in a panic. The thought of being detained here at the hospital is making me so anxious I feel like I'm hyperventilating.

"Floor Two Hundred Five," the voice says as the door slides open. "Frontal lobe critical care."

Otherwise known as the psych ward. My mom has been doing rotations so long I've gotten to know the lingo.

My mom waves her passcard in front of a sensor, her hand shaking. A face appears on the oversize InstaComm above the empty nurses' desk: a woman who's at least sixty. My mom mentioned that the hospital was eliminating some full-time administrative personnel, replacing them with freelancers and bringing them in when necessary through InstaComm.

"Welcome, Regan," she says. Her eyes flick up toward my mom. "Please proceed to room A-Twenty-Four."

My mom gives the image a quick nod before it disappears. The hall is deserted, just a series of closed doors. I wonder what's behind them. Other patients, just like me? Locked inside, with no way out?

"I found his passcard," I say. "And it hadn't been deactivated. Why would he leave it behind? How could he have started that plane without it?"

My mom stops cold. She has to know how suspicious that is. Actually, her stunned reaction makes me wish I'd thought to tell Patrick. If my brain hadn't been in such a fog after coming out of Elusion, maybe I would have. No one goes anywhere without their passcard. It not only contains their identification, but it accesses all their bank accounts, works as the key to all locks—everything.

"If that's true, why didn't you show it to me as soon as you found it?" my mom asks. "Or afterward, when you confessed to breaking into Patrick's office?"

"Because . . ." I'd made a promise to Josh. That we would keep the card a secret so we could have some leverage in case we ever needed it. Even now, I can't betray his trust. "I should have. I'm sorry."

The wheelchair moves forward again, taking me farther and farther away from the exit. The only noise is the sound of the wheels rolling along the floor. God, I can't get stuck in here.

"There's proof. His passcard is—"

"Your father is gone," she says, firmly.

The wheelchair comes to a stop. My mom presses her pass-card against the lockpad for room A24, and the door slides open. The room is empty, and the walls are made of reflective glass, mirroring our images. It's the first time I've seen myself since I returned from Elusion, and my appearance is alarming. My eyes are completely bloodshot. I'm wearing the same jeans and T-shirt I wore to search the abandoned house in the Quartz Sector, so my clothes are dirty and covered in soot. All in all, my looks aren't helping things.

"I can't lose you too. I won't." She attaches an IV to my arm and bites her lip. As the liquid inside the bag begins to flow, she presses a button on a nearby panel and a keyboard lights up. She types in a code and then pulls out her tab from her pocket, examining it quickly. "I'm being paged. I'll be right back. I have to get someone to cover my shift."

The moment my mother steps out of the room, an image of a woman in a light blue lab coat appears on the InstaComm wall to my left. She's holding a tab in her hand and appears to be looking directly at me.

"Hello, Regan. I'm Dr. Randall. Can you tell me if your head is hurting and, if so, where?"

"My head is fine," I say. I feel a warm, fuzzy sensation spreading through my limbs. I know it's coming from the IV draining into my arm, but as nice as it feels, I can't afford to give in to the meds. "Please," I say, stumbling over my words, the sedative taking effect. "I'm not crazy, Doctor. I just . . ."

I know better than to tell her the truth. If my own mother and best friend won't believe me, this stranger certainly will not. I have to switch tactics and convince her of my sanity. In other words, I have to do what I should've done the moment I saw my mom waiting for me with those two goons.

I have to lie.

"I think I'm just confused. It's probably the Aftershock. Maybe if I went home and got some rest, I'd feel better."

"Maybe," the doctor says with a patronizing smile. "But before we release you, we need to run a couple of tests, okay? We have to do some blood work and run a brain scan just to make sure everything checks out."

"Can I come back for the tests another time?" I ask, trying to reason with her, but there's no point.

"This won't take long," the doctor says, the smile still plastered on her face.

If I had to take a guess, I'd bet she's lying too.

My mom comes back into the room and immediately begins busying herself with the keyboard on the wall. A rush of resentment floods my mind as I watch her typing all sorts of background information on me. I was there for her when she needed me most. I took care of her when she couldn't take care of herself. I would've thought those months of dedication had earned her trust, but instead she believes the worst—that even though I was fully aware of the danger, I'd hijacked Elusion like an addict.

"As soon as she's resting comfortably," the doctor says,

looking at my mother, "you can take her down for the scans." The screen goes dark.

My mother inserts another needle into my arm, but I can barely feel it as she withdraws a tube full of blood.

"You've always been such a strong, responsible girl," my mom says, tears streaming down her cheeks. The top part of the wheelchair reclines, turning itself into a bed. She presses her passcard against the glass wall, and a drawer pops open. She pulls out a blanket and drapes it over me. "I think you were crying out to me for help last night, but I didn't realize it . . . until it was too late."

Last night. She'd come home and found me working on the anagram, and begged me not to use Elusion.

"I know you're scared," she says. "I know I let you down after your dad died. But you don't have to be afraid anymore. I'm going to take care of you. The way I should have been all along."

It's the apology I've been waiting for. But as much as I appreciate the sentiment, my mom is completely misguided, and her mistake could have deadly consequences.

But I can no longer argue with her. I'm having trouble moving my mouth, and my head feels heavy, like it's weighted to the pillow.

"I love you so much," she says, sitting on the edge of the chair that has become my bed. I notice her pallid skin, the circles under her eyes. "We're going to get through this, you and me together. I'm not going to disappoint you again."

She presses her lips gently to my forehead.

I hate to upset her and cause her more pain, but I have no choice.

I'm going to break out of here.

EIGHT

WHERE AM I?

I can't see, blind from protective contacts that scrape against my eyes like sand. I'm lying on something hard and stiff, my arms and legs restrained.

"Did you get the frontal scans?" I hear a deep, male voice ask.

"Let me check," says another voice, a woman with a hint of an accent. A pause as I'm rotated around and lifted. "Hmm. Yep. Frontal lobe—temporal. It's clear. There's no bleeding, at least none that I can see. Where are we sending the results?"

I try to speak, to call out to them, but I can't. There are tubes in my nose and mouth, filling my lungs with air.

"I gave you the name. The doctor is in California. A specialist."

"What's she in here for?" the tech asks. I know she's refer-ring to me.

"Rapid-onset psychosis. At least that's what it says here. But I heard it might be due to Elusion."

"You really believe that stuff? I think it's just rumors to drive vlog traffic. That's what the company is saying. And Elusion is CIT approved. Seems like if it was that dangerous they'd take if off the market."

"I don't know. I saw on the Net that another girl was found dead today. In LA, I think. And she had the same Equip marks as that Caldwell kid."

Another dead girl?

I think about Claire, dissolving in front of my eyes, and a chill runs down my spine.

Please don't let them be talking about her.

"I don't believe it," the woman says. "I've been there a mil-lion times and nothing. And so has everyone I know. Never had a problem. I think this whole thing is going to blow over."

"So what do you think is wrong with her?"

I know that by "her," they mean me.

"Drugs, probably. Same as the rest of them. But this patient's mom works here. And she doesn't want to believe it. That's why we had to work her up."

The machine flips over so that I'm facing the floor. I can feel the heat from the scan on the back of my head.

"Nice to have connections, huh?" one of them says.

The machine stops, and I'm flipped on my back again.

"That's it. Last scan. Think we can leave her alone in here so we can go start on the next one? I'd love to get out of here on time for once."

"Yeah. Looks like they gave her a megadose of alprazolam not too long ago. She should be out for a while. I think her mom is getting her admitted. I'll call her to come and fetch her."

There's a pause. I hear a click and then silence. I'm alone.

Alone and locked in a brain-scanning machine with tubes in my nose and throat, blinded from the contact lenses. Still, I can wiggle my body. And although my head is still foggy, my mind is coming back into focus. Enough so that I know I need to get out of here before they come back.

My fingers curl around the restraints. They're leather, unlike the metal ones that so firmly clamped me into the wheelchair. I adjust my shoulders so that I can move my hand ever so slightly. I feel the bottom of a metallic clip. I'm not locked in. These restraints weren't designed to prevent patients from escaping but to hold them in place while being scanned.

I pull my shoulders up one at a time until I can wrench an arm free. I swipe the contacts out of my eyes, but my vision is still blurry, my eyes sore. I grab the tubes attached to my nose and throat and gently slide them out, stifling a coughing fit with my hand.

The scanning machine isn't big enough for me to sit up straight, so I curl myself into a ball and get on my knees. I crawl toward the opening, peeking my head out to make sure I'm alone. I wince in the bright light and stick my head back in the tube. I wiggle myself around so that I'm sitting on the edge of the platform and swing my legs over the side, the industrial tiles dancing beneath my feet. I'm too dizzy to move. I blink several more times, my vision coming back into focus as it adjusts to the bright light of the room.

How long have I been here?

I'm dressed in a white T-shirt and blue drawstring pants. I have paper flip-flops on my feet.

As my brain comes out of its medicinal fog, images of my dad and Josh float through my mind. I have to help them.

Think, Regan.

I'm obviously in the radiology unit. It's only a few floors below the psych ward and isn't heavily staffed. My mom is always complaining about how old the building is and how the security system is so crappy she doesn't feel safe. In fact, they just started a major renovation to upgrade the building a month ago.

But I'm still going to have to get down the elevator and stairs without the aid of a passcard or tab, both of which were in the pocket of my clothes. And I can hardly walk out the front door in an outfit that practically screams "mental patient." How will I get through the lobby?

I look around the room until my eyes fix on the InstaComm panel on the wall. I wobble toward it and press the screen. It lights up, the hospital insignia flashing before allowing me access to the Net. It's almost three in the morning. I've been here for hours. Who knows how many Escapes the people in Etherworld have attacked, and how much danger they've seen in that time?

I need to get help—someone who can pick me up and take me to Orexis.

Avery. While she still thinks my dad is responsible for what happened to Nora and is overjoyed I've been committed, she has probably revived Josh by now. Maybe he could help me get out of here.

I tap into my TabTalk account. I have one new text, sent about forty-five minutes ago, but it's not from Avery. I sent her two messages and she hasn't responded to either one. Where the hell is she?

I click on the message, telling myself that Avery is too busy helping Josh to get back to me, because I can't afford to believe anything else right now.

You okay?

It's from Zoe. The last time I saw her was at Patrick's house, the night we found out about the first Elusion victim, Anthony. It was no secret she was interested in Patrick, and they had obviously hooked up that night. But even though Zoe goes to my school and her dad is one of the biggest stockholders in Orexis, I don't know her that well. Would she help me? Even if she knew the guy she was dating had committed me?

Probably not.

But she texted me in the middle of the night to ask if I was okay. And I really don't have anyone else to turn to.

I'm at the hospital with my mom, I write. *Could use a ride home. Can you pick me up?*

I press Send, feeling a little bad for not really telling her what the situation is, but then I realize that if she's talked to Patrick in the last hour or two, chances are he's already told her what happened.

Within a few seconds, a reply flashes on the screen.

Can you make it to the freight entrance in 15?

Apparently, she knows. But why is she willing to risk her neck, coming out here to get me?

But I don't have time to guess the answer. All I have is fifteen minutes.

I'll be there.

I close out of the session and the hospital logo appears on the screen once more. I walk over to the door and stand behind it, taking a few seconds to figure out my next move. How can I get out of this room without a passcard? And how can I get out of the building dressed like a patient?

I hear voices outside the room. I duck behind a rolling cart as the door slides open and two janitorial workers head toward a supply closet.

I have to move. *Now.* Before the door closes behind them.

Sneaking out from behind the cart, I slink out, my paper slippers soundless. I'm in a hallway, a few feet away from a nurses' desk, where a solitary employee stands in front of an Insta-Comm. Several people—also hospital employees, from the look of their blue scrubs—are milling about, checking their tabs.

The elevator bank is at the opposite end of the hall from the room I just exited. To get there, I have to walk past at least ten other rooms. The doors are made of some kind of transparent faux-glass material, so I can see that some of the rooms have patients and lab techs inside.

Although the elevator is passcard enabled, someone is waiting for it: a woman wearing a lab coat. Maybe I can hitch a ride with her? I look around and notice that someone has left a MealFreeze container on the edge of the nurses' desk. Luckily, the man stationed there gets up to answer a page, so I walk over, grab it, and head toward the elevators. I figure I can act my way through this, and pretend to be an elective-surgery patient who happened to wander onto the wrong floor.

The elevator doors open.

"Hold that elevator, please," I call out politely. I glance over my shoulder and see that the nurse hasn't returned to his station. No one else seems to notice me either. Despite what I'm wearing, it's almost like I'm invisible.

I step inside, hoping the woman next to me won't notice my flip-flops or my hospital clothes and that I'll be able to walk right out of here. She looks up from her tab just long enough to swipe her passcard and activate the elevator.

"Floor?" she inquires.

There's a ding as the neighboring elevator opens. My mom steps out and heads right toward the nurses' desk, just a few feet away.

"Lobby," I say as quietly as I can, moving toward the back of the elevator.

But I'm not quiet enough. At the sound of my voice, my mom turns. Her eyes lock on mine, and I see her surprise. But before she can move, the elevator doors slam shut. My stomach dips as the elevator begins its rapid descent.

We speed downward, dropping almost fifty floors in seconds before the elevator catches itself and rolls to a stop. The woman steps off, still staring at her tab. I press the lit-up *L*, hoping the rest of my descent will be as easy.

The elevator goes down one more floor and stops. The doors open as a crowd of people push their way in.

No one seems to notice me except for a woman in orange scrubs. "Are you a patient?" she asks, staring at my paper flip-flops.

The doors have shut and the elevator is moving, hurtling toward the ground floor.

I force myself to take a sip of the lukewarm MealFreeze, trying not to gag. "I was just in radiology. Got a little turned around. I need to get back to the OR prep unit."

"That's the twenty-fourth floor," a short, balding man says. His eyes shift to the elevator control panel. "It looks like you're headed to the lobby."

Shit.

"Can I see your passcard?" the woman asks.

"I left it in my clothes," I say, calmly taking another sip of my MealFreeze, hoping that she doesn't notice that my hands are starting to shake.

"By the way, you're not supposed to eat before surgery," the balding man says, his eyes narrowing at me.

Shit. Shit.

"What's your name?" the woman in the scrubs snaps.

My eyes focus on the numbers lighting on top of the elevator doors. 24, 23, 22 . . .

When I don't answer, the man's voice becomes even gruffer. "What's your name, miss?"

Everyone else in the elevator is staring now. As if on cue, all their tablets begin buzzing, and a small red warning light begins to blink on the elevator ceiling.

Great.

My mom has sounded the alarm. Everyone knows a psych patient has escaped, and here I am, wandering around the hospital alone.

I mentally prepare myself for someone to pull out a little needle and stab me just like before. But instead I hear a familiar ding, and the elevator doors open. Twenty-first floor.

"Someone grab her!" the woman says, reaching for me. I toss my MealFreeze down on the ground. As it splits open, everyone jumps back, trying to avoid the splatter. I take advantage of the commotion to lunge out of the elevator. And then I begin to run.

The two nurses behind the reception desk look up in time to see me speed past them, skirting the handful of medical personnel as I make my way toward the open exit at the end of the hall. An automated maintenance device is stuck in the door, sweeping the floor in front of it with swirling brushes.

I slip past it before the device swings free and the door slides shut. I begin running down a flight of stairs, pausing at the next landing and praying the door will open automatically, but without a passcard, it doesn't budge. Despite my mom's complaints, the hospital seems pretty secure to me.

"Stop!" a female guard yells from the landing above me.

I wedge my hip on the iron banister, putting my weight against the railing. I slide down like I was told not to as a kid, moving faster and faster, going from one floor to the next.

A flash of electricity ricochets off the banister, nearly hitting me as the acrid smell of smoke fills the air. Another guard is standing a floor beneath, pointing some sort of Taser at me, his finger on the trigger. I land on my feet and head toward an open door covered in yellow construction tape. As the guard charges in my direction, I break through the tape and run inside.

The cavernous space is dark, lit only by the red emergency lights on the wall. Still, I can see that the air is thick with drywall dust. The entire floor has been gutted down to its cement walls, and large piles of construction debris are scattered throughout. The freight elevator is on the other side of the lobby, so it should be opposite where I'm standing right now. I make my way through, accidentally stepping on a discarded nail. I lean over to inspect the wound and hear the stairwell exit door squeak open. I squat down, curl myself into a ball, and hide underneath a large scrap of metal.

"She's got to be in here," says a husky voice, as someone charges into the space. A beam of light bounces across the room, narrowly missing me.

"The stairwell leads to the front entrance. We've got that covered."

I hold my breath. I know a Taser can't kill you, but it knocks you unconscious and your body reportedly hurts like hell for weeks because of the shock to your nervous system.

"I doubt she'd be in here in those paper shoes." The female guard kicks a piece of metal and it clangs across the floor, stopping inches away from my hiding spot. "Get cut to shreds."

She's even closer now, so close I can smell the peanut butter on her breath. I hear a scraping noise beside me. Two tiny red eyes peer at me through the dark.

A rat.

I swallow. I've had to deal with a man-eating worm in Etherworld; surely I can handle this furry little thing.

"Did you hear that?" the female guard asks, turning and staring in my direction. I can see her clearly now. She's tall, with long brown braids. She's holding her Taser in front of her, as if I'm a violent criminal.

I'm not about to have a rat give away my hiding space. My fingers fold around a block of wood and I poke it toward the gray, whiskered creature. The rat jumps and scurries out from underneath our hiding place, knocking down more debris as it runs away, heading toward the open door.

"That way!" the male guard says as he follows the noise. "Hurry—she's headed toward the south stairwell."

I hold my breath as they follow the rat, the thudding of their feet getting softer and softer. I push myself up and head in the opposite direction, away from the door. I move as quickly as I can, making my way around the construction, walking on my tiptoes to avoid the nails that are scattered around the floor.

I head past another set of elevators, this time roped off with yellow tape. There's no way I'd try them anyway. I need a more discreet exit, like a stairwell.

But before I'm past them, I hear a ding and the door slides open. I'm staring into the eyes of another security guard. I jump as he points his flashlight in my direction. His mouth drops in surprise as he takes a step toward me, his other hand reaching for his Taser.

I run, weaving in and out of the huge piles of construction debris. The guard is older and overweight, and he's struggling to keep up. I reach the middle of the room, where a tarp is stretched from wall to wall, acting as a barrier. I skid to a stop, drop down to my belly, and slide underneath.

I hear a grunt as the guard smashes into the tarp. As he attempts to get under it, I see the oversize passcard-operated elevator. It's right next to an open stairwell, behind a mound of drywall. I'm guessing they both lead to the freight entrance.

I'm so close to freedom.

I climb over the drywall and make my way toward the steps.

I'm out of breath when I reach the ground floor of the hospital. The entire area outside the elevator is deserted. I lean over and put my hands on my knees, trying to suck as much air into my lungs as possible. When I catch my breath, I walk over to the huge sliding doors that lead to a loading dock outside. My stomach drops when I scan the area and don't see Zoe or her car anywhere.

I cross my arms over my chest and start pacing, mostly so I don't panic. I reassure myself that if I keep moving—even if it's just in a circle—I will get out of here and find Josh. But then I hear a humming sound, followed by a slight insect-like buzzing. My feet come to a stop and my eyes dance around the room, searching for the source. When I spot a silver security camera, zooming in on me, my mouth drops open.

I duck and plaster myself behind a pillar, but the lens adjusts and continues to track me. I roll my eyes when I think about how outdated the technology is—there are plenty of undetectable surveillance cams—but then fear takes over once more. I have no idea if someone is watching the footage live from a control room.

I have to take care of that camera before it records any more.

I lean out from behind the pillar and peer around the place. There are stacks of sealed boxes and metal pallets, a few automated dollies and conveyor belts. The camera buzzes again, and I will it to shift to the other side of the room.

No dice. It's still fixed on me.

I duck back around the pillar, praying that I'll figure a way out of this mess, when I see something miraculous in the reflection of the doors. A large piece of industrial piping, tilted up against one of the smaller conveyor belts.

I have to make this quick. Zoe could be here any minute.

After taking a deep breath and getting into a ready-set lunge, I sprint toward the pipe. The camera hums louder as it tries to keep up with me. I grab the pipe, and it nearly slips through my fingers; my palms are soaked in sweat. I frantically tuck the pipe in between my knees and wipe my hands on my pants.

The only problem is that the pipe weighs a lot more than I expect it to. When I lift it up, my biceps simultaneously tighten and twinge. I walk over to the camera, clutching the pipe hard, even though my arms aren't faring well under the pressure. Once I'm in swinging range, I lift and angle the pipe, propping one end on my shoulder. When I put my legs into a wide stance and thrust the top of the heavy pipe toward the camera, my arms feel like they might snap in half.

The pipe hits the wall behind the camera, smashing a hole in the plaster. I pull it back and try again. With another wobbly swing, I manage to connect with the camera, crushing the lens as shards of glass and plastic rain down on me.

I have to admit, destroying that thing felt pretty damn good.

But hearing a car horn coming from outside feels even better.

I turn and look through the glass doors. Even though the sun is a couple of hours away from rising, I can make out Zoe behind the wheel of a sporty red coupe. She's waving at me, signaling that the coast is all clear. I run over to the sliding doors and . . .

They don't open.

I pound on the doors with my fists in a fit of frustration.

Zoe steps out of the car, dashing toward me. As she reaches the door, the motion-sensor lights flash on, dousing her in harsh yellow light. She's not wearing her O2 shield and is dressed in all black, as if she's trying to blend into the night.

She places her gloved hands on the glass, mirroring mine. A sudden breeze ruffles her long raven-colored hair, and now she looks like a cat burglar turned runway model—although if she's caught breaking me out of the hospital, we can add juvenile offender to that list.

She gives me a look of grim determination as she says, "We're going to get you out of there."

"How? I don't have my passcard." And even if I did, it wouldn't unlock these doors.

Zoe leans forward, looking inside the room.

"What about the boxes behind you? Are those medical supplies?"

They're either stamped or labeled, so there's at least some sort of information about the contents.

"Yeah, seems like it," I reply.

"Try to find one that might have something sharp and metal in it, like scissors."

"Why?"

"Just hurry up and do it," she says.

I dart over to a stack of boxes and begin to hunt for anything that might be marked for the emergency room or the trauma unit. The box at the bottom of the stack is just what I'm looking for. It's covered in quick-seal, which can only be opened with a laser pen, but when I push the box on its side, I see a small hole in the corner. I shove my pointer finger through the hole so I can make it even wider. Once the hole is big enough to fit a couple more fingers, I'm able to tear off the side of the box.

A whole mess of objects come spilling out. I grab the first pair of medical scissors I see, peel them out of their sterilized packaging, and dart back to the sliding doors.

"Are these good?" I say, holding them up for Zoe's inspection.

"Perfect," she says. "Now take them and stab the sharp end really hard into the lockpad."

"Anywhere, or someplace specific?"

Zoe squints as she stares at the lockpad from the other side of the door. "There should be a magnetic strip on the top. That's your target."

I scramble over to the lockpad and check. I force the point of the scissors into it and a tiny spark flares and then fizzles.

Nothing happens.

I'm trying to decide where to stab next when the doors suddenly slide open.

"Let's get out of here," Zoe says.

We dash toward the car, Zoe's grip on my arm tightening with every step. As soon as we strap ourselves in, Zoe swipes her passcard and the engine purrs to life.

"How'd you know how to open that door?" I ask her, my voice shaking with relief.

"That's a story for later." She gives me the once-over. "Nice outfit." She leans closer, pointing to the white powder on my arm. "And what are you covered in?"

"Drywall," I say.

She reaches into the backseat and tosses me a sweatshirt. "Put this on."

I still have no idea why she's here, risking her ass for me, but whatever the reason, I'm grateful. Even if she's planning on taking me to Patrick, I'd prefer that to the hospital.

"We have to get out of here fast," Zoe says.

"Do you think we can use the private access tunnels?" I ask her.

"I think so. My father has privileges. You just need a specific code and a remote to enter them." Zoe snatches her tab, which is plugged into the car's console. "Let me see if—"

Slam!

Two fists pound on the windshield of Zoe's car. A tall security guard, standing right outside my door.

"Get out of the car. Now!" the man orders, clenching his teeth.

Another set of hands starts slapping Zoe's window. A female guard has joined in, trying to stop us from leaving.

"There's nowhere for you to go," the woman says. "We've alerted the authorities and we're blocking off the exits."

Zoe and I look at each other. We don't say anything, but it's like each of us understands what the other person is thinking. I give her a small nod, a move I hope neither of the guards notices. Then Zoe puts the car into reverse and presses her foot down on the gas. We move backward at such a high speed that both guards fall to the ground. Zoe looks over her shoulder, spinning the steering wheel in a circle with the palms of her hands until the back of the coupe fishtails around. She puts the car in drive and we blast off.

I glance in the side mirror as the guards sprint toward a white van.

"Hurry," I say to Zoe. "They're going to follow us!"

Zoe doesn't even flinch. She just keeps her eyes trained ahead. "Take my tab and do a search for the closest access tunnel for I-75."

"Can't I just use the AutoComm for that?" I ask.

Zoe swerves to avoid a patron walking toward the hospital and barely misses hitting him. My stomach practically drops to the floor.

"Forget it. The sync function is broken," she answers.

I pull the tab off the port where it connects to the console. As soon as I start typing on the touch screen, I hear sirens. While the tab calculates the quickest route to the access tunnel, I check the mirror and see a white van behind us.

Zoe slams on the brakes as another white van yanks in front of us. My harness digs into my shoulders as I fly forward.

"Hang on!" Zoe says as she accelerates, cranking the wheel. The maneuver gets us past the other set of guards, but now we have two vans behind us, and the sirens are getting louder.

"Once we get off the grounds, make a right," I say. "A mile

down the road, there's an on-ramp to the tunnel."

"Good," Zoe says, but her tiny bit of relief is sucked away when we see that the chain-link gates to the closest hospital exit have been closed off. Her foot eases off the gas.

"Don't slow down," I say. "Those vans are going to smash into us!"

Zoe shrugs. "What do you want me to do? Drive right through the gate?"

"If we have to, yeah."

A look of confusion clouds Zoe's face. I can't tell if she's squeamish because she doesn't want to damage her sports car, or if she's worried we're going to get killed performing this ridiculous stunt. But then she narrows her eyes and the coupe starts flying toward the gate.

The sound of metal crushing metal is louder than our screams. The car breaks through and skids off the road. Horns blare behind us, the vans stuck behind the crushed gate. Zoe regains control and speeds away, the headlights from the security vans fading into the night.

NINE

AS ZOE'S CAR BARRELS DOWN THE
expressway, I clutch the leather armrests, holding on tight.
Even though we haven't seen any sign of the white vans or the
police, she's still driving at a breakneck speed.

"Where to?" Zoe asks.

"Thirty-Two Flat Rock Road," I reply. "Quartz Sector."

Zoe makes a sharp left, the seat harness digging into my
shoulder. "Why are you helping me?" I ask.

Zoe's eyes flick over to me for a split second, and they're
shimmering with energy. "I know you think there's something
wrong with Elusion. Yesterday I overheard my dad talking on
his tab with some other stockholder. Things got pretty heated.
He was on some rant about something called nanopsychosis.
Saying that he wasn't going to dump his shares until there was

real proof Elusion caused it. I don't think I've ever seen him that angry."

Finally, word of Elusion's dangerous flaw is making it through the corporate ranks. "Did you ask him about it?"

"Hell yeah, I did. But of course he blew me off, like he always does. So I said I was meeting some friends in Elusion, and he yanked my Equip away from me and forbade me to use it. When I called Patrick, he was pretty cagey too, but eventually he admitted that you were suffering from this weird sickness. After that, I had to see what was going on for myself, so I texted you." She looks at me sideways and smirks. "For the record, you don't look sick to me."

"Thanks," I say. "I'm not."

"That's what I thought. So are you going to tell me what's going on?"

I begin to talk, explaining everything. She listens, only asking questions when necessary. By the time I've finished, the streets have narrowed and are lined with ugly little steel trailers, evacuated houses, and uncollected trash. We're closing in on the Quartz Sector, the dilapidated area that was hit by a severe storm ages ago and pretty much left to rot.

Zoe is quiet, her gloved fingers gripping the steering wheel. For a minute, it seems like she's trying to gauge her feelings, or trying to figure out whose story to trust. "We have to help those people who are still stuck in Elusion."

My thoughts reel back to the night Avery, Josh, and I went in search of Nora—how we rescued Maureen, the frail girl in the basement of that broken-down house, who repeated my father's words back to me. And how Claire disintegrated in the rapids, screaming out in pain.

"Are there any more details on that girl who was just found?" I ask.

"Why don't you check the Net? You can use my tab."

I reach for her tab, which is on the floor near my feet. The car chase had sent it flying out of my lap. I try to access the search function after waking it up from sleep mode, but there's a passcode preventing me from getting past the home screen.

"Oh. Type in 'bitchypants,'" Zoe says.

I raise my eyebrows at her and laugh a little. "Seriously?"

"It's an inside joke." She shrugs, without saying the name of the other person who's in on it.

I put in Zoe's passcode and then look up a reliable news site on the Net.

The headline pops on the screen: *College Star Athlete Succumbs to Unusual Brain Injury.*

My hand begins to shake as I click on the link. A well-dressed male reporter stands outside the gate of a beautiful mansion surrounded by palm trees. The volume is muted, and I'm about to adjust the settings when the image of the reporter recedes and a graduation picture appears on-screen.

It's a girl with white-blond hair, pulled back in a ponytail, and bright green eyes.

Claire.

"Did you find something?" I hear Zoe say.

I don't respond. I just stare at the picture of Claire, imagining all the things the reporter must be saying about her in his rehearsed yet sympathetic voice-over: what a great athlete she was, how she loved doing anything to challenge herself, and what a loyal friend she could be, even to someone she hardly knew.

My head falls forward.

"You okay?" Zoe asks. I'm trembling, my body shaking along with my hand. A wave of sadness threatens to sink me, but I can't let it, because then I won't be able to help anyone.

"Yeah," I respond, giving her a quick reply. If I say any more, I'll lose it.

Zoe respects my silence, leaving me alone as I do a quick scan, checking on the progress of the other Etherworld survivors who followed Anthony. There are a slew of updates, including one posted late last night about how the authorities are still searching for the kids Claire was last seen with: Wyatt Krissoff and Piper Lewis. There are mentions of Cole Rankin and Anderson Schmidt, the two kids from Miami—who are still in comas—and reports from physicians who still haven't found anything definitive connecting these brain injuries to the use of Elusion but are warning parents not to let their children access the app until they know for sure.

And then I see a fresh headline that makes my stomach churn.

Daughter of Original Elusion Inventor Admitted to—
and Escaped from—Psych Ward of Inner Sector Medical.

I click on it and watch the video of Patrick leading me into the medical pavilion. Thankfully, my face is only partially visible, which means the public might find it hard to identify me. But all anyone would have to do to catch a good glimpse of me is look my name up on the Net and download any number of social media photos, like the ones that were taken at the Elusion release party at the Simmons estate less than a week ago.

Now there's a target on my back, on top of everything else.

"Finally." Zoe slams on the brakes and undoes her harness in one sharp movement. "Let's go."

My head jerks back up and a few stray tears land on my knees. I wipe off my wet cheeks and get out of my harness, and I'm staring now at the front door of Josh's trailer. I was just here a couple of days ago, but it feels like a lifetime. He and I were still strangers then, trying to determine whether or not we could trust each other. And now I'm praying he's here with Avery, up and around and plotting how we're going to break into Orexis again.

"Come on, Regan," Zoe urges, as she reaches into the trunk and grabs a canvas tote.

"What's that?"

"Clothes," she says. "You need to get cleaned up and changed."

"Thanks."

As we sprint up the steps, I envision a reunion with Josh that begins with him smiling, then grabbing me and pulling me into a tight hug. My pulse is skyrocketing as the front door slides open.

"What the hell happened to you?" Avery asks. As usual, she's wearing her vintage army jacket. Her red, curly hair is tied in a messy knot on top of her head, and her glasses are slipping down the tip of her nose.

I never thought I'd say this, but thank God she's here.

"She was in a psych ward, among other places," Zoe answers for me.

"Guess what? I don't care," Avery says, and my gratitude is suddenly reduced to zero.

"Well, what have you been doing all night?" I counter. "You didn't answer any of my texts."

Avery crosses her arms in front of her chest. "I stayed at the hospital for a few hours, waiting for that girl to come out of surgery. I thought if she woke up, she might be able to tell us something about Nora. I didn't realize that there wasn't a signal on my tab until—"

"Wait, you didn't have a signal that whole time? When did you get my messages?" My voice is really high-pitched, like I'm trying to squeeze the words out of my tightening throat.

Avery casts her eyes down to her scuffed black boots, so she doesn't have to look at me when she makes her admission. "About twenty minutes ago. I'm sorry. I would have been here sooner, but . . . I didn't know."

"Are you saying Josh is still unconscious?" Zoe asks, because I'm standing here in stunned silence.

Avery nods.

I push past Avery and into the trailer. The InstaComm is blaring some ninja movie marathon, which Josh was probably watching before he surprised Patrick and me in Elusion. There's an unfinished MealFreeze sitting on the kitchenette counter, right next to the photocube I looked at when I first came here.

"Did you try pushing his emergency button?" I ask Avery. He's been under trypnosis five hours longer than me. I have no idea what that means for his cortisol levels and if they're high enough to cause the stimulus overdose that my dad warned me about.

"Yeah, but it didn't work."

"You didn't disconnect him, did you?"

"No way. When I was at the hospital, I overheard some doctors saying that they thought Maureen's brain injury might've been caused by taking off her Equip abruptly instead of weaning her off trypnosis slowly," Avery says. "I don't know if they're right, but I didn't want to take a chance and do something that could make things worse."

As I run to Josh's room, Avery shouts, "Will somebody please tell me what the hell is going on?"

Zoe begins retelling the whole saga I recounted in the car, but when I see Josh lying on his bed, his eyes covered with the visor, an IV drip in one arm, the other arm dangling off the mattress, I can't hear anything but my heartbeat thudding inside my ears.

I get down on my knees so I can hold Josh's hand. I move my other hand up to his face, my fingers trailing down the side of his cheek. He doesn't respond to my touch at all, and for a moment I try to convince myself that he's just taking a nap, tired from a long day.

Any minute now, he'll wake up, I think.

But seconds tick by without any motion, except for the scrambling footsteps that flood the trailer. Soon Zoe and Avery are both in Josh's room with me. When I turn around, I can tell by the frozen look on Avery's face that she's been blindsided by everything she just learned.

"You saw Nora?" she asks me.

"Yes," I reply.

Avery kneels down next to me. "Is she okay? How did she look? Do you know where she is?"

"The last time I saw her, she seemed fine, but . . ." I swallow hard. "She never told me where she was when she disappeared."

Avery's shoulders slump forward; her lower lip trembles. We're both silent, not knowing what to do next. Thankfully Zoe is here to keep us moving, even though sitting with Josh feels like all that I can manage.

"Avery, did you hook Josh up to this IV?" she asks.

"Yeah, I was hoping that getting some fluids in him would help," Avery replies, her voice softer than I've ever known it to be.

"Great idea. Where did you find an IV?" Zoe places her hand on Avery's shoulder, as if trying to help her get her strength back.

"Nora had a few in her room," she explains. "And I watched a tutorial on the Net to figure out how to use it."

I think back to the first time Josh took me to the warehouse out by the HyperSoar hangars, where he tried to show me evidence that would convince me that people were becoming addicted to Elusion, overriding the safety mechanisms and hooking themselves up to IVs so that they could stay in there for hours—sometimes days. Nora had been one of them.

I press my lips to Josh's forehead, willing him to wake. "Come back to me, please," I whisper.

"He hasn't moved or said anything, but his pulse seems strong." Avery stands back up again, adjusting her jacket as if it will help her regain her composure. "He could be in worse shape, so that has to be a good sign."

She could be right. I remember what my dad said when we were at the mines—once the destruction protocol was complete, everyone would be released from Elusion's powerful trance. Josh is going to be okay; I know it. He'll walk away from this once my father's attack plans are carried out. But until then, we'll have to keep him as safe and protected as possible.

"So what now?" Zoe asks. "Do we take him to the hospital?"

"The doctors still haven't figured out a treatment," Avery says, annoyed. "And even with all these incidents, they can't prove that Elusion caused any of it."

"That might not matter," Zoe explains. "My father got a call from another investor who told him about nanopsychosis. Word is spreading. Who knows, they could pull the app off the market any minute now."

Avery coughs up a sarcastic laugh. "Oh, really? Then why did Cathryn give a statement herself last night assuring everyone that Elusion is safe and they're releasing it nationally as planned? The bastards at the CIT were right there with her, standing by her side."

"So *you* weren't the one who released the info from the memo?" I ask.

Avery shakes her head. "I wanted to, but I always check with Josh first. I tried texting him earlier, but he didn't answer, so I just thought he was tied up with you."

Patrick. He has to be the one alerting the stockholders to what's really happening. Maybe he's plotting some kind of sneak attack on Orexis that will force them to stop the national release of Elusion in a couple of days?

"What do you want to do, Regan?" Zoe asks.

"I think we need to keep Josh here, hooked up to the Equip, and monitor him closely." I place my hand on his chest and feel the rhythm of his heart under my palm. "My dad says that once the program is destroyed, everyone who is trapped in this trance state will wake up."

Avery props her hands on her hips. "So we just sit here and wait?"

"I can't stay." I slowly pull myself away from Josh and stand up, my legs unsteady. "My dad is being held hostage at Orexis. I have to find him."

"Good idea. Then the police will get involved and blow this whole scandal wide open," Zoe says.

"Yeah, and maybe the cops will do more to help us find the missing," Avery says hopefully. Then she gives me the once-over and scowls. "But how're you going to get into Orexis covered in dust and wearing your pajamas?"

"I brought her some clothes, Avery, so chill." Zoe smiles and holds up the tote.

"What I don't have is a passcard," I say. I used my dad's to sneak in once before, but it's at my house, and I can't go back there now. Mom will be looking for me, and so will the police.

"I have a passcard with clearance," Zoe says, pulling one out of her jeans. "All I had to do was dig through two suit pockets."

"Wait, are you saying you—?"

"Borrowed this from my father? Yeah, sure. That works."

I'm amazed by Zoe's abundance of foresight. She is coming through in ways I never would have imagined.

"I hate to piss on this happy moment," Avery says, smirking at Zoe, "but your dad's passcard is only going to get Regan into the building. I doubt he'll have access to the room she needs."

Zoe's face falls as she realizes that Avery has a point. "Where is your father exactly?" she asks me.

"He's in one of the research labs."

"Shit," Zoe says. "Dad's card is probably only good for the executive suites and some of the conference rooms."

"If I can get inside, maybe I can steal a passcard from someone else," I say. It sounds ludicrous, but I can't afford to lose faith now.

"That's the worst plan in the world," Avery says, right on cue. "And even if you found someone else who has access to the labs, Cathryn probably had Bryce integrate some kind of special code into the lockpad."

"Look, we all know how great you are at shooting ideas down, but why don't you try coming up with a solution for once?" I snap.

"You want a solution? I'll give you a solution." Avery pulls her tab out of her jeans. "I'm going to call Giblin."

"Who the hell is Giblin?" Zoe asks.

"A guy I know," she replies. "He's got connections that we could use right now, and he owes me one, so he'll help us out." She wanders out into the hall, typing on her tab, and I glance over at Josh, my stomach tying into a knot. I try to remember that Avery is his friend, and that without her, we never would have decrypted the files on the QuTap I used to hack into Patrick's quantum computer at Orexis the other day. I try to remember when he told me that we were going to get through this together.

The room seems empty all of a sudden, even though Zoe is standing next to me, watching me stare at Josh. But then the quiet is smashed when I hear Avery calling out to me from the other room, her voice booming.

"Congratulations! I just saved your ass!"

Ten minutes later, I go into the small bathroom at the end of the trailer and change into Zoe's clothes, yanking on a pair of jeans that are about a size too small and an inch too long. The hooded knit sweater she gave me doesn't fit right either—there's a lot of room in the chest—but at least the fabric is extra soft and almost like fur. The boots she lent me are perfect, but the heel makes them a little impractical. I'm just glad not to be in paper shoes and pajamas anymore.

I glance at my reflection. It's funny—I've spent a good chunk of the last eight hours unconscious from either trypnosis or hospital drugs, and yet I don't think I've ever been this tired. I could probably curl up on the floor right here and fall asleep for days, but I won't let the fatigue set in. I pinch my cheeks so hard I turn them pink. My eyes snap open a little more too, as my thoughts wander back to the last time I was holed up in a bathroom.

It was the other night. At my house.

Josh and I had just returned from our first trip to the Mount Arvon Escape, where we'd shared a kiss inside an ice cave that looked as if it had been built out of frozen emeralds.

I touch my mouth, remembering how it felt to have his lips pressed against mine, his hands gripping my waist, the warmth of his breath on my face. I'm startled by a hard knock on the door, followed by the loud roar of a truck's engine.

"Hurry up," Avery barks. "He's here."

I step out of the bathroom, expecting to see Avery outside, waiting to harass me some more, but she's already welcoming Giblin, a tall, lanky, baby-faced guy with a ponytail longer than mine. He's wearing a ratty blue T-shirt and has ink-black hair, a piercing in his left eyebrow, and a tattoo of a Chinese dragon on his forearm. In his hand is an industrial-size brown duffel bag that could easily fit a dead body.

He notices me and juts his chin out, which I guess is his version of a hello. "Did you order the house call?" he asks, his voice not as rough as I thought it might be.

"I guess," I say.

Avery waves me over, and I come a little closer as he sets his huge bag down on the floor. "Gib, this is Regan Wel—"

"I know," he says, locking eyes with me. "I saw that video of you and that billionaire on the Net. What's life like in the nuthouse?"

"Uh, pretty awful." I glare at Avery. The last thing we need is someone knowing who and where I am, but she just shakes her head at me like she's certain he won't tell anyone.

"I brought the Turbo. It should only take a minute to warm up, and less than five to make the piece," he says, crouching down and unzipping the bag. Then he pulls out a big insulated box, which he opens very delicately. Inside is a thin, sleek, rectangular machine that he places on Josh's coffee table.

"Nice 3D printer," I say, kneeling in front of it to get a better look. "That's the smallest one I've ever seen."

"This one isn't even out on the market yet," Giblin brags.

I squint at him. "Then how'd you get it?"

Avery swats me on the arm. "Rule number one: never ask Gib how he gets anything."

"Is there a rule number two?" I ask.

"The less you know about me, the better," he replies, smiling. "So Avery says you need a fake passcard with a custom semiconductor chip. That right?"

I look at Avery and she's standing there with a smug grin on her face, but it doesn't bother me one bit. In fact, I smile back at her, grateful that she thought of this. Additive manufacturing is everywhere these days, but making phony passcards with 3Ds is illegal, especially ones with embedded chips that have the power to do things like crack lockpad codes. Possession of a fake passcard is a felony. Still, it's the best way to get inside Orexis and to the lab where my dad is being held, so taking this risk is totally worth it.

"Yeah, that's right," I say.

Giblin presses a couple of buttons on the printer and a low humming sound begins to emanate from the machine. Then he pulls out his tab from his back pocket and begins typing on it.

"Okay, let's talk credits," he says. "I'm thinking two thousand will cover it."

"Two *thousand*?" Avery says, aghast. "What the hell, Gib? Are you trying to price-gouge us?"

"Sorry, but that's the cost of high demand." He sets his tab down next to the printer and then cracks his knuckles. "You're going to pay extra for an express order and at-home delivery."

"This is bullshit. You know you owe me a favor," Avery says.

He shrugs. "I can knock off five hundred, but that's the best I can do."

I tug on the sleeve of Avery's jacket and we take a few steps back while Giblin inspects the printer.

"Do it," I say. "I'll figure out a way to get him the money."

"That's really steep," she says.

"There are lives on the line here. I don't care. I'll get the money somehow."

Avery nods and heads over to Giblin, sticking out her hand. "Okay, we're in for fifteen hundred. Deal?"

"Deal." Giblin gives her a shake and me a polite nod. "Now comes the fun part."

He reaches into the insulated box and brings out an egg-shaped container filled with wet, cream-colored putty. It's the compound that makes the mold. Giblin puts it into a tray in the back of the printer and closes it. He digs in the box again and takes out a cellophane envelope containing the gold semiconductor chip, which is so tiny I can barely see it. He puts that into another compartment and uploads the product design with his tab, and then we watch as the printing process begins. The low hum raises an octave or two, but the machine is much quieter than any other 3D I've seen.

"So here's the thing," Giblin says as the printer goes to work. "This will be state-of-the-art merchandise, and I can guarantee it will get the job done. But some lockpads might have codes that are harder to bypass, so it might take anywhere from thirty seconds to a minute for the card to crack it, depending on the tech sophistication."

"That's no good," Avery says. "She needs instant access, not this time-delay crap."

Giblin raises a pierced eyebrow at me. "Instant access, huh?"

I don't even bother responding. I just keep my eyes on the printer and envision myself walking into room 5020, like my father hoped I would do a week ago. I feel a surge of determination rising within me.

This is going to work.

"The chip is top quality. It'll worm it's way through some nasty stuff, so don't worry," Giblin reassures us.

"What about security systems? Will the semiconductor set off any kind of alarms?" Avery asks.

"No, it should be undetectable," he says. "Like me."

Minutes later, a tray slowly opens from the front of the printer, presenting us with a fresh, new, white passcard that looks completely real. Giblin takes it and gives it to me, the plastic warm in my hands.

"You can wire me the credits. Avery has my info. If I don't have the payment in the next two hours, I'll send someone to look for you. And he won't be as friendly as I am," he says, narrowing his dark eyes at me.

"Consider it done," Zoe says, walking into the room. "I just wired the credits to Avery. She'll make sure you get them."

"Zoe . . . ," I protest.

"It was nothing," she says. "Seriously. My dad can pay me back. It's the least he can do."

"Thank you," I say.

"The pleasure was mine," Giblin says, quickly packing up all his equipment into his duffel bag and throwing it over his shoulder. "Avery, nice seeing you again."

"But you were never here, right?" she replies.

He smirks and says, "You know me. I'm never anywhere."

Then he darts out the front door of the trailer and into his truck, which growls to life and speeds off into the early morning darkness.

TEN

ZOE PATS ME ON THE LEG. "SO ONCE WE get to the building, you're going to use the side door, right?"

We left Zoe's car with Avery and we're sitting side by side on the Traxx, zooming over patches of pre–Standard 7 shift traffic. I'm attempting to disguise myself by wearing Zoe's obnoxiously large Florapetro glasses, but it doesn't seem to matter. Even though it's only five in the morning, and the train is already half full of people, they're zoned out, eyes closed with Equips on, their bodies swaying with the turn of the train.

"Right," I reply. We're going to use the door where I met up with Cathryn the other night. It's the most hidden of all the building entrances, and because it's rarely used and not open to the public, it's not guarded. I glance nervously out the window. The Renaissance Center looms in front of us, the tower lights at the top of the titanium building gleaming in the black sky.

"Thanks again for the whole Giblin thing," I say.

"Of course. What are friends for, right?"

"Yeah," I say with a nod and slight smile. Up until today I wouldn't have referred to Zoe as a friend, but she's proving herself to be just that. "Do you think Avery will be able to hack into the security cameras?" I ask, getting back to the matter at hand.

While disabling the entry point is key, I'm more worried about getting to the elevators and the research lab floors without detection.

Zoe shrugs. "I don't know. She's good, but taking down an entire network from her tab is asking a lot."

I fidget with the safety harness as I continue to stare out the window, turning my attention across the river toward Canada, catching an occasional glimpse of Windsor's lit skyline through the oily clouds. My mind is spinning like it did when I was in the car with Patrick and thought we were headed toward Orexis: I'm excited about finding my dad but terrified I'll screw things up.

"If worse comes to worst, I can just hide out in a closet or something until I can get lost in the morning rush," I say.

"That might be a bad idea. The longer you're in there, the better chance you have of getting caught and hauled away again. I'm not sure I can jailbreak you a second time."

I'm realizing just how crazy this stunt is. Yesterday, when my mom confronted me about sneaking into Patrick's office with the QuTap, she was shocked. If she could see me now, armed with an illegal semiconductor-enhanced passcard in my pocket and ready to storm back into Orexis, she'd think I was nothing short of insane. But when I get to room 5020 and find my father there, she and everyone else will understand why this was worth the risk.

And all the lies will finally be revealed.

The train screeches to a stop at the Inner Sector. We exit into the darkness of the early morning, walking on a platform hundreds of feet up, in front of a gigantic electronic billboard for *The Must-Have New Product of the Year—Elusion! Don't You Deserve to Escape?* Zoe pauses, giving the sign the middle finger, and I grin, making my way toward the giant aerial spiderweb of escalators.

"Don't forget your O2 shield." Zoe hands me one as she motions toward the air quality reports on the information screens.

I fasten it over my face as we step onto the escalator and begin to descend, the lights of the inner-city skyline vanishing as the escalator zooms toward the ground. I think about Josh, still unconscious, his mind still trapped in Elusion. The possibility of him—or my dad or anyone else—not being able to return makes my blood turn to ice.

We step off and weave our way through the crowd, heading toward one of the pedestrian bridges that funnel through the Orexis complex.

We arrive at company headquarters, not far from the exact

spot where I saw Cathryn trying to avoid the media the other day. I cringe as I remember how naive I was that night. During our ride to the Merch Sector, she chatted cozily with me, giving me advice like a second mother. She seemed so . . . normal. How could she have looked me in the eye, knowing full well my dad was still alive and locked away under her orders? How did I not see through her?

I look around. From what I can see, the crowd of media has grown significantly—at least a hundred more people are huddled in the floodlights, breathing into their O2 shields. I'm tempted to run out and give them the scoop of a lifetime, but I know it won't do any good. No one is going to believe my dad is alive until they see him for themselves, especially since all of Detroit knows I was in the nuthouse, as Giblin put it.

"I think I should go in with you," I hear Zoe say, my eyes still glued to the buzzing of the crowd. "If we spot Patrick, I can keep him occupied while you head to the lab."

"No, we should stick to the plan. Talk to your dad. Tell him everything that happened to me; tell him what you saw with"—I swallow hard—"Josh. Maybe you can get him to agree to help us, or at least delay the release."

She taps me on the shoulder, and when I turn to her, her brown eyes are glistening. For a second, I think she might lean over and give me a hug. Instead, she rummages through her bag and then hands me a small silver tab.

"Zoe, I can't," I say, backing away a little. She's done so much for me already, including loaning me those fifteen hundred credits to cover the passcard.

"Just take it. I have two, so this one's a spare. The benefits of having divorced parents." She winks.

"Thank you," I say, gratefully accepting the tab. "For everything."

"After you find your dad and call the police, take all the video you can. Record him and the room too—from every angle. Talk into the mic about what the camera can't pick up," she instructs.

"I will," I say. Her other tab chirps and she pulls it out of her purse. "Avery just texted. The cam on the door is down but . . . damn it, that's all she could do."

"The other security cameras are still live?"

Zoe nods. "She also told me to tell you to hold the passcard in front of the lockpad for an extra second or two. Just to make sure it can access the codes."

"Okay, will do."

With Avery coaching me via Zoe, I think back to how Josh talked me through placing the QuTap on Patrick's computer, how he was there with me every step of the way. Suddenly, my chest feels heavy and it's a little hard to breathe.

Once I walk through this door, I'll be totally and completely alone.

"One more thing," she adds.

"Yeah?"

"If someone tries to grab you or anything, use this." She flashes me a grin as she pulls out a miniature bottle of OC spray from her back pocket. "Avery wanted you to have it. She says it's potent, but won't do any real long-term damage."

"Thanks." My hands shake a little when I take it from her.

"Good luck," she says.

I put up my hood, dart toward the side of the building, and hold Giblin's custom passcard over the lockpad near the door for a full ten seconds.

Then the door magically slides open, and I'm in.

Unlike the grand entrance to Orexis, with its soaring ceiling and heavily guarded reception desk, this lobby is stark—there's just a black mat on a marble floor, and one solitary elevator facing me, against the opposite wall. I walk across the lobby and swipe the passcard through the scanner. The doors open and I enter the elevator, pressing the button for the fiftieth floor as I tuck the passcard and Zoe's tab in my pocket.

When the doors close, the space feels so small, almost like I'm in a brightly lit coffin. There are no mirrors on the walls, just white panels, and although it's a smooth ride, the elevator car moves much slower than the ones in the main building.

Flashes of heat creep up the back of my neck. I try to busy myself by pulling out Zoe's tab and toying with its video function. Oddly enough, it's the same model as the one Patrick bought for me the other day. I wonder if he expects me to show up here, since I'm sure he's heard about my escape from the hospital. I know he thinks he was acting in my best interests, but I'm still hurt that he didn't believe me.

But if he's here, I'll deal with him. I know what his

intentions are now, and there's no way I'm letting him take me back to the hospital.

My fingers swipe across the touchpad, but they're trembling, and the tab isn't responding well to my commands. Like Zoe said, aside from the semiconductor card, this tab is my best weapon against Orexis. I have to know how to operate it by the time I get into that lab. I try again, but no matter what I do, I can't seem to figure it out. I start to spiral into full-blown panic mode, but then I breathe in deep. I have to pull it together.

With only five floors left, I try to give myself a pep talk.

I'm the only one who can do this.

There isn't anyone else.

I can't fail my dad now.

A rush of cold air blows through a vent in the ceiling, knocking my hood back and sending my hair flying. It makes me shiver and yet it rejuvenates me, kind of like a brisk shower. With my nerves temporarily frozen and my fears numbed, I look at the tab again, channeling the same determination I felt when I snuck into Patrick's office with the QuTap. When I'm done studying the video app, I reach into my right pocket and grip the semiconductor passcard tightly, knowing without a doubt that I'm going to succeed.

This is exactly how my dad wanted me and the other survivors to feel before going to battle in Etherworld.

The elevator comes to a stop, and the second I step out into the hall I'm inhaling the strong scent of cleaning fluids.

I pause, looking in either direction to see if anyone is waiting in ambush. But the floor seems empty. Still, Zoe said Avery couldn't get to the cameras inside the building, so the quiet doesn't mean the security guards aren't aware I'm here.

I have to be quick.

I begin to walk, glancing at the numbers above the doors. Everything seems clean and new: the floor tiles and ceiling all made of white, marble-looking glass that practically sparkles with my reflection. The heels of the boots I borrowed from Zoe click along the floor as I veer toward the corner, moving faster and faster, the thought of being reunited with my dad spurring me on.

I pull out the semiconductor passcard, getting ready. I'm practically running now. 5010, 5012 . . .

I whip around the corner, and stop.

Cathryn is here, walking right toward me, wearing a slim-fitting red suit and typing something on her tab, her pale-blond hair tucked behind her ears. I didn't expect her here this early. I know from Patrick that she usually doesn't make it to her office until after the massive crush of the seven a.m. commute.

I shove my hand back into my pocket, hiding the passcard. She looks up from her tab and comes to a halt, her perfectly shaped eyebrows arching in confusion. "Regan? What are you doing here?"

Behind her is room 5020, the numbers etched in the glass above the door.

There hasn't been a lot of time to think about what I might

say to Cathryn if I ever ran into her again, but I don't think I could have predicted that I would actually just stand in front of her and draw a complete blank. I don't know why I'm this stunned. Maybe it's because now that she's only a few feet away from me, I see a woman I've known my entire life—someone who made me popcorn on sleepovers, and held my hand during my dad's memorial service.

The mother of my best friend.

"I need to get into that room."

Cathryn stands there frozen for a second, taken aback by my demanding tone. Her lips twitch a little, like she's annoyed that she has to deal with me right now, and then she corrects herself, her face softening a bit.

"Why? What's wrong, sweetheart?"

I hesitate, my other hand retreating into the pocket with the OC bottle.

"I saw my dad in Elusion. He told me—he said he's in room fifty-twenty," I say, still struggling to find the right words.

She clutches her tab to her chest, staring at me like I'm some kind of basket case. "I don't understand. You saw . . . your dad?"

Her "playing dumb" act snaps me out of my confusion, unleashing a geyser of anger within me. How can she look me in the eye and pretend? After everything she's put my family through and the lies she's told and all the people she's placed in danger?

"I know. I know *everything*. You've had him trapped here for months," I say, my jaw clenched.

"My God," she says, shaking her head. "Patrick said you were sick. I guess I didn't want to believe it."

"Stop acting like you care about me!" I bark at her.

"Regan?" I hear a tense voice calling out from behind me. Patrick is running down the hall, out of breath. "What the hell is going on? How did you get in here?"

"It's all right, Patrick. Calm down," his mother says, her voice pinched. "Regan and I are just talking."

"It's not all right. That's what I've been trying to tell you. The safeguards against nanopsychosis aren't working," Patrick says. He looks like he hasn't slept all night. My hope is that he's been secretly making those calls to the stockholders, trying to throw up a roadblock to Elusion's national release in two days, because we're all running out of time.

"People are becoming addicted to trypnosis and having hallucinations," he continues. "That's what's happening to Regan."

"I'm not hallucinating!" I shout. "And I can prove I don't have nanopsychosis if you just open this door!"

There's no way I'm going to let Cathryn know I have the semiconductor in my pocket and can open it myself. It's too valuable to lose. Besides, with Patrick here, there's a good chance he'll force the issue.

But she's already finding a way to get rid of me.

"Security needed on the fiftieth floor. Immediately," she says into her tab.

"Mom!" Patrick yells at Cathryn. "Call off security. I can handle this!"

When she doesn't respond, Patrick looks into my eyes and then lunges toward the door, pressing his passcard against the lockpad. He stands back, waiting for the door to slide open, but nothing happens.

"Mom?" Patrick says, touching his passcard on the lockpad again. "Why can't I get in?"

Her lips tighten, like she is really irritated that all this drama has occurred before her morning coffee. "I don't have the faintest idea."

He hesitates a beat as he steps away from me, his gaze fixed on his mother. "Why don't you try your passcard? If that doesn't work, I'll get someone in security to override the system."

"Of course." She presses her card against the lockpad.

The light above the door flashes green as it swooshes open. This is the moment where all the lies finally stop. This is the moment that changes everything.

I push past Patrick and Cathryn, and dash inside with Zoe's tab at the ready, holding my breath.

But once the autosensor lights flicker on, there's nothing to see.

It's just a regular tech lab filled with quantum computers, tall glass tables assembled into two half circles, stainless steel cabinets lining the walls, and two InstaComm screens looming over it all.

I step inside the room, still holding on to Zoe's tab. There are no signs that my dad was ever here. Not a used IV bag or an Equip component discarded on the floor. Every surface is gleaming and spotless.

My stomach lurches, and I steady myself on the cabinet, my hands clutching the edges like my life depends on it. My dad seemed so sure he was being held here, but from the looks of things, Cathryn either moved him, or . . .

Killed him.

Patrick enters the room and puts an arm around me. "I know what you're feeling seems real, but it's not. Your mind is playing tricks on you."

"Where is he?" I murmur, turning toward the door, where Cathryn is standing, perfectly poised. "What have you done with my dad?"

"I don't know what you're talking about," she says, looking down at her tab and mindlessly typing away.

He can't be dead. Cathryn may be many terrible things, but a ruthless, cold-blooded murderer? Is she really capable of that? She's had months to kill my dad, and up until now she has kept him alive. Why would she kill him after all this time? Is it because she knew I was onto her?

"He was here; I know he was." I pull away from Patrick and charge toward Cathryn. "He was in this room and you're trying to cover it up."

Patrick chases after me and tries to get in between us. Then he says to me, "Ree, your dad died. Four months ago. In the plane crash, remember?"

An image of Josh suddenly pops into my mind. He's leaning

over me in the Red Canyon Escape, his face collapsing with horror as he watches me disappear right in front of him. That's how I feel right now. Like I'm watching someone vanish and there's nothing I can do to help. If I can't find my father, how can I save Josh? What will happen to the rest of the survivors?

"No, he's alive," I say. "I just saw him. And your mother has taken him away!"

"Drive her home. She needs some rest," Cathryn says to Patrick, though her attention is still focused on her tab. "Poor thing. I think this has all been too much for her."

"Home?" he says angrily.

Cathryn looks up from her tab.

"Regan needs to go back to the hospital," Patrick continues. "And we need to find these hackers who are hijacking the signal, and—"

"Our researchers have looked into that," Cathryn interrupts. "They couldn't find anything wrong with the signal between the Equips."

"Well, they're wrong!" Patrick follows her into the hall. "Look at what's happened to Regan. What more proof do you need?"

I trail behind him, standing by his side as he confronts his mom. Cathryn's eyes flick over to me, and for a moment, I see a bit of warmth shining through, as if she actually cares.

"Regan's problems have nothing to do with Elusion," she says softly. "She's suffered a horrendous loss, and her mother . . . Well, it's no secret that she's been very unstable since losing David."

I cannot believe she went there. True, my mom has had a rough time since my dad "died," but who could blame her? Cathryn is responsible for all the pain and suffering my mother has endured over the past four months, and she's trying to spin it so that no one will take me or my mom seriously?

"You destroyed my family," I say with conviction. "And by putting Elusion on the market, you're about to destroy millions more."

"Why can't we temporarily halt production and do a product recall? At least until we get all this under control?" Patrick pleads with Cathryn.

"It's too late for that," she says. "We have millions of orders to fill."

"It's not too late," he urges. "If we can make some changes, then—"

"No!" Cathryn says sternly. "We've already made enough changes."

"But none of them are working, are they?" I say. Her left eye twitches slightly, hinting at the stress of her deception. "My dad knew the sodium pentothal wasn't a good solution. He knew that users would build up a resistance to it eventually. But you and Bryce submitted it to the CIT behind his back. When he found out, he was furious, and that's when you both trapped him in Elu—"

The back of her hand comes around and hits my cheek, the crack resounding through the air as her rings dig into my skin.

"Mom!" Patrick yells, rushing to my aid. Cathryn stands

still, as if she's just as surprised as we are. I bring my hand up to my cheek. It feels wet. I look at my fingers. Blood is trickling down them.

Patrick turns back toward his mother, furious. "What is wrong with you?"

"I'm sorry," she says. "I just couldn't stand here and listen to her accusations anymore."

"That's it," Patrick says. "I'm going to the board of directors and demanding an immediate recall."

"Don't be ridiculous. You don't have the authority to call a board meeting," Cathryn says.

"I don't give a shit! This has gone on too long. And if you try and stop me, I'll go straight to the press," he says. For the first time I can remember, he's going against his mother's wishes.

"If you make any public statement about Elusion, it won't be as an employee of Orexis," she counters.

"What's that supposed to mean?" Patrick asks.

Cathryn opens her mouth, but nothing comes out. It's almost as though she's having second thoughts, and whatever monster she has become is still capable of having some kind of maternal instincts.

But then she clears her throat and says, "If you're not willing to defend the product that David created, which the CIT has certified and approved, then I think you need to resign. There are plenty other product designers here who are willing to step in and stand by our work and protect David's legacy."

I take a step toward her, fists clenched. "How dare you!"

Patrick grabs my arm, pushing me back as he takes the lead. "So you're giving me an ultimatum? If I say anything, you're going to fire me?"

"Don't throw your future away like this," she says to him. "You've spent your entire life preparing to be a major part of Orexis. Think about how hard you've worked."

Patrick is still holding on to my arm, standing in front of me, his body acting as a barricade between me and his mother.

"If you want to run this company one day, you have to be a leader," she goes on. "You have to make tough decisions. Your father couldn't handle it. Can you?"

Patrick's eyes soften. For a split second it looks like he's going to agree with her.

"Pat," I whisper. "Please. You've got to help me."

He winces and closes his eyes as he runs his free hand through his hair. "I'm sorry, Mom," he says. "I'm not putting my career above people's safety."

Cathryn drops her head as Patrick steers me away from her, toward the main elevator bank, on the opposite side of the building from the private elevator I used to get up here. We turn the corner, leaving Cathryn behind, but two burly guards are racing down the hallway, ready to cut us off at the pass.

"Mr. Simmons," says the bearded one. "We have instructions to escort you directly to your car."

Patrick's neck is suddenly covered in red blotches, so he takes a deep, calming breath. It's obvious now that his mom was sending messages to security and contacting HR from her tab a few moments ago. The whole line about Patrick needing to resign was just BS. She decided to fire him the moment he forced Cathryn to open the lab door for me.

I guess she sees him as a liability now. And for my sake, I hope she's right.

Patrick turns toward the guards and flashes them a brilliant smile, raising his hands in protest. "Hey, guys. No need to get excited over a family argument," he says. "Besides, we're leaving. When my mom gets in one of her moods, it's best to stay out of her way until she calms down. I'd advise you to do the same."

His congenial response seems to confuse them, and they hesitate. The elevator door opens and we all step in, tension still circling around us. Unlike the private elevator, this one is huge, its walls covered in mirrored glass. I turn toward the wall and see a light bruise and a small cut on my cheek from where Cathryn hit me, but I couldn't care less. My father's plan has all gone to hell. I have no idea where he is, or if he's even still alive.

No, I can't allow myself to think like that, or I'm going to lose it.

"I have to go to my office before we leave," Patrick announces as he presses the button for the seventy-third floor.

"I'm sorry, Mr. Simmons. I don't think we can do that," says the bearded guard. Even though he's twice Patrick's size, he flashes another nervous glance at his clean-shaven, round-faced partner. "Our orders were to escort you and Ms. Welch out of the building immediately."

"I need to grab my coat and my O2 shield," Patrick explains.

The guards exchange a worried look. "What am I going to do? Steal something?" Patrick adds, grinning good-naturedly. Although he appears relaxed, his neck is still red, a clue as to how anxious he really is.

"Sir, no one thinks you're going to steal—"

"Listen, I'm sorry you guys have to be in the middle of all this," Patrick interrupts. "I'd appreciate your discretion. My mom's been under a lot of pressure lately and she's not thinking clearly right now." He rolls down his sleeves, buttoning the cuffs. "This will blow over within the next hour or so, and when it does, she's going to be upset if I can't do my job because I've come down with a Florapetro flu. I'd hate for her to harbor a grudge toward anyone. You've been with our company since before I was born."

The elevator continues to zoom upward, and I know Patrick's words are getting to them. After all, they have a ring of truth. So much so that I'm wondering if Patrick himself really believes what he's saying.

"I have to escort you into your office," the round-faced guard says.

"Sure," Patrick says. "And when my mom cools off, we'll all have a good laugh over this."

Then he turns back to me, his eyes widening.

"Hey, you're bleeding," he says, handing me a cloth out of his pocket, his gaze pained.

"What's this?" I ask, taking the piece of silky fabric and holding it to my cheek.

"It's a handkerchief."

"And you just happen to carry it around because . . . ," I ask.

"I don't know. Your dad had one. And I thought . . . it was cool," he says with a shrug, embarrassed.

As I look at him, I can't help but feel a little bit sorry. He's still the same awkward guy I've cared about for years. And I know how much he loves my dad. He thinks he's lost him. And now he thinks he's lost me too. I just have to prove otherwise. "Thanks," I say.

The elevator dings and the doors open on the executive floor, but the desk area is empty, the familiar receptionist, Estelle, not yet at work.

"She stays here," the bearded guard says, stepping in front of me as I attempt to follow Patrick.

Patrick gives me a quick nod of reassurance before disappearing into the executive hall, the other guard following. I move toward the wall of windows, looking across the river at Canada. To think I was standing right here a few days ago, and my father was in a room only twenty floors below.

I could've rescued him then. But now . . .

I snap my eyes shut, willing my doubts away.

My dad is alive. I found him once and I will find him again.

"Ready?" Patrick appears, carrying his suit jacket, an O2 shield, and a light silver briefcase.

The bearded guard swipes his passcard and presses the button for the lobby. None of us say a word as the elevator drops, sliding to a halt at the lowest sublevel.

"I'm sorry about this, Mr. Simmons," the other guard says, his shoulders drooping.

"No problem," Patrick says cheerfully as we step into the small foyer that leads to the underground parking structure. "I could use some time off anyway."

The doors shut, locking us inside the hermetically protected garage.

Patrick's fake smile and happy demeanor fade.

"Come on," he says, moving toward his car and motioning for me to follow him.

"I'm not going with you," I say. "I'm not going back to the hospital."

"I'm not taking you to the hospital." He holds up his briefcase and pats it affectionately. "We need to go to my place and have a look at something on my quantum."

"Why?" I ask. "What's on it?"

"The security footage for the research hall." He stares at me, his eyes searching mine. "Maybe there's something on it that can show what was in that room and why my passcard couldn't open the door."

"Does this mean that you finally believe me?" I ask.

"I don't know what it means," Patrick says, sighing. "I just . . . I want to believe you're okay, Ree. I really do. But if you don't have nanopsychosis and everything you're telling me is true . . ." He trails off and then his lips tighten, like he's trying to stop himself from yelling. "I can't believe she hit you like that. She's never struck anyone in her life. And firing me for standing up to her? How vindictive can she be?"

It's good to see Patrick get angry like this. He's finally beginning to come around. If he still needs more evidence that his mother isn't just vindictive but part of a conspiracy that's threatening the lives of millions, then he's right, we should go to his place and confirm it. Besides, there might be some kind of clue on there that explains what Cathryn has done with my father.

I hurry toward Patrick's car, pushing away any suspicion that he might trick me again and take me back to the hospital.

"We need to make this fast," I say. "Josh is still . . ."

With my dad gone and no idea if he's even okay, I can't bring myself to admit that Josh is in his bedroom, attached to his Equip, unable to be ejected with his emergency button. The whole time I was in Etherworld, I never allowed myself to think about what my life would be like if I lost them both, and now that I'm in the real world, I might have no choice but to face that possibility.

But I won't do it. At least not yet.

Patrick opens the car door with his passcard and we both get in. He touches my knee and I turn to him, hoping to find my best friend sitting next to me. Not Patrick the billionaire or Cathryn Simmons's genius son or my father's protégé.

I need my best friend. Now more than ever.

"Just one more thing," he says as the engine rumbles and the headlights come on. "If you're right, I'll stand by you. I'll do whatever it takes. This will be *our* fight, okay?"

I take his hand in mine and give it a hard, desperate squeeze. I'm so relieved to hear him profess his loyalty like this, to know that he won't abandon me. That is, if the security footage turns up enough proof.

And it has to. Or we're all screwed.

"If I'm right, that means Josh is in real trouble," I say. "And you have to promise you'll help me figure out a way to save him."

Patrick doesn't look at me, I think because he hears my voice trembling and he can tell how terrified I am. Which means my feelings for Josh are probably more intense than he realized. But I believe him when he nods in affirmation.

Then he slams his foot on the gas, and his tires spin against the concrete, making a high-pitched squeal that rings in my ears for miles.

TabTalk Message
From: Unknown user
To: Leavenworth, Avery
5:52 a.m.
Hey, it's Regan. Zoe gave me a new tab. Any news on J?

TabTalk Message
From: Leavenworth, Avery
To: Unknown user
5:53 a.m.
No change. Will keep trying. What about u? Did u find ur dad?

TabTalk Message
From: Unknown user
To: Leavenworth, Avery
5:54 a.m.
No. When I got to the room, he was gone.

TabTalk Message
From: Leavenworth, Avery
To: Unknown user
5:54 a.m.
Shit. What now?

TabTalk Message
From: Unknown user
To: Leavenworth, Avery
5:55 a.m.
Just wait. Be there as soon as I can.

ELEVEN

A HALF HOUR LATER, THE SUN RISES behind the spire of the Erebus Tower, the most exclusive hotel and apartment complex in Detroit. The last time I was here, the mob of reporters was so thick I barely made it inside. But fortunately, there's no swarm of journalists blocking the entrance, or security guards roaming out front. I can't get caught on camera again, not with the police looking for me.

I press my palm against my cheek and feel a small round divot in my skin, still sore to the touch. Since we left Orexis, a ball of rage has been forming in my chest, and I'm glad. When I saw that empty lab, it felt as if someone punched a hole through me—causing my determination to seep out, drop by drop. But the anger is helping me regain my momentum.

Patrick drives past the building and shifts gears, suddenly swerving onto a small access road. It's a dead end, with nothing but a row of tall, thick bushes looming in front of us. But instead of slowing down, the car speeds up.

"What are you doing?" I ask, clutching the armrests.

"Parking structure," he says. "Those shrubs are just a computerized image. No one likes to look at a garage."

No sooner does he finish speaking then the bushes begin to shimmer, every green leaf disappearing before my eyes. The car zooms inside a concrete maze, the virtual foliage closing behind us. We begin to spiral around floors lined with tightly packed cars until we reach the top. Patrick pulls into a prime spot designated as *Penthouse Suite 1950AB*

My door unlocks and opens automatically.

"Where are all the reporters?" I ask, stepping into the lot.

"The condo's lawyers were able to get an injunction. They can't get within a block of here." He exits the car and briskly walks to the entrance that leads to the building's main elevators.

Within a few minutes, we're inside his apartment. I was just here two nights ago, but now it looks totally different. He hasn't gotten rid of his stylish, sleek furniture or replaced his ugly art, but it looks warmer and more comfortable. Maybe it's because the unusually bright sun is shining through the huge windows, casting everything around us in a happy glow. I sit on the edge of a boomerang-shaped couch while he walks over to the kitchen.

"Are you hungry or anything?" Patrick retrieves a carafe of orange juice from the refrigerator. He doesn't bother getting a glass, and instead sips directly from the bottle. He takes a breath and then another two big gulps.

"No, thanks." I haven't had anything to eat since dinner last night, but after everything I've been through, I don't have much of an appetite.

"I have plenty if you change your mind," Patrick says, setting the juice on the pristine countertop. "Be right back."

When he heads down the corridor, I spot a light yellow cardigan, tossed on top of one of the black-striped accent chairs. It definitely belongs to Zoe. It's strange, thinking about the other night, when I walked in on her and Patrick. I'd been worried about Zoe getting too involved with him, yet today she risked so much for me, and she's out there right now, trying to convince her father to pull rank with the Orexis stockholders.

I text her to see how she's doing.

Any luck?

The light on my tab flashes a few seconds later.

He's not at home. Still trying to track him down. Did u find your dad?

I'm about to write back when Patrick appears beside me, balancing a blue bottle, a box of cotton swabs, and his quantum laptop against his chest. "Is everything all right?" he asks, glancing at my tab.

"It's Zoe," I say. "She just wanted to know if I was okay."

"Zoe? How is she involved in all this?" Patrick sets the items down on the coffee table and picks up his tab. He types on the keypad, and suddenly the drapes begin to close around the wall of windows, darkening the room.

When I don't answer, he puts down his tab and says, "She helped you escape from the hospital, didn't she?" When I neither confirm nor deny it, he adds, "Come on, Ree. What else did she do? I need to know."

"Why? So you can yell at her?"

"I'm not angry, I'm just . . . frustrated, that's all. She should mind her own business. She doesn't understand what's going on right now."

"And you do?" I ask.

He grabs the small blue bottle, popping open the cap. "We should put some Dermastitch on your cut."

"Thanks, but I'm fine," I say, pulling away a little.

"I don't want it to get infected." He dips one of the swabs inside and holds the little ball of wet cotton up to my cheek. "May I?"

"The security footage," I insist.

"As soon as I take care of this."

While Patrick tends to the abrasion on my cheek, a wistful grin slowly appears on his lips. "Remember the wok incident?" he says. "I think that took about five years off your dad's life."

"If you hadn't bandaged my entire head with the gauze from that old first aid kit, we probably could have hidden that burn from him," I say as the Dermastitch fizzes near my ear. I'm trying hard not to smile.

"I was eight. Secrecy wasn't something I was good at back

then." He blows on my wounded skin, his lips close to my cheek and his breath smelling like oranges. My mind flashes back to our comet ride in Elusion and how he leaned in for that awkward kiss, and an uncomfortable chill runs down my spine.

"Okay, stop. I'm good," I say, craning my neck back and waving his hand away. I stand up and tuck my hair behind my ears, my cut still stinging. I watch Patrick's grin dissolve, and I realize how stupid it is to hurt his feelings just as it seems he's beginning to trust me. But I belong somewhere else, with someone else. And the longer we stay here, the longer it will take for us to get to Josh . . . and my father, wherever he may be.

"Let's just focus on what we came for, all right?" I say.

He sets down the swab and turns his attention to the laptop without saying another word. Once he logs on, I sit back down next to him, trying to ignore the tension between us. I lean over so I can see the screen, but he inches away from me.

I don't want this to turn into an ugly argument like the one we had in this very room two nights ago, when it became not only obvious that Patrick knew more about Elusion's problems than he was letting on, but that I didn't return his romantic feelings.

"I'm sorry if I'm being abrupt," I say.

"Forget it," he says, cutting me off. He logs on to his quantum and begins accessing Orexis's network remotely. "I'm bringing up the security logs now. This shouldn't take long."

Patrick begins to type, his fingers whizzing across the touch screen. Then a passcode prompt pops up, requesting special clearance. Patrick enters a bunch of numbers and symbols into the text box, and we land on an Orexis splash page. He keys in more digits, taking us to the Office Services section of the company directory, complete with a list of rooms and labs in the entire building.

"Here we go." Patrick clicks on a link that takes us to what looks like a user history of all the public labs in Orexis. Once he zeroes in on room 5020, groupings of numbers appear on the screen, one on top of the other.

"Are those employee IDs?" I say, pointing to the five-digit clusters.

He makes some enhancements on the screen so that the list is magnified. "Yeah, and this is really weird. The number 37194 is appearing over and over again. No one else has been in this room for months. They haven't missed a day," Patrick says.

"Until yesterday," I add, looking at the screen. "Maybe that's when my father was moved."

"But wouldn't security have picked that up?" Patrick clicks on a V-shaped icon at the bottom of his screen. His brow furrows in confusion when he hits a brick wall with an error message. "Shit. The video surveillance on this whole floor has been disabled."

"I take it that's not normal."

"No, it's not."

"Can we figure out who the ID belongs to?" I ask.

"Yeah. We just need to burrow into the HR database," he says.

Patrick minimizes the current window we're looking at and opens up another one, issuing a series of commands. It only takes a few moments for him to bypass the security of the Orexis human resources department.

Enter Orexis ID Number

Patrick keys in 37194.

Williams, Bryce M.

Project Engineer and Research Specialist

Security Clearance Level—11A

Years Employed—15

Citations—0

Promotions—7

I can't look away from Bryce's unassuming company photo. His eyes are partially closed, and his dark skin is ashen, with deep lines running across his forehead. He has a goatee, and there's a small ink mark on the pocket of his pale blue shirt. He looks so ordinary.

"This is bizarre," Patrick says. "Bryce Williams? This lab isn't even designated to his group."

"I told you he was involved," I reply, vindication seeping through my voice. Although we haven't found anything that can pinpoint what Cathryn might have done with my dad, knowing that Bryce was in that room less than eight hours ago seems like proof enough.

I think another thing has also been ruled out.

"I don't have nanopsychosis. I never did," I say.

"I believe you," he says. He pushes his laptop away and looks at me. "I couldn't have loved your dad more if he was my own father. And this whole time my mother and Bryce were plotting against him? And faking his death? It's just so . . . unreal."

"It's real," I say. "And we have to do something to stop them."

"You're right," he says, bolting forward and grabbing his tab. "I'm going to call Estelle and have her track down Bryce."

"Do you think she'll be there? It's not seven yet."

He holds his tab up to his ear. "Trust me, she's always early."

A second or two later Estelle picks up, and Patrick launches into a bunch of questions about Bryce and what's happening at the office. From the frustrated one-word responses on Patrick's end, it's clear the conversation is not going well.

I pull out my tab and check the Net. The sites are all buzzing with news of Patrick's resignation and contain a statement from Cathryn:

> *It is with great sadness that I report the resignation of my son, Patrick Simmons. Although we at Orexis are grateful for his contribution as chief product designer, we respect his decision to focus on his significant health issues. Orexis has always placed a premium on the well-being of our employees. The Simmons family asks for privacy as they deal with this delicate family matter.*

It's official. Cathryn fired her own son, humiliating him with some lie about health problems. Not that it matters, now that he's going to help me bring her whole world tumbling down.

"Bryce hasn't come in yet. Estelle tried his tab, but he didn't pick up," Patrick says, his gaze floating back to the screen of his laptop. "All of his personal information is included in this profile, though, including his home address. So we should just go straight over there."

"Not yet. There's someone we need to help first."

"Who?" Patrick asks. "Someone you love?" he mumbles half sarcastically as he refers to Josh.

I'm so surprised by what Patrick has just said that I don't answer at first. I've known Josh for a week. Is it possible I love him already?

"Josh is a good guy," I say. "Life hasn't been easy for him, but even though he has every reason to be angry at the world, he's not. He'd do anything for his family—or for me. He believed me when no one else did."

Patrick hesitates, the weight of my nonanswer sinking in. But then his clear blue eyes meet mine, and he nods. "All right. Take me to him."

When Patrick and I enter Josh's trailer, my nerves are fried. Driving over here during the start of the Standard 7 shift was a big mistake—traffic was at a standstill and it took us hours to get here. I complained to Patrick that it would have been faster to take the Traxx, but then he pointed out that the freedom of getting around in a car was what we would need in the long run.

"You!" Avery shouts at Patrick, her voice raw from desperation. "You did this to him. If it weren't for you, none of this would be happening!"

"We don't have time for this!" I say.

I try to move forward, but Avery is blocking the door to Josh's room, glaring at Patrick like she plans to tackle him at any moment.

"I thought you said there was nothing we could do if the emergency button didn't work," Avery snaps. "That's why I've been sitting here with my thumb up my ass."

"I know," I say, "but Patrick helped design Elusion. Maybe there's something he can do to help Josh."

On the way over here, I told Patrick about my father's warnings and what I knew about the destruction protocol. Patrick didn't say much, but he recorded it all on his tab so we could refer to it any time we needed to.

Avery doesn't see anything remotely positive about Patrick being here, and I didn't think she would—which is why I didn't tell her when I texted to say I was on my way back to the trailer.

"Tough shit. He's not welcome here," Avery says, standing her ground.

"Move aside!" I say, staring her down.

After a beat of hesitation, she backs up against the wall and crosses her arms, allowing us to squeeze past. Josh lives with his uncle, but there's no sign of him, which makes me wonder if he's merely a ghost in his nephew's life—how could he not come home for two full days? No wonder Nora was able to disappear without anyone really noticing.

When we enter the bedroom, Josh is as I left him, sprawled out on his thin mattress, his eyes still covered by the sleek black visor. I kneel next to the bed and touch Josh's arm. His body isn't as warm as it was a few hours ago. In fact, it's like he's caught some kind of chill.

"Avery, hand me a blanket. He's cold," I say, panic flooding me.

As Avery goes to the closet, Patrick rushes to Josh's side, picks up his hand, and checks the face of his wristband. "So his emergency button isn't working?" he asks.

"I just said that a minute ago, idiot," Avery mutters. She drapes a blanket over Josh's legs and pulls it up to his waist, then takes a few steps back.

I know that Patrick's worried. Ever since we were kids, he would shut down and become very quiet when he was most afraid. This is one of those moments for him, and a part of me wishes that I were a million miles from here—or even back in Elusion. Then at least I'd get that temporary wave of euphoria before my world splits apart.

Patrick types a few numbers into the chrome keypad on Josh's wrist. As he studies the silver face of the wristband, his brow wrinkles in concern.

"I'm trying to reboot his system, but it's displaying the same error code yours was. I might be able to use the Escape's coordinates to override the Equip signal . . . ," he says, looking at the screen of Josh's tab. Then he curses under his breath.

I try to get a peek at what he's doing, but before I can see the screen, he sets it down and says, "I need my quantum."

As Patrick dashes out of the room and to his car to grab his computer, I stay next to Josh and try not to let myself get lost in dark, frantic thoughts. I pick up his tab and examine it. The blue status bar is flashing along the bottom of the screen, as if attempting to engage the program.

ELUSION© Escape 010402 is experiencing difficulties.
Please try again.

"Did you see this?" I ask Avery. The codes for the Escapes are basic. The first two digits are always the same—01, the master program for Elusion. The second two numbers stand for the specific Escape within Elusion, and the last digits, usually a complicated and lengthy collection of letters and numbers, mark the user's identity. I've never seen an Escape code so short.

"That's so weird. It was all zeros a minute ago," she says.

Patrick bursts back into the room, his quantum already open. He's breathing hard, but I can't tell if he's excited, like a brilliant idea has come to him, or just plain scared. He sets his quantum on the edge of the bed beside me and squats in front of it. He begins to type.

"What's going on?" I ask him.

"Remember last week when I explained to you how Elusion was set up? Dumps with basic codes of security programs in them? Grouped together, they make up the master program for Elusion, which becomes active when someone turns on the app."

"Which explains the first two numbers," I say. "And the next two are the Escape number. But the last ones—that's what I can't figure out. It's supposed to be the user's code, right?"

"Yeah, but all user codes begin with the same two numbers: zero two. The rest are digits that define the user, in terms of quantities produced."

"But there's no other code here," I say.

"I know," Patrick says, typing away. "It's like Josh is using your dad's tab—like he's inside his domain. But that's . . . impossible."

"No, it's not," I argue. "I told you, everyone in Etherworld got there through my dad's domain. Zared made the chip and cracked the algorithm—"

"I know what you told me, but it doesn't make any sense," Patrick says, frustrated. "How could a homemade chip get into a state-of-the-art, government-approved security system? There's no way he could get through the fractal encryption!"

"I don't know what fractal encryption is, but all I can tell you is that everyone broke into Etherworld. And to do that, they had to be in my dad's domain." I motion toward Josh's wristband. "The code on here proves it," I say to Patrick.

"You and Josh didn't break in," he points out. "You were both in my domain, not David's. So how did you get into your dad's?"

"I don't know." I clutch Josh's hand, remembering our small argument outside the Great Space when my father hadn't come back from the ping tunnel. "Josh thought that maybe the Escapes that were still under construction were somehow connected to it."

Patrick shakes his head at me. "Well, he's wrong. They're not."

"Are you sure?" I ask.

"We don't have time to debate this. Just read me the Elusion access code in the corner of the screen," he says.

I read off the string of letters and numbers from Josh's tab, stumbling more than a few times, as Patrick types. I'm so rattled by his refutation of Josh's theory about how we got to Etherworld. It seemed like such a reasonable explanation, but Patrick's denial and utter confusion over it all has me thinking that we're stumbling onto an even bigger mystery— one that my father might have been trying to keep us from figuring out.

"Try the ejection button again," Patrick says as he finishes typing.

I push my forefinger against the red button, and we all stare at Josh, watching his reaction.

Nothing.

Patrick bites his lip as he looks back down at his quantum. He hesitates a minute and then begins to type again. He stops as rows of complicated code scroll across the screen. Every now and then Patrick trails his finger along the list, pausing to enlarge something before whisking it away.

"What are you doing?" Avery asks, leaning in for a better view.

"I'm looking for a weakness inside the programming of David's domain. I might be able to open up a hole in the firewall and disrupt the signal long enough for the emergency ejection button to work."

A silence falls over the room. I keep my eyes focused on Josh, trying to reassure myself that he's going to be okay.

Patrick yelps with excitement. "Yes! I found something!"

He types a few more digits and then says, "Hit his emergency button! Now!"

Holding Josh's wrist in my hands, I push my finger against the red button once more. The numbers on Josh's wristband flash in unison and then suddenly disappear, replaced by one word:

Good-bye.

"He's out. Help me get his Equip off," Patrick says, reaching for Josh's visor as I take out his earbuds and pull off his wristband. For a second I think I see Josh's lips parting, as though he's about to call out my name, but my eyes are playing tricks on me.

"Josh!" Patrick says, giving him a shake. "Can you hear me?"

"Josh, please, wake up," I whisper, pressing my lips against his ear.

Nothing happens until Avery begins to take the IV out of his arm and we see his thumb and index finger twitch.

"It's working," I murmur.

"Thank God," Patrick says. "It could take a while for him to fully come around. He's been under trypnosis for over twelve hours. We just have to be patient."

And so we wait, the clock on Patrick's tab monitoring the time closely. Every few seconds, my anticipation surges as Josh gives us another small sign of life—his eyelids fluttering, his leg shifting, his head slumping to the side, his body temperature rising. When we reach the fifteen-minute mark, he still hasn't regained consciousness.

"What the hell? Why is this taking so long?" Avery says, bolting off the floor.

"I'm starting to get worried, Pat," I say.

I can tell by Patrick's solemn face that he doesn't have any reassurances left to offer. But luckily we won't need them. Josh's hand grazes my arm, and when I look down at him, his eyes are open.

"He's awake!" I breathe excitedly.

I take his hand and bring it to my lips. The corners of his mouth twitch a little, almost as if he's attempting to smile, and I bend forward and kiss him.

"We're not out of the woods yet, are we?" Avery says.

"No, not yet," Patrick replies. "Josh? Squeeze Regan's hand if you understand me, okay?"

Josh's fingers press against my skin, very lightly, but even so, that's something.

"Good," I say. "Can you talk?"

Josh tries to open his mouth and force something out, but he fails.

Patrick turns to Avery. "I know you gave him a lot of fluids, but maybe a glass of water might help?"

Avery runs to the kitchen, and when she comes back, I give Josh a few sips. The water trickles down his face a bit, since he doesn't have much control over his muscles—but within a few more minutes, his jaw is moving easily and he's able to drink almost the whole glass.

"Regan," he murmurs. It's faint, but there's no mistaking my name. "I didn't think . . . you'd made it," he says, delivering his words through long breaths. "What . . . happened?"

I sit up and motion toward Patrick, who's retreated to the corner of the room. "Patrick pulled me out of Elusion. And he just did the same with you."

Josh glances over at Patrick, confused. Then he looks back at me. "But what about . . . the mission? I was in . . . the Alaskan Shore Escape . . . with your dad," he says.

"My dad's still alive?" I say, relieved.

If Cathryn had gotten rid of my father, there would be no way he could still be inside Elusion, fighting the program with Josh. But where is he? And what does Cathryn have planned for him?

Patrick takes a few steps forward, his hands stuffed in his pockets. "It was too risky to leave you attached to the Equip. You were under trypnosis for over twelve hours."

"Okay." Josh is squinting, like he's trying to figure out what's going on, and I hold his hand, hoping that will help comfort him a bit.

"He should probably take it easy for a while," Patrick suggests. "Maybe we should all go into the other room and let him rest."

"No, we can't let him rest," Avery says, squatting down at the foot of the bed, her brows still knitted together with worry. "Josh, do you know where Nora is?"

He nods, wincing in pain.

"Tell me," Avery pleads. "We have to bring her back."

"Island . . . Sector," Josh says, swallowing hard. "Near Hennepin . . . Point."

"That's just a few minutes away," I say.

"Yeah, but what the hell is she doing over there?" Avery murmurs.

Even though they're only separated by the Thorofare Canal, the Island Sector is totally unlike the dilapidated Quartz Sector. It's filled with beautiful, historic houses and old summer enclaves that have been handed down through the generations.

Avery bolts up and points at Patrick. "You're giving me a ride over there. And you're going to help me wake her up. Right now."

"Of course," Patrick says. "Whatever I can do to help."

Avery rolls her eyes, but at least she doesn't say something antagonizing.

"I'm coming . . . with you," Josh says, trying to sit up. He moves his legs slightly so they hang off the bed, and he tries to stand, but his legs begin to shake and he flops back down on the mattress.

"Josh, you're weak," I say.

It takes all his strength to push himself up again. "No one's . . . going anywhere . . . without me."

He stands up and takes a wobbly step. Avery and I both reach out to him before he falls, but Patrick is there in a blink of an eye, grabbing Josh and propping him up in one quick motion. He takes Josh's arm and flings it around his shoulder, helping to steady him, and I do the same.

"Will you take my stuff to the car?" Patrick says to Avery.

She retrieves his quantum and tab off Josh's dresser, then dashes out of the room, her boots clunking against the floor.

Patrick and I help Josh, our legs moving in unison, one step at a time.

TWELVE

JOSH AND I ARE SCRUNCHED IN THE BACK of Patrick's car as it idles twenty feet in front of the long glass-encased bridge, its two red barriers preventing us from going any farther. In our rush to get here, we completely forgot that getting across would require having the appropriate clearance.

"What are you stopping for?" Avery says. She's sitting in the front with Patrick, leaning forward with both hands on the dashboard, ready to jump out and find Nora herself.

"There's no way to get over the bridge without residency codes, remember?" A horn wails behind him, so Patrick presses a button and his window comes down a little. He waves the vehicle around us.

"Well, can't you make a few calls or something? You're famous, for Christ's sake. You can pay off somebody in bridge security, or maybe someone who lives here," Avery says, shoving him in the shoulder.

"Stop it, Avery. You're not helping," Josh says, his voice still faint. I can tell his strength is slowly coming back to him, though, just by holding his hand. His grip is getting tighter around my fingers; his arm muscles feel less slack. The redness is beginning to fade from his eyes a little too, but he has a way to go before he's back to normal.

Avery turns around in her seat and glares at Josh, her cheeks flushed with fear. "How did Nora get here, anyway?"

She has a point. It's a private island with a private bridge. There are no special access tunnels leading here, and swimming across the canal is out of the question. Even though it's not as polluted as the river, the water still has toxins in it that could kill anyone who might accidentally ingest it.

Josh looks like he's about to say something, but before he can, Avery twists around, facing me directly. "The semiconductor chip. Do you still have it?" she asks, looking at me through her dark-rimmed glasses.

Of course, the passcard. If it can unlock any door, maybe it can get us through the bridge's sensors.

I take it out of my sweater pocket with my free hand and give the card to Avery, who holds on to it like it's some kind of crystal ball that will show her where exactly Nora is and how she's doing.

"Where did you get that?" Patrick asks, his blue eyes flicking back to me in the rearview mirror. The blotches on his neck confirm what I've already assumed—he's upset with me again. This is the second time I've broken the law this week, and while I know I had no other options, it's clear Patrick doesn't understand just how far I'm willing to go.

"Does that even matter?" I ask, tipping my head at Avery, trying to be reassuring. "We can try and use it to get across the bridge."

Josh squeezes my hand and I turn to him.

"It matters," he says, swallowing hard. "If the chip isn't compatible . . . it could cause—"

"A huge shortage that could shut down the power grid on the island—which would be yet another felony to add to the list," Patrick interjects. He's still staring at me through the mirror, and I see how he's sweating. "There are cameras every-where too, so chances are we'll get caught if this doesn't work."

"I don't care how many laws we break," I say.

"Me either," Josh says.

"That makes three of us," Avery chimes in. She practically flings the card at Patrick, who catches it in his right hand, and stares him down.

"Fine," he says, putting the car into gear.

We slowly advance toward the red barrier. Patrick raises the passcard right before the wheels roll to another stop, just a few inches away from the bridge's entrance. A yellow beam of light flashes down from a sensor embedded in the barrier and fixes on the passcard.

Suddenly there's a beeping sound, and the barriers open

wide so that we can drive onto the bridge. Avery lets out a joyous yelp that fills the car with a surprising sense of hope, which we all desperately need. Patrick floors the gas, the canal passing below us in a hazy green-brown blur.

"Do you know the address?" he asks Josh, keeping his gaze on the road for now.

"Lakeshore Road," Josh says through a cough. "The only red house on the block."

"Plug the street name into your tab. Reporters have hacked into everything I've got, including my AutoComm," Patrick tells Avery, who does exactly what he says.

I lean back in my seat, tugging on Josh's arm and signaling that he should do the same. "How are you feeling?"

"Better," he says. "My legs aren't as numb as before."

"Do you think we'll be able to get to Nora in time?" I whisper, not wanting to worry Avery more than she already is.

Josh looks at Avery and whispers back when he sees that she's preoccupied with getting directions. "I hope so. The Alaskan Shore Escape was huge. We couldn't find the triggers. . . ."

"We have to get her out before she leaves Elusion. We can't pull people out of Etherworld," I say.

"It's possible she's still there. There aren't that many of us left, so it's taking us longer to destroy the Escapes," Josh says, lowering his eyes. "We've destroyed about half of them but we've lost so many people. They've all been sent back just like Claire." He leans forward and his forehead touches mine. "Do you know what happened to her? Or the others?"

"Claire didn't . . . she didn't make it."

His face falls, the grim truth seeping in. "I was so scared that you'd . . ." He closes his eyes. "But you're okay."

"Yes," I say. I touch my fingers to his cheek and then pull back a little when I notice that Patrick is glancing at us in the rearview mirror, his eyes filled with resignation.

The car crosses the island and onto Lakeshore Road, which travels north toward Hennepin Point, where large Victorian homes and remodeled summer estates dot the coastline. Avery almost has her nose pressed against the window in anticipation, waiting for a red house to come into view. Josh shifted his gaze to the passing scenery as soon as I told him what happened to Claire, and my stomach is twisting into a knot.

And it only twists tighter as Avery shouts, "There it is!"

Patrick pulls the car in front of a partially refurbished red colonial-style house with a huge wraparound porch. There's a tarp over the roof, as if the house is undergoing renovations.

"Doesn't look like anyone lives here," Patrick says.

Josh jumps out of the back without any assistance, his legs a lot sturdier than when he got into the car twenty minutes ago. But before anyone can run toward the steps, Josh walks around the car and moves in front of Avery, blocking her.

"You should wait outside," he says firmly.

"Are you kidding? No way," Avery says, turning toward the house.

Josh grabs her arm. "Just do it, okay? It's what Nora wants.

She told me she's hurt you enough. She doesn't want you to see her like this."

I glance at Patrick, wondering if he has any idea what's going on, but he only shrugs.

"I'm going to hurt *you* if you don't get out of my way. And it won't be too hard—you're an easy target," Avery says, her jaw clenched.

Josh backs off, and we follow Avery up the porch stairs. She turns around at the front door and waves her hand at Patrick.

"Gimme the passcard," she says.

He hands it over and Avery holds it in front of the lockpad, and after a few seconds the tiny green light on the front blinks.

Avery barges inside, mindlessly calling out Nora's name even though we all know there's no way she can respond. We follow her, glancing around the foyer and heading into the expansive kitchen filled with all the latest appliances. As soon as we see that Nora isn't there, we file into the living room, where the furniture is covered in drop cloths. There's no sign of Nora.

"What's this?" Avery asks as she grabs a dusty photocube off the mantel. She shakes it, revealing a flurry of pictures of a family, including a person who is all too familiar—to everyone but Patrick, that is.

"Maureen," I murmur as an image of a girl hugging a German shepherd puppy floats in front of me. She's the same girl we found with Nora's tab inside an abandoned house in the Quartz Sector. The same girl Avery took to the hospital and waited with while she was rushed into brain surgery.

And then another photo rises to the surface. One of Nora and Maureen, in the very room we're standing in, their arms around each other, laughing.

"Is that someone you know? From Etherworld?" Patrick asks me.

Avery's eyes begin to water as she turns to Josh. "Is this Maureen's house? Was Nora staying here with her?" When he doesn't answer, she shouts, "Tell me, Josh!"

"It's not what it looks like," he says. "They're just friends. They met each other through this Stealth group and got hooked on Elusion together. They used to hijack their Equips here, that's all."

Avery looks at him, shaking her head. It's the first and only time I've ever seen her at a loss for words. I know she's wondering the same thing I am: Maybe Nora ran away for a reason. Maybe she was cheating on Avery.

Avery starts shaking, and the photocube drops to the floor. I need to defuse the situation before Avery has a meltdown. All that matters right now is that we find Nora and bring her home.

"Let's start with the top floor," I say. "We can worry about everything else once we make sure she's okay."

Avery follows me up the stairs to the second floor in silence. There are at least five open doors, so we all split up, with me running down the hall toward the very last room and Josh taking the first one, limping as he walks.

As soon as I enter, I hear Patrick calling out to us, "She's not here!"

"I've got nothing!" Josh shouts from the other end of the hallway.

I'm about to say the same thing, since all I see is a bare mattress on a platform-bed frame and an InstaComm wall. But then I walk in a little farther and see that there's a suite off to the left. A big inhalation for courage, and I turn the corner.

The emaciated girl lying on the gray couch barely resembles the Nora I met in Etherworld. She's dressed in jeans and an old T-shirt; her hair is longer than it was in Elusion. A dusty visor covers her eyes, resting against her sunken cheeks, and there's an empty IV on the floor, the needle from the tube taped to the inside of her wrist. There's a tab lying near her right leg, and even from here I can see the blue status bar zipping along the bottom. It's still active.

There's a chance we can help her.

"She's here!" I yell at the top of my lungs.

A thud of footsteps echoes from outside the room as I walk toward the couch and sit beside Nora, gently picking up her hand to look at her wristband. It reads:

Error.

I grab the beat-up silver tab and check it, too.

ELUSION© Escape 010402 is experiencing difficulties.

Please try again.

"No, no, no," Avery cries, her voice full of anguish as she enters the suite alcove and heads toward Nora. Josh grabs her by the shoulders, restraining her. Patrick follows close behind, stopping short when he spots Josh's sister.

"She's still in Elusion," I say to him. "You can get her back, can't you?"

Patrick pulls out his tab and begins typing. "I need the Elusion access control number. Can you read that to me off her tab?"

"That's not Nora's tab," Avery mumbles. "Maureen had it. We don't know why."

Josh gives me a look of affirmation that's become second nature to us.

He knows why.

"It doesn't matter. I need the access code from the tab she's using," Patrick says.

Avery kneels next to Nora, gently taking her lifeless hand. "Wake up," she says quietly. "Please wake up."

Josh crosses his arms, his eyes never leaving his sister. I hug his waist, as if trying to absorb some of his pain.

After a few moments, Avery looks at Patrick. "What's happening?"

"I've identified the weakness, so it should be a matter of simply—" Patrick stops midsentence. He leans in toward his screen, his brow creased in confusion. "This isn't possible," he murmurs.

"What's wrong?" I ask.

"The hole in the firewall. The code that I used to get through it—it's, it's . . ."

I let Josh go and he limps over to Patrick, staring at the screen. "What kind of programming language is that?"

"I don't know. I've never seen it before. It's as if the hole has been repaired and the code rewritten. What's even weirder is that I can see chunks of my original code, like the new code was written right over it."

"Do you think someone else is altering the program?" Josh asks.

"No," Patrick says, frantically typing. "All my reconfigurations are getting rewritten as I type. This looks like a . . . system error or something. No person would be able to make changes this fast. It's not . . . possible." Patrick looks up, scared. "I'm sorry. I can't do anything."

His words suck all the air out of the room, and for a second it's like none of us can breathe.

"Yes, you can," Avery says to Patrick, cupping Nora's cheek with her hand. "You have to."

"There's nothing more he can do, Ave," Josh says, his voice cracking a little. "She needs more fluids, though. I think we should take her to the hospital and tell them not to disconnect her Equip."

"Maybe we should take her to the doctors who are taking care of Maureen," I say. "Weren't they already making the connection between the comas and Equips?"

"I think it might be better to use my family's private medical service," Patrick says. "There's a doctor on duty. He'll have the ambulance pick her up and he can oversee her treatment. I trust him to take care of her and to be discreet."

"Good," Avery says. "We need to protect Nora's identity as long as we can; otherwise the police will get involved. And they'll never believe us. Everyone knows Patrick got fired from Orexis for 'health reasons' and Regan just escaped from the loony bin. They'll detain us all, and we'll never be able to destroy Elusion."

"What do you mean you escaped from the loony bin?" Josh asks me, alarmed. I realize there's so much he doesn't know yet. Everything that happened at the Orexis lab—my showdown with Cathryn, discovering that my father's body is missing—and what Patrick and I learned about Bryce at Patrick's apartment. But now that Nora's life is hanging in the balance, how can I unload all of that onto him?

"Patrick had Regan admitted to the psych ward because he thought she was batshit crazy. Then Zoe helped her break out, and the cops are looking all over Detroit for her, so Regan's on the run from the law now too," Avery answers for me, as poetic as ever.

Josh turns around and glares at Patrick, who's still on his tab arranging for the medical service to pick up Nora. "You had her incarcerated?" he asks, his voice full of disgust. "How could you do that?"

"It's okay," I say. "Let's deal with that later."

Josh touches my cheek and then focuses back on Avery, who can't tear herself away from the girl she loves, no matter how upset she is about what might have been going on with Maureen.

"You guys go take down Elusion," Avery says. "I'll take care of Nora."

Josh and I are sitting across from each other on board Patrick's seventy-foot luxury yacht, motoring out from the Detroit River into a muck-filled Lake Erie. A new weather system is blowing in, pelting the glass-enclosed cabin with big drops of dingy rain.

"I wonder what's taking so long. Pat's been down on the lower deck forever," I say.

Josh stares at the built-in touch-screen monitor on the table that separates us. It's displaying our coordinates, which Patrick entered in not long after we launched. A red line is moving along charts filled with latitudes and longitudes, carefully monitoring our progress.

"I don't know," Josh says, distracted. His thoughts are with Nora, like mine are with my father.

We all decided that Patrick's leisure cruiser was the best place to regroup and come up with the next step. Usually it's anchored outside the Detroit Yacht Club, but under the circumstances, we thought it best to take it out onto the lake.

"Do you want to go check on him or something?" Josh asks, tapping his fingers impatiently. On the way over here, Patrick and I filled Josh in on everything he missed, and it's obvious from the clipped way Josh is referring to Patrick that he's furious with him.

"He said he'd be right back," I reply.

"That's his MO, though, isn't it? Say one thing and do another?"

"He's made some mistakes," I say, "but he's trying to make things right."

"By pulling you out of Elusion and then throwing you in the hospital when you asked for his help? Do you have any idea how bad things could have gotten if you hadn't escaped?" Josh asks.

"He thought I had nanopsychosis," I reply. "That why he didn't believe—"

"Don't defend him," Josh says quietly, cutting me off. "He's supposed to be your friend. He's supposed to help you. Instead he keeps making things worse, and he never apologizes for any of it. And all that hero stuff with my sister? He's just trying to save his own ass. He doesn't think about anyone but himself."

"I know it seems that way, but give him a chance, please," I say, taking Josh's hand. "He's on our side now, I swear to you."

Before Josh can pledge allegiance to my best friend, the door to the lift slides open and Patrick appears, carrying a few high-end protein drinks in his hands. He places them down on the table in front of me.

"Any word from Avery about Nora?" Patrick asks.

Josh shakes his head, narrowing his eyes at him.

Patrick hesitates and then walks to the other end of the table and starts examining the navigation charts. "Look, Josh, if I could turn back time and change everything, I would. But I can't."

Josh shoves his chair and stands up, walking toward the window. "How could you do that to her?" he asks, nodding in my direction. "How could you put her in a psych ward? Don't you know her at all? You don't even know when she's telling you the truth?"

"I know you're mad. You have every right to be. But how about we try to put it behind us?" Patrick says, his eyes still trained on the ship's electronic charts.

"Regan told you what was going on and you refused to believe her. You just . . . treated her like some little girl who needed protection."

"How dare you talk about my relationship with Regan?" Patrick says. "I've known her for years and you just met her last week!"

"That's right. And I could see the kind of person she was the minute I met her. You've known her all this time and you have no idea who she is or what she's capable of."

I know I should interject, but I'm stunned by Josh's analysis of the situation. He's right. He did seem to understand me from the get-go. I trusted him for a good reason.

"You've hurt the people I care the most about," Josh says, angrily. "You're going to have to earn my trust back."

"Saving your life isn't enough?" Patrick finally looks up, his face red.

"*Regan* saved my life. Not you!" Josh argues.

"Stop!" I shout, standing up. "We don't have time for this. We have to move forward and work together. Nora and my dad are still in Elusion, and Orexis is picking people off one by one. Arguing isn't going to solve anything."

Josh's eyes meet mine, the anger in his face softening as he flashes me a smile, kind of like he's proud of me. Patrick runs his fingers through his hair and plops down next to me as Josh takes a seat across from us.

I breathe in deep and begin doing what we came here to accomplish. "Let's review the facts, the best we can."

"Regan's dad is alive and is hooked up to an Equip, probably somewhere in Detroit," Josh says, looking into my eyes. "He and his followers are carrying out an attack plan on Elusion so that it will self-destruct."

"They're also using Etherworld as a refuge, so their brains will be protected from an overdose of stimulus," I add.

"Okay, stop right there," Patrick insists. "Regan says that everyone entered Etherworld through David's domain using some kind of algorithm that gave them the destination codes."

"Everyone but us," Josh says. "I told her about the possible connection between—"

"The Phase Two Escape and David's domain? Good guess, but it's not possible," says Patrick. "Every app contains safety protocols to protect the user and prevent anyone who's not specifically invited from getting in. David's safety protocols weren't touched."

"So how did we get there?" Josh asks.

"That's the question," Patrick replies. "And what was causing the program to rewrite itself like that?"

"You mean when you were trying to bring Nora back?" asks Josh.

Patrick nods.

"What about Bryce? Maybe he was behind it," I say.

"I told you, no person could do that," Patrick says. "It was too fast, and I've never seen that code before. Besides, why would Bryce—or my mother, for that matter—want to trap kids in Elusion? Kids that neither of them have even met before? The bad publicity is hurting sales."

Silence fills the room, except for the sound of the boat's Florapetro-fueled engine whirring in the background. Patrick is right. Cathryn and her partner in crime are trying to cover up the danger. They wouldn't want to make it worse.

"Elusion was built to adapt," Patrick continues. "For instance, the ExSet feature was designed to provide the user with an exhilarating experience: climbing, swimming, rafting, and so on. Each time the user returns to the app, the experience needs to be more exciting. The wristband is monitoring the user's biosigns and the visor the visual response; then the data is sent to the program, which tabulates the information so that it can provide the best experience for the user. But there are limits to how it can react, and it can only make a certain amount of choices based on the data it's receiving."

"But what does that have to do with the rewritten codes?" I ask.

"David once told me that Elusion's like a tree, in a constant state of development. And like a living organism, it's made up of a series of codes, like DNA sequencing," Patrick explains. "But what I just saw in that house back there . . . was impossible. In between me freeing Josh and trying to break Nora out of Elusion, the DNA markers in your father's domain didn't change. They were replaced. The entire firewall was rebuilt. There's no way I can break through that."

"Back up," I say. "Did you refer to Elusion as a living organism?"

"Just in theory," Patrick says quickly. "No system contains the seven characteristics of life. At least, not yet."

"Wait, you mean the traits we learned about in basic bio?" Josh asks.

"Right." Patrick taps the glass table and types something into the touch pad that appears on the screen. The oceanographic chart quickly changes into a diagram labeled *The Seven Characteristics of Life*. The word "life" is in the center in red, with black arrows around it leading to seven other terms in green.

"Organization, metabolism, adaptation . . . ," I say, reading.

"Growth, response to stimuli, homeostasis, and reproduction," Patrick finishes.

"Elusion is organized," Josh begins.

"By dumps made up of basic code," Patrick adds.

"But Elusion doesn't have a metabolism," I say.

"Actually, it kind of does," Patrick says. "It's fed by electromagnetic radiation, just like all other Net systems. Unlike other systems, though, it creates new simulations, gets more users, and takes in more power."

"We know it responds to stimuli," Josh says, staring at the screen. "That's an inherent part of the way the app and the Equip respond to the user. And that might even explain—"

"The reaction of high responders," Patrick breathes. "And

that leads us to . . ." Patrick types on the screen, and the word "adaptation" flashes in bold. "I woke Josh up by exploiting a weakness in the code, momentarily disrupting the system. What if Elusion figured out what I did and compensated? What if Elusion fixed itself?"

"So Elusion is growing," Josh says.

Patrick nods.

"What are you suggesting, Pat?" I ask, with a nervous laugh. "That Elusion is alive?"

The boat plunges into a wave, and we all grab onto the table to steady ourselves. I'm nauseated not only from the sudden motion but from the realization that Elusion might be more powerful than any of us could have imagined.

"I'm not suggesting it has a heartbeat," Patrick says. "You have to think outside the box. Elusion was created to adapt. Maybe it's taken that adaptability to the next level."

"Are you saying it can make its own decisions?" I ask.

"Spontaneous cognition," Josh mumbles. "When a machine actually begins to think for itself."

None of us speak for a moment.

"Maybe Elusion took us to your dad's domain because it knew how much we wanted to find him," Josh says. "It went beyond the program's original boundaries to give us the best possible experience."

I can't help but wonder if this piece of the puzzle is what my dad might have been keeping from me and the other Elusion survivors.

"But if my dad knew Elusion was capable of something like that, why would he keep it a secret? Wouldn't he want us to know what we were up against?"

"Not necessarily," Patrick says. "If we're right, and Elusion is sentient, knowing the truth might have put all of you in danger. The moment you set foot in an Escape, the program would be able to tap into your thoughts, and use everything you know to its advantage."

I think back to my dad's instructions at the mines, about believing we could accomplish our mission. Would any of us have been able to do that if we were aware of how powerful Elusion had actually become?

Patrick is right. My dad had been trying to protect me and everyone else in Etherworld. But what about his safety?

"Claire was . . ." I pause, remembering how she dissolved right in front of me. "She was sent back right after she hit the target. Do you think it's possible Elusion did that on purpose?"

The three of us exchange a worried glance. "We should track down Bryce. He was the last person who saw David alive in that lab," Josh says.

"You're right, we should. But it's going to be tough to get Bryce to tell us anything," Patrick says. "He takes corporate confidentiality pretty seriously."

"We'll need some pretty good leverage, then," Josh replies.

"Do you think Cathryn might be paying him for his silence?" I ask.

"Maybe," Josh says. "We could check his bank statements.

See if there's anything suspicious."

"Do you think Avery might be able to hack into his quantum? Get his financials that way?" Patrick asks Josh.

"Let's hope," Josh says, getting out his tab to text her.

"Will she get the message? She didn't have a signal at the hospital before," I say.

"She told me she'd find a place outside to check her tab," he says.

"Tell her to look at everything," Patrick instructs. "Bank statements, paper trails, and any deposits that look suspicious. If Regan's right, and my mother's giving him hush money, we need to have some kind of proof that will make him sweat."

"Got it," Josh says, typing away.

"So what do we do in the meantime?" I ask Patrick.

"There's still one more characteristic of life we need to prove. And to figure that out—"

"We have to go back into Elusion," I say, reading his mind.

"And not just to a domain," he replies. "We need to get into the master program."

THIRTEEN

WHEN I OPEN MY EYES ABOUT AN HOUR later, I'm flat on my back, lying on the cold, hard ground. A gigantic arch looms over me, its fluorescent yellow tendrils pulsating with the regularity of a heartbeat. I prop myself up. We're inside a room with sleek, curved walls that are embedded with thousands of glowing blue letters and numbers.

"Patrick? Are you okay?" I ask, my voice encased in a strange echo.

"Yeah," he answers. "You?" He's lying beside me, both of us dressed exactly as we were in the real world.

"Good," I say.

Good, yes, but not even close to what I'm used to feeling in Elusion. Just like the Prairie Escape—the last destination Patrick and I were in together—this master program isn't triggering the intoxicating feelings Elusion is known for. In fact,

I can still detect traces of the shock I felt the moment Patrick suggested that the app might be developing an awareness of its own.

He stands up and offers me his hand, helping me to my feet. "This is where it all begins, Ree. These are the basic source codes that build every Escape."

"So this is the framework of each destination?" I ask, trying to focus on what appears to be a string of complex programming language.

"Exactly." Patrick takes a couple of steps back and begins to follow the curve of the wall, glancing in all different directions.

If Josh were here, he would be amazed by this place. It's too soon for him to go back into Elusion, so he had to stay behind. "So what are we looking for?" I say.

"Irregularities." Patrick walks over to one of the walls, examining all the symbols that are fixed in place like brick and mortar.

"How can you even read that? All the characters are overlapping each other."

"Like this," Patrick says. He waves his hands in front of the wall, and the code moves out of the wall and into the air, numbers and letters hovering above us. Patrick gazes up at them, the glowing symbols casting a soft blue light on his face.

"We need to find the code that was used to override my changes to the firewall," he says.

"And how do we do that?" I ask.

"We have to search for any errant syntax. It should show

up as a different color." Patrick gestures to his right. "Want to take that section?"

I head over to the other side of the wall and shift my hand in front of it like Patrick did. As the code breaks away and floats around me, I try to look for anything suspicious.

I continue on, canvassing the side of the wall. It feels like the room is expanding, but the ceiling is dropping at the same time, the arch of neon-yellow tendrils getting closer. I've looked at so much code that everything is becoming a bit of a blur, the symbols losing shape and flickering like a strobe light. I also feel a strange buzzing in my head, like something is crawling into my mind and mining it for thoughts. And suddenly, I'm thinking about the first time I went to Elusion with my father. We jumped off the edge of that cliff and went hang gliding at sunset—ecstatic as we soared into the clouds together.

It's one of the last happy memories I have of my dad, and I don't want to let go.

"It looks like everything's okay," Patrick says.

My hand reaches out to touch one of the electric-blue letters dangling in front of me. I'm not sure why I'm compelled to do this, but I can't stop myself.

"Maybe," Patrick says, continuing, "the code I saw was just an isolated occurrence that—"

Boom!

As my fingers make contact, the code explodes, the entire room shaking as blue debris rains down around us. Thick wires bleed out from the wall and snake toward the top of the arch, where the fluorescent tendrils have all but dissolved.

"What did you do?" Patrick doesn't sound mean and accusatory, just genuinely baffled.

"I . . . I just touched one of the characters," I explain.

Above us, a piece of orange code begins transforming itself into a beautiful, vibrant sun.

"Oh my God," he murmurs. "What's happening?"

But neither of us knows.

The walls begin to fade as the remaining code spins around us, expanding and then morphing into elements of a world that seems eerily familiar. Patchy bits of green appear under my feet. Another piece of code loses its shape and bends itself until it reemerges as the same gleaming hang gliders that my dad and I used. The remaining symbols begin to intertwine and blend together until the sky is a vibrant blue and a sea of white mist is floating up from the ground.

When it clears, Patrick and I are perched at the edge of a rocky cliff. Down below there are miles and miles of dark green forest. In the distance is a chain of majestic mountains with snowcapped peaks, which border a large body of water made up of shimmering swirls of turquoise and jade. Everything is subtly outlined with a translucent glitter, almost like fairy dust.

"This was the first Escape your dad created," Patrick says. "It's not even in existence anymore. The source code was erased a long time ago. It never even went into production."

I'm filled with a sudden burst of euphoria. How could I even think about destroying this? I turn my face toward the sun, sweet electricity being absorbed by all my nerve endings.

"I was just thinking about it before I—"

"Touched the code," he says, his voice lilting like this craziness is beginning to make sense to him.

I take a step toward the ledge. The deep cavern below doesn't scare me. I don't need the hang gliders. If I just open my arms and jump, I can fly.

The ground begins to rumble.

"Regan!" Patrick yells, pulling me back as the edge of the cliff gives way, the spot where I was just standing crumbling into the forest below.

I look back toward the glider, but it's turning white, fading into thin air. The corners of the land below are also fading, a sea of white flowing toward the center. Patrick and I are standing on the edge of the precipice, staring down into a crevice so deep I can't see the bottom.

Maybe I should be nervous, or worried, but I'm not. I remember my dad taking me here as one of the best moments of my life. And that's enough to remind me that this is where I belong.

"Time to go," Patrick says. Before I can stop him, he grabs my hand and presses the ejection button on my wrist.

"No!" I protest, wrenching away. But I'm too late. A blinding light consumes me, sending me home.

* ° * °

Everything hurts—my hands, my legs, even my teeth.

I'm sitting in a reclining chair, unable to move, but inside me, every neuron is firing with adrenaline, making me want to jump out of my skin. My vision is out of focus, and even though I hear Patrick and Josh talking, it sounds like they're underwater.

The ground beneath me shifts and sways, and I realize I'm still on Patrick's yacht. Other than that, my mind is scarily blank, like something erased the last few minutes of my life.

"What's going on, Patrick?" I hear Josh say. "You said the master program wouldn't cause any Aftershock."

"It shouldn't. The trypnosis at that level barely has any effects on the brain."

Aftershock. Escapes.

Elusion's source code blowing up the moment I touched it.

It's all coming back to me now.

Rough lips brush against my forehead. "Regan?" Josh says quietly. "Hold on; this'll all be over soon."

And he's right. Within a few silent moments, the pain begins to subside and I can make out the details of Josh's face—his weary eyes and clenched jaw. I stretch my fingers and he picks them up, grasping them firmly. I give him a slight nod of acknowledgment as I whisper, "I'm okay."

Patrick appears on the other side of the chair, crouches down, and presses his right thumb against my wrist. "Breathe slowly," he says. "Your pulse is racing."

"What the hell happened?" Josh asks him. "You weren't even gone the full hour."

"We had to leave," Patrick says, swallowing hard. "Somehow the master program started creating new code and was able to generate a fully designed Escape—one that we discontinued before the app was distributed to the test markets."

Josh locks eyes with me. "Holy shit."

"Homeostasis. Elusion is functioning independent of its environment. And it was able to conjure up an Escape that's no longer in existence," says Patrick, "that means it's found a way to—"

"Reproduce," I say.

Even though we have solid evidence now, and even though we've proven that Elusion has acquired the final characteristic of life, it still doesn't seem possible that a system like Elusion, an app and an Equip, has learned how to think for itself. That it's, by definition at least, alive. But there's more—I haven't told either of them about that kinetic pulling sensation I experienced. I felt it just before images of my dad's Escape burrowed into my mind.

I lean forward, still feeling a little unsteady, but Josh grabs me and helps me up. A beeping sound comes from the Insta-Comm wall, located on the left-hand side of the room, followed by a 3D image of our boat's position on the lake. There's a ticker running across the bottom of the screen, estimating our time of arrival at the dock in Detroit as well as the weather conditions for our trip back. Patrick must have reconfigured everything while I was still coming out of Aftershock.

"Why would the app do something so random, like bring

back an outdated Escape?" Josh asks.

"It wasn't random. I went there with my dad on my first trip to Elusion," I explain.

"So it's like we thought. Elusion is anticipating the user's desires and trying to fulfill them in any way possible, even if it's outside the programming limits," Josh says.

"Or maybe it raided Regan's user profile, indexed that trip to Elusion, and proliferated from there?" Patrick suggests.

"No, that's not it," I say. Josh puts his arm around me, and I lean against him, still weak. "There was this buzzing sensation at the base of my neck. It felt like Elusion was trying to tap into my thoughts. Not to fulfill my wishes, but . . . I don't know . . . to control them somehow."

"And that's when you touched the code, right?" Patrick asks.

"Yes," I say. Josh looks from me to Patrick, trying to catch up on everything he missed.

"It felt like someone was picking through my brain, searching for information," I explain. "And then, once the Escape formed, I felt . . . serene. Like nothing bad could ever happen to me there."

"Did you feel any of that?" Josh asks Patrick.

"No, I didn't," he says.

"Maybe that's because Pat's not a high responder," I say, pulling away from Josh a little, since I'm feeling a bit steadier on my feet. "But the two of us are."

"I'd agree with you, but don't forget I had that strong reaction while we were in the Prairie Escape together," Patrick says. "My emotions were totally out of control."

"But what if that had nothing to do with Elusion?" I ask.

"So you're saying the rage was real?" says Patrick, looking down.

"You were angry as hell about me and Regan," Josh says. "I can't say I blame you."

Patrick hesitates, surprised. Josh is offering him an olive branch.

Suddenly the InstaComm wall flashes an incoming call message.

Meredith Welch awaiting connection. Accept or deny?

All of us look at one another, the color from our faces draining quickly.

"What should I do, Ree?" Patrick asks. "Do you want me to block her? Or do you want to talk to her?"

I reach for Josh's hand and hold it tightly. As the seconds tick away, I think about my options: I could attempt to tell my mom the truth again, but I doubt she'd believe me, even with Josh and Patrick on my side. In fact, it might just makes things worse, even inspire her to confront Cathryn, which is the last thing I want. Cathryn imprisoned my dad for threatening to stop Elusion's release—what would she do to my mom if she thought she was in her way?

No. As much as I hate to keep my mom in the dark, I really don't have much of a choice. This is the safest option for her right now.

"I can't let her know where I am. Not yet, anyway," I say.

"Maybe you could talk to her for a minute or two, and reassure her somehow? I'm sure she's really upset."

"Okay," he says, taking a few deep breaths before he accepts my mother's call. Josh and I step outside the cabin. The doors automatically open and close behind us, so we won't be seen, but there's a sliver of window that will allow us to look on as Patrick stonewalls her.

As the boat's location chart disappears and my mom's face begins to materialize on the screen, he tucks in his shirt, making himself presentable. But when she comes into full view, I cover my mouth to hide the gasp that's building in my throat. Her reddened eyes, her runny nose—she looks exactly the way she did the day of my father's memorial service.

Then I hear her panicked voice.

"Patrick, thank God! I've been trying to reach you for hours!"

I bet she was trying to contact him at the office, at the apartment, and on his tab; but since he's been avoiding talking to anyone since the story about Anthony's death went live, maybe he hasn't been checking his call logs or texts that carefully.

"Sorry. I've shut down my tab. There's been some trouble at work."

"I heard. Are you all right? That statement said something about you being sick," my mom says.

"I'm fine. The whole thing is a big misunderstanding," Patrick says, straightening his posture as if it might get him through his lie without detection.

"I'm worried about Regan," she says. "Has she tried to contact you? She left the hospital this morning. No one has seen her since."

"I know. I've been trying to track her down too, but I haven't had any luck," Patrick replies.

"Do you think she's going to believe him?" Josh whispers.

I shrug, and try to shake off a huge wave of guilt.

"I'm so, so sorry. I wish I knew where she was." Patrick lowers his eyes, like he can't bring himself to continue lying to her. My mom is visibly shaking as she dabs at her cheek with a tissue. The signs of strength I have seen the past week are completely gone.

Because of me.

"We have to find her, Pat. We have to get Regan back to the hospital," she pleads.

"Have the police come up with any leads?"

"No," my mom says. "The police are stationed at our house and at school. They said security guards saw Regan get into a car with another girl. Do you know who she was with or where she might have gone?"

Shit. They're onto Zoe now. I wonder how long it will be before they identify her and drag her off to some precinct for questioning.

"I don't know, but we're going to get to the bottom of this. You should just wait at home; maybe she's on her way back there."

"But I can't sit still anymore," my mom says through a sob. "I feel so helpless."

I cast my eyes to the floor for a moment, not wanting to look at the worry and pain that are eating her up inside.

"I promise you, she's going to be okay."

"If you hear anything, please call me."

"I will," Patrick says.

The screen fades to black as I bury my face in Josh's chest. Even though I asked Patrick to do what he could to get my mom off our scent, I guess I didn't expect to feel this horrible.

"Are you okay?" Josh says, gently stroking my hair. "That must have been hard to watch."

"I never thought I'd betray her like this," I say.

He holds me tighter. "You haven't betrayed her. You're—"

"Please don't say I'm trying to protect her."

"Actually, I was going to say you had to do it to protect *us*. And that you're really brave."

I look up at him, and he gives me a small smile I just can't return. Not this time. "I don't feel brave, Josh. I feel . . . lost."

Before Josh can answer me, the cabin door slides open and we pull away from each other. Patrick is standing there, holding his tab, his face hard as stone.

"I just got a message from Bryce," he says. "He wants to see us."

TabTalk Message
From: Heywood, Josh
To: Leavenworth, Avery
1:45 p.m.
How's Nora? What did the drs say?

TabTalk Message
From: Leavenworth, Avery
To: Heywood, Josh
1:52 p.m.
Stable for now. Drs monitoring closely. They brought in a bioengineering specialist.

TabTalk Message
From: Heywood, Josh
To: Leavenworth, Avery
1:56 p.m.
Good. No media, right? Still flying under the radar?

TabTalk Message
From: Leavenworth, Avery
To: Heywood, Josh
1:56 p.m.
No press leaks. For now.

TabTalk Message
From: Heywood, Josh

To: Leavenworth, Avery
1:57 p.m.
On our way to Bryce's. Got any info on him?

TabTalk Message
From: Leavenworth, Avery
To: Heywood, Josh
1:57 p.m.
Found sketchy Swiss bank accounts. Lots of weird transactions.

TabTalk Message
From: Heywood, Josh
To: Leavenworth, Avery
1:57 p.m.
Send me the acct statements asap.

TabTalk Message
From: Leavenworth, Avery
To: Heywood, Josh
1:58 p.m.
OK. But this is the last favor until we talk about Maureen.

FOURTEEN

"GIVE ME ONE GOOD REASON WHY I shouldn't punch this asshole the minute we see him?" Josh says.

We're standing near Patrick's car, parked in the middle of a cul-de-sac in the Woods Sector, the most exclusive suburb of Detroit. Each one of the nearly fifty homes is encapsulated in its own individual protective Zeoform "bubble" that lets the owner regulate air quality and temperature. Even though we're directly in front of Bryce's driveway, we can't go any farther, blocked by the clear yet impenetrable wall of the bubble. Behind the three-story granite house, I can make out deck chairs and a glimmering infinity pool.

"He deserves worse than that." Patrick pushes his hair out of his eyes, and then narrows them on Bryce's house.

"Do you think he has David hidden somewhere on the grounds?" Josh asks.

"Doubtful. If my mom really is involved in this, there's no way she'd keep David in close range," Patrick says, "especially if she thought people were on to them."

"Also, doesn't Bryce have a wife and kids?" I ask. "I don't think he'd want to get his family involved."

"He's going through a divorce, but still, you're right," Patrick says. "What kind of person doesn't want to protect his own family?"

Patrick's tone is resigned, and I know he's thinking about his own mother when he says that.

"The gate's wireless biometric," Josh says, pointing toward a thin line in the plastic. It forms a large half circle, big enough for a moving van to squeeze through. On the other side of the dome is a winding stone drive, surrounded by more leafy green trees.

"Is there a visitor access button anywhere?" I ask.

"No. He included an access code in his text," Patrick says, pulling out his tab and typing something in.

The half circle becomes more obvious and the gate lifts, sliding into the plastic above. We enter the terrarium-like space, and as the gate shuts behind us, we take off our O2 shields, hook them onto our belt loops, and breathe in the purified air.

We head toward the front door fast and determined, with me in the lead, spurred on by a nervous energy that makes me feel more awake than I have in days. While I'd like nothing more than to level Bryce with all my outrage, another approach might work better.

"I know you guys want to kick Bryce's ass, and believe me, I do too." I climb up the front steps and take a deep breath. "But the mission here is to find out everything we can about my dad and Elusion. Roughing him up isn't going to help. After all, he must have asked us here for a reason. So we have to try and be calm, okay?"

"Fine," Patrick says through a frustrated sigh.

"Avery sent me the statements from those Swiss banks, so we have that in our back pocket if he doesn't come clean," says Josh, placing a warm, comforting hand on my lower back.

"And if he does, I'll make sure I get it all on my tab." Patrick pulls the device out of his pocket, turns on the audio recording function, and slips it back into his pocket, where it could remainin undetected.

But before we can request entry to the house or finalize any more interrogation tactics, the door slides open. Bryce is standing in front of us, holding a tulip-shaped glass in his left hand and reeking of alcohol. His dark brown eyes are puffy around the rims and his face is unshaven. He's wearing a faded sweatshirt that has the Orexis logo emblazoned near the left shoulder and a pair of beat-up moccasins—a far cry from the suits I've seen him in at the office.

"Come in, come in," Bryce says, waving at us and slurring his words. "Please excuse the mess. I'm sorry, terribly sorry. I just didn't have time to clean up."

When Bryce gives us a warm smile, I glance at Josh, who looks just as confused as I am. It's as if Bryce is acting like we're here for some kind of social call.

Bryce moves away from the door and Patrick lunges at him, but Josh holds him back. "Remember what Regan said," Josh whispers.

We step inside a grand foyer with a crystal chandelier and follow Bryce down a hallway. A photo wall comes to life, unleashing a cascade of family pictures—his two sons playing basketball on an indoor court; his ex-wife dancing with him at a wedding; a professional portrait of everyone, taken behind the dining table at Thanksgiving.

It seems too hard to believe. How could such a family man hurt anyone, especially one of his coworkers and a bunch of innocent kids?

Bryce staggers into a room and points toward a sleek couch. "Go on, have a seat," he says, kicking aside one of the many tall-neck bottles that are littering the carpet.

"We don't want to sit down," Josh says.

"Are you sure? You've come a long way and everything." Bryce takes another sip of his drink. "Guests should be comfortable, right?"

"Where's my dad?" I ask.

Bryce bows his head, not wanting to hold my gaze. "Cathryn said you found out what we've done somehow, and I . . . I feel so, so horrible. About everything. It's . . . unforgivable.

231

Completely unforgivable." He swallows. "Your dad is at Orexis. Room fifty-twenty—"

"We checked this morning," Patrick says. "He's not there."

"It's just an empty lab," I say.

"He was there last night," Bryce says, a little surprised. "I was monitoring his vitals and I saw something . . ." His voice trails off. "I went to talk to Cathryn. She and I argued, and then she fired me." He shakes his head, as if he still can't believe it. "Had security walk me out. I haven't been back in that room since."

"And you expect us to believe that?" Josh says. "You were in charge of this whole operation. You were in that lab every day. And suddenly you're just out of the picture?"

Bryce sets his glass down on the marble mantel of the fireplace, his fingers trembling a little. "I was never in charge. Just hired help, constantly overlooked and underappreciated."

"We don't have time for this," I say to Josh and Patrick. "I think we should search his house, just to be sure my dad's not here."

"Look all you want," Bryce says. "*Mi casa es su casa.*"

Patrick stands guard over Bryce, making sure he doesn't do anything to surprise us—though that would be a miracle, given the state he's in.

I take Josh's arm and lead him out into the foyer. Then we duck into the living room, where the entire back of the house is open to the pool—part of the lush, protected world within the dome. I scan the wide, empty spaces surrounding the modern furniture, as if my dad might suddenly materialize, but as we move out of the living room and on to the next room and the next, it's obvious that he isn't here. If Bryce is telling the truth, he may have vanished for real this time. Josh wraps an arm around me, but it doesn't help.

When we return, Bryce shoots us a smile that sends a chill through me. "How could you do this?" I say, my voice cracking. "My dad trusted you."

"I used to deserve that trust," Bryce says wistfully. "I was a good person. And I would've stayed that way, if I'd never worked at Orexis."

"What do you mean?" asks Josh.

"I was doing all this research on trypnosis. Groundbreaking research. Research that was changing science and technology. But Patrick and David were the ones getting all the credit," Bryce explains, his words tumbling over one another. "They were the faces of the product. They were the ones calling all the shots. It was tearing me apart, watching everything I did go unnoticed. Tore my marriage apart too." Bryce sighs. "Cathryn was the only one who saw how unhappy I was, and Jesus, did she take advantage of that."

Patrick gets right in his face. "How?"

"She promised to promote me," he replies. "I'd be VP of the entire company if I got Elusion through CIT and helped her keep David under control. I just . . . I had no idea it was going to go this far. I was just supposed to lock him in Elusion until we found a way to stop the malware. Everything else that

233

happened wasn't exactly planned."

"That's no excuse for what you've done," I say. "You've ruined so many lives. People have *died*. You never went to the police. You did nothing to help him."

"I know. I wanted to put an end to all this, but I was in too deep. I had to think about my family, and what the truth might do to them," he says. "And now we're too late."

"What do you mean?" I ask.

"We might be able to defeat a person. But Elusion, well, that's something else. And make no mistake—Cathryn may be helping, but Elusion is calling the shots."

Patrick's eyes get big when Bryce starts talking about Elusion like it's human—and for a moment they stare at each other, a look of recognition passing between them. All the theories that we've been formulating have finally been verified.

"How long have you known?" Patrick asks.

"That Elusion was sentient? Since you told me that Regan saw David in the Thai Beach Escape." Bryce gets up and wanders over to a black cabinet that automatically opens when he steps in front of it, revealing a huge selection of liquor. "I did the troubleshooting you asked me to do and saw how Elusion had overridden the programming code and sent Regan into David's domain."

Bryce grabs a bottle out of the cabinet—and I yank it out of his hand.

"But that doesn't explain why Josh and I were locked in

there," I say. "Or why it was trying to kill us when we were looking for the portal into the firewall."

"All I can tell you is that if Elusion wanted to kill you, it would have. I think Elusion locked you in there for the same reason it sent you there: user data suggested you wanted to see him." Bryce stares at the bottle in my hands, but doesn't reach for it.

"Josh and I weren't alone," I say. "Other kids are stuck in there, too. They said they got into his domain by creating a chip that cracked the algorithm—"

"Wait," Bryce interrupts. "A bunch of kids broke through the fractal encryption code?"

"That's what they think, at least," Patrick says.

"It's possible that when they entered David's domain, something was triggered inside Elusion that accelerated its evolution," Bryce says.

"So you're saying the chip might have been—" Patrick begins.

"Divine inspiration?" Bryce asks. "Possibly. It might have planted a seed of independent knowledge in Elusion, which was all it needed."

"They taught Elusion how to send people to my dad's domain by hacking in?" I ask.

"Not just anyone. A high responder, someone who was more susceptible to trypnosis. Someone who had been into David's domain before and wanted to see him more than anything else. Like you," Bryce says, looking at me, his eyes wild. "This is . . . this is incredible."

"Incredible?" Josh growls. "People are dying and others are fighting for their lives!"

Bryce looks down at the floor, as if ashamed. "I need to show you something," he says, heading toward his quantum. We gather behind him, staring at the screen.

"I've been monitoring David's brain activity while he's been hooked up to Elusion," Bryce says. "It's been almost nonexistent."

"That's because David and the others are taking refuge inside a low-stimulus area on the other side of the firewall," Josh says.

"David built a fail-safe into his domain?" Bryce asks as he stops typing.

"He built Etherworld to protect people from too much trypnosis exposure," Josh says.

"That helps to explain some of what I saw last night," Bryce says, typing again. A straight, green line appears on-screen. "This is his level of brain activity at ten fifty-eight."

I feel a flash of heat wash over me. Right now, this line is the only thing I have left of my dad, at least in the real world. I reach for Josh's hand.

"And look at what happens less than one minute later," he says. The green line spikes again and again, each time higher than the one before. "I wasn't sure what was causing the spike in brain activity. But then I checked his blood levels and saw he was suffering from a dangerous increase in cortisol."

"That's when I was pulled out," I say. "We were in Elusion."

"Your dad had a big spike less than an hour before, although not quite as intense. It was right before we lost one of his Escapes."

"He's hooked up to an autotimer that pulls him back to Etherworld when the danger to his brain is high," I explain.

"David also warned us that entering an Escape would cause our wristbands to reactivate," Josh adds. "And that safety settings could go off, sending us home before the Escape was destroyed."

"And how exactly were you supposed to destroy the Escape?" Bryce asks.

We all hesitate, not sure we can trust him.

"In order to help you, I need the facts," he says, raising his hands in the air as if surrendering.

After a pause I say, "He's hidden bombs behind the firewall. They have to be connected with triggers inside the Escapes in order to detonate."

"Of course," he says. "Two separate mechanisms, two separate sets of coding. No wonder I couldn't find them."

"And he told us that no one should be removed from their Equip before the protocol was complete," I add.

"He's right about that," Bryce says, pushing himself away from the desk. "Cortisol is a stress hormone, so pulling someone off their Equip in the middle of an increase is dangerous."

"Do you think that's what happened to Claire?" Josh asks.

"No," I blurt out. "When she died, her bomb had just hit the trigger. It felt like . . . Elusion specifically targeted her."

"Is that possible?" Patrick asks Bryce. "Do you think Elusion is increasing their cortisol production intentionally?"

"Elusion might be trying to protect itself," Bryce suggests.

"It's trying to kill us before we can kill it," I say, my voice just above a whisper.

"Yes," Bryce says. "If that's what it takes for it to survive."

I don't know how many minutes tick by before someone speaks again. Patrick finally lets out a breath and buckles over, placing his hands on his knees. "We have to get them out of there," he says.

"No, we have to go back inside the program and help them finish this. Or else Nora is going to . . ." Josh pauses. "If the program lives, she dies." He turns toward me. "Regan, what do you think?"

"Sorry, everyone," Bryce says. "But Cathryn is one step ahead."

"What do you mean?" I ask.

"For the past few months, Cathryn had me working on an antiviral program to help Elusion build immunity and teach it how to fight back against sabotage."

"What kind?" Patrick asks.

"It's an inoculation program, similar to David's malware. But this is made up of minigrenades, not bombs. They operate without a trigger and launch through David's domain one Escape at a time. If it works, the Escapes will be immune to his destruction protocol."

"How long will the immunization process take?" Josh asks, his eyes darkening.

"It should be finished at midnight," Bryce replies.

I swallow hard, thinking about how little time we have left. "And then what happens?"

"Since Elusion can replicate itself, eventually it won't need the Equip anymore," Patrick says, interrupting. "It will be able to attach itself to any network it wants, so whenever anyone uses an electronic device, Elusion will be activated."

"So . . . as long as Elusion has access to an electromagnetic signal, it will be able to access people's minds and take them into its virtual world, whether they want to go or not?" I ask.

"Yes," Bryce mumbles.

"Are you crazy?" I shout. "Why didn't you stop it when you had a chance?"

"I'm sorry," Bryce murmurs, his shoulders shaking. "I'm so, so sorry."

"But not sorry enough to send back the shitloads of money that Cathryn diverted into those Swiss bank accounts," Josh says.

"If Elusion becomes immune to the malware, it's a death sentence for anyone else who's still in Etherworld," Patrick says.

"You can speed up the destruction," Bryce says quietly. "Then you might have a good chance of beating the inoculation program."

"How?" I ask.

"I'm guessing David has to keep returning to Etherworld after each Escape is eliminated?" Bryce asks.

"Yes," I say.

"So you need to figure out what Escapes are left and open a ping tunnel between them. Then he'll be able to get from one to the other more quickly," he says. "But you need to do it all from outside the program somehow, or Elusion might detect it."

"But you said you couldn't even change the code, because Elusion was shutting you out," Patrick reminds him. "I had the same problem when I tried to revive Nora."

"Elusion is probably using up a lot of energy defending itself against David's bombs while absorbing the antiviral, so you might be able to find a weakness somewhere."

"But how do we figure out what's going on in my father's domain without going back there ourselves?" I ask.

"An optical imaging plate," Patrick says, his blue eyes lighting up. "It would create a hologram of David's domain."

"So you can see inside it, like a crystal ball?" I say.

"No, it's kind of a cross between architectural blueprints and a satellite image. But it would be enough for us to determine which Escapes have been destroyed," Josh says. "I think I can locate one."

Josh stares Bryce down for moment and walks away, motioning for Patrick and me to fall in behind him. "Let's go, guys. We have work to do."

"One more thing. I might have a lead on where Cathryn took your dad." Bryce begins typing on his quantum. "Orexis has been buying up real estate in the Oak Sector, commercial stuff like old shopping malls. According to the purchase orders, it was for company expansion, satellite branches outside of the city, that kind of thing. As of last week, Cathryn had cleared out parts of several floors in multiple buildings for renovations. I just sent Patrick her listing of real estate holdings. Maybe your dad's in one of those buildings."

I look at Josh and Patrick as I motion toward the door. It's time to go.

"This is far from over," Patrick says to Bryce. "I'm sending some personal security units over here to watch your house in case you try to run."

"I know you want justice," Bryce says. "You deserve it. And when the time is right, you're going to get it, trust me."

"Trust you?" I ask. I shake my head, the thought ridiculous. "I feel sorry for your sons. They're going to find out what kind of man their father is, and they're going to be ashamed."

As I leave, Bryce stops me, grabbing my wrist. Before I can protest, he sets something in my hand. It's an antique watch with a mother-of-pearl face and a silver band. My breath catches and I turn it over, reading the inscription.

Love you Dad
XO, Regan

I gave this to him on his birthday two years ago.

"It stopped working one day when . . . we were in the lab,"

Bryce murmurs. "I wanted to get it fixed. So I took it off your dad and . . ." There's an awkward pause, and his eyes start to well up. "You can give it back when you see him again. Okay?"

My fingers close around the watch, the steel cold as ice. Then I leave, with Josh and Patrick marching like soldiers on either side of me, hoping to never set eyes on Bryce again.

FIFTEEN

"DID YOU GET IT?" I ASK AS AVERY STORMS through the front door. It's after six, and we're running out of time.

She breezes past me and squares off against Josh, who's sitting at the dining room table, hovering over his tab as he studies Cathryn's recent real estate ventures.

"I thought I told you no more favors," she says. "Not until we talk about Maureen."

"Sit down and we'll talk," Josh says, kicking out the chair next to him.

Avery slumps in the seat, glaring at him. "I'm waiting?" But before they can even get started, they're interrupted by a cheery voice coming from the kitchen.

"Pizza pockets will be ready in a minute!" Zoe calls out, like she's about to host a dinner party.

It's all very sweet of her, but since Josh, Patrick, and I have made plans to return to Elusion in a few hours, these pizza pockets could actually be our last meal.

After we left Bryce's house, Zoe set us up in the Heights Sector, in a corporate townhouse that belongs to her father's company and is typically used as temporary housing for high-level executives moving to Detroit.

We all talked about going to the cops with Patrick's recording, but Josh pointed out that Bryce's drunken state didn't exactly make him a reliable source. Without proof of his claims, would the police even bother listening to his ramblings? So we're going to finish what we started, on our own.

"First tell me what's going on at the hospital," Josh says to Avery. "Is Nora . . . ?"

"There hasn't been any change," she says.

I join them at the table and rest my head against the back of the chair. I'm exhausted, my head spinning. As relieved as I am that we finally got the truth about Elusion from Bryce, I'm scared.

Elusion is murdering people.

And my dad is stuck inside it, desperately trying to protect the remaining survivors.

I take a deep breath as I glance over my shoulder toward Patrick. For the last couple of hours, he's been hiding out in the sunken den, quietly buried in work. He didn't say much on the way here, and I'm worried about him.

"That's good, right?" Josh says, hopeful. "It means she's not getting any worse."

Avery's leg is bouncing up and down, the heel of her boot making an annoying tapping sound. "I want to know what her relationship is with Maureen."

"There isn't much of a story," Josh begins.

"Great. Then this should be a short conversation, and I'll hand over the imaging plate you all want," Avery snaps back. "Was she cheating on me?"

"No!" Josh crosses his arms in front of his chest. "When we were in Etherworld, Nora told me about all the problems you guys were having. That you were fighting all the time. She said that you were threatening to break up with her for weeks."

Avery's cheeks turn pink, I think from embarrassment. It doesn't seem like she expected that Nora would confide in Josh about their relationship, at least not this intimately.

"What was I supposed to do?" she says. She doesn't sound angry anymore. Instead she sounds sad, almost defeated. "Nora was acting like a different person. Hanging out with all of those E-fiends, putting herself in dangerous situations. I tried to convince her to stop, but nothing worked. So I told her that I was going to break up with her."

When Avery's head dips and she begins biting her bottom lip, Josh reaches over and pats her on the knee.

"I didn't mean any of it. I . . . just wanted to scare her a little," she explains. "Just enough that she'd quit what she was doing."

"I know," Josh says. "And she does too. But when things

got tough, Nora started leaning on Maureen. I guess Maureen was in the same situation with her boyfriend and could relate."

Avery fixes her eyes on him, eager to hear more. I lean in too, waiting for Josh to continue.

"So then they started going to Elusion together, searching for David like the others—but still in secret because both their families and friends knew it was having a negative effect on them," he explains. "One night they made a plan to hang out and go to David's Escape, but there was some kind of miscommunication about what sector they were meeting up in, and they had accidentally taken each other's tabs."

"So there was nothing else?" Avery murmurs. "You swear it?"

"Nora loves you, Avery. Sometimes I don't know why, but she does," Josh says, chuckling in spite of his serious look.

Then, out of the blue, Avery and I both laugh a little too, the happy sound seeming so foreign and strange to me. She pulls her right hand out of her pocket and opens it, revealing a tiny, round, mirrored magnetic plate.

"You don't need a quantum," she says. "It can be used with a tab."

"Where'd you get it?" I ask, wondering if she contacted Giblin again and how many credits he might charge us for this kind of equipment.

"My dad had this in his office," she says. "It's not that impressive. Architects use them to create 3D hologram blueprints. And so do a lot of program designers."

"Okay, here we go. Food is fuel, people," Zoe says as she

enters the room holding a steaming plate piled high with crusty dough. The smell of melted cheese must have wafted into the other room, because Patrick finally joins us at the table, his eyes bloodshot.

Avery reaches over and grabs a pizza pocket. "You ready to give us a show or what?"

"More than ready," Patrick says, holding up his tab. "I was able to find the location information for David's domain through some programming logs I archived right after I took over for him."

"So the plate will be able to show us what's happening there?" I ask.

"To a certain degree," Patrick says. "It's going to be more of an accurate map of the current layout, but it won't give us any information on who's left helping him, or details about how well your dad's mind is functioning, or anything like that."

I reach into Zoe's sweater pocket and pull out my father's antique watch, gently running my fingers over the face.

Josh stands up and hands Patrick the imaging plate. Patrick studies it for a moment, then places the plate on his tab.

"Zoe, could you hit the lights? It'll be easier to see," he asks.

Once it's dark, Patrick points his tab toward the center of the room, and a holographic image—several feet long and wide—instantly appears. It looks like my old science fair project, where I attempted to demonstrate the construction of an atom. In the middle of the giant hologram are four deep-red globes the size of my hand, pulsating as if they're actually sending energy through the structure. They're framed by two rings, outside of which float black, bulbous-looking marbles. The rings and the nucleus are linked together with strands of red and black piping.

"It looks like these Escapes have all been destroyed," Patrick says, stepping directly through one of the black balls until he's standing in front of the red pulsating globes in the middle. "And while there are six remaining," he adds, "four of them are the core of Elusion." He points toward the thick red piping. "These red pipes are the ping tunnels that are still functioning, but as you can see, they are pretty far away from each other. All the black ones are ping tunnels that have been shut down."

"There haven't been any reports of Elusion becoming faulty, though," Avery says. "If so many Escapes have been destroyed, why is the app still working?"

"Because David's domain still has functioning Escapes. We need to destroy every single one of his Escapes to stop Elusion," Patrick replies.

"So how long will it take to create tunnels to link these Escapes together?" I say, still holding Dad's watch tightly in my hand.

"I don't know. Two hours, three at the most," Patrick says, shutting off the hologram. "I'm going back to my place to see if there's a way to locate the antiviral too."

I put my dad's watch on my wrist, snapping the latch of the band closed. It's big and dangles a bit, so I push it up until it fits around my forearm. It kind of feels like a shield, and since we're all about to go off into battle, I couldn't need it more than I do now.

"Josh, why don't you and Avery go back to the hospital and stay with Nora for a bit while Zoe and I go look for my father?" I say, glancing at my tab and the real estate info. There are at least ten old strip malls that Cathryn purchased under the guise of setting up satellite offices, and over the next couple of hours, we're going to search every one until we find him.

"No, Ree," Patrick says. "If you and Josh want to come back to Elusion with me, then you both need to eat and rest. If your immune systems are compromised in any way, the trypnosis might affect you even more than before."

"No," I protest. "If Cathryn has my dad hidden in one of these buildings, we have to start searching the area. Oak is a big sector; it will take hours to—"

"Regan, I can start looking for him," Zoe says, placing a hand on my elbow. "Pizza pockets can't be my last contribution to the cause."

"Shouldn't you be keeping a low profile?" Patrick asks. "The cops have a description of your car."

"I borrowed my dad's hybrid, so I can team up with Zoe," Avery offers. "I made a nurse promise to keep me updated on Nora. If anything happens, good or bad, I'll let you guys know."

"So . . . that's it? We just stay here and hang out?" I ask, glancing at Josh, who just shrugs awkwardly.

"That's it," Patrick says, grabbing his suit jacket off one of the dining room chairs. "Although I suggest you get some sleep."

"Are you sure? This seems so . . . stupid. Like we could be helping more."

And yet the moment I say that, I stifle a huge yawn that practically sucks all the energy out of me. As much as I don't want to admit it, the fatigue I was feeling on my way to Orexis early this morning is beginning to catch up with me. I see the stress building up in Josh too.

"If you two want to go back to Elusion and finish destroying this damn thing," Patrick says, "then getting some rest *is* helping. I'll text you when I'm leaving my apartment." He gives Zoe a little smile. "You'll let us know if you and Avery find anything?" he asks her.

"Yes," she says. "We will."

Patrick moves toward the front door and I grab his hand, giving it a squeeze. I feel like this is a turning point in our relationship, an admission that we will never be more than just friends. He pauses for a minute, hesitating as if he's about to say something, but instead one by one his fingers fall away from mine, until he fully lets go.

Once Patrick has left the apartment and Avery has gone into the kitchen to get us something to drink, Zoe turns her attention to Josh and me. "Okay, let me show you guys the upstairs. My dad's company is in the process of redecorating, so only one of the bedrooms is functional."

We follow her down a hallway. She opens up a small linen closet and pulls out a comforter and a set of sheets.

One of each.

For both of us.

I turn toward Josh, and he's staring at me so intently, my face grows hot. Our eyes lock for a moment, and then he turns his head away and pretends to examine the molding at the corner of the ceiling.

"There are some rules to crashing here," she says, handing all the linens to Josh. "The neighbors are super nosy, and the last thing we want is to land on their radar, so keep the lights low or totally off. And don't make too much noise, either."

"Right," I say. "Got it."

She waves us over to an open automated lift and we all get on the platform, which slowly rises until we reach the second floor. Josh and I step onto the landing while Zoe stays put. However, she isn't done with her instructions.

"The bedroom is the last door on your right. Oh, and try not to touch anything. We don't need your prints all over the place," she says.

"What about downstairs?" Josh asks.

"I'm going to wipe everything off with a microfiber cloth real quick before Avery and I head out in a few minutes," she tells us, the perfect picture of calm. "And don't worry about us; we can handle the Oak Sector."

Without thinking about how she might react, I spring toward Zoe and give her a big hug. She wraps her arms around me and hugs me back, but just when she's about to pull away, I whisper in her ear, "You're amazing."

"I know." She grins.

About fifteen minutes later, Zoe gets into Avery's car and they drive away with Giblin's passcard in her back pocket. Now Josh and I are here alone inside the bedroom, with only the dim light from one of the apps on his tab. It casts the room in a gauzy haze, and I'm whipped back to that moment in Elusion when I was fading away from Josh, my father, and the canyon that surrounded us. I'm filled with a fear that the world is about to end.

I can't breathe. I grab Josh by the wrist, and when I feel his skin against mine, the grip on my throat eases a little. I can barely make out the outline of his face—the blackout window shades covering the sunset make it seem like the middle of the night. I sense he's looking at me, and I desperately want to know what he's thinking.

Is he afraid we're going to fail? Is he worried that when we return to Elusion, we might never see the light of day—or each other—ever again? Is he aware that we might be living our last moments?

I can't bring myself to ask.

Josh steps directly in front of me, close enough to kiss. I hold his hands as his lips graze my cheek. "Everything's going to be okay," he says, his voice low and comforting.

I tug him toward me and throw my arms around his neck. "How can you be so sure?"

"I'm not. That's what you're supposed to say when you're scared shitless."

I laugh so hard my shoulders shake. "I'm impressed by your confidence," I say.

"Guess I owe it all to my military training."

I close my eyes and lean my head against his chest, wishing that this tiny pocket of warmth between us would last forever.

"We should get some sleep, like Patrick said," he says. "You can have the bed. I'll crash on the couch in the lounge at the end of the hall, okay?"

"Oh, sure," I say, more than a bit disappointed he's not going to be staying with me.

"Let's get you settled," Josh says, opening up a fresh sheet and spreading it across the bed's mattress.

As he tucks the sheet under the corners of the bed, the knowledge that I might spend my last hours of life alone twists my stomach into a knot of regret. I start thinking about my mom, and how she looked this afternoon on Patrick's Insta-Comm: devastated and scared. She has no idea if I'm dead or alive. What will she do if I don't come home?

I'm overcome with guilt, thinking about what this quest of ours might do to her. It must show on my face, because Josh stops what he's doing and asks, "What's wrong?"

"I keep thinking about my mom. If something happens to us . . . to me, I don't think she'll be able to cope. She doesn't deserve to be hurt like this."

"What about sending her a video message?" Josh's hands slip off my back and he reaches for his tab, which is sitting on a nightstand. "I can help you make it."

My lips curl up into a smile. "Great idea." I run my fingers through my hair so I won't look like such a mess. "What do you think I should say?"

"Speak from your heart. You can't go wrong," he says, turning up the light on his tab so the video app can function properly. "Ready?"

"Ready."

Josh counts down from three and then gives me a thumbs-up when he's recording. There's a long silence as I try to decide how to begin, but once I do, everything comes pouring out.

"Mom, I can't tell you how sorry I am. I know you're worried, and probably angry too," I say, my voice cracking. "But what I'm doing right now is the most important thing I've ever done, and if all goes well, Dad and I will be home soon."

Josh gives me the okay sign with his fingers, encouraging me to go on. So I take a deep breath, because the hard part is coming up.

"But if something does go wrong, and I don't make it back, then I want you to know how much I love you." I wipe away a tear as my bottom lip starts to quiver. "I know you think that you haven't been strong the last few months, but no matter what, I've always thought of you as the person who made us a family. I hope you can forgive me for leaving you behind, for hurting you like this. I hope you can find a way to heal. Because you deserve to be happy."

By now, my cheeks are streaked with tears and I can barely

talk, so I dip my head down and shield my face with my hands.

"I'm putting the tab away," I hear Josh say.

His footsteps grow closer, and I feel his arms loop around me. I lean into his chest, his T-shirt soaking up the wetness from my eyes.

"She's going to hate me if I die on her," I whisper.

"You're not going to die." Josh kisses my forehead and then my nose.

"Are you scared?" I ask.

"A little." He cups my face in his hands. "Want to know what scares me the most?"

I nod, staring into his eyes.

"The thought of never seeing you again." He tucks a strand of hair behind my ear. "We're new to each other, but . . . you make me dream about the future. Happy dreams. Know how good that feels?"

"I do," I say, taking one of his hands and lacing my fingers through his. I stand on my tiptoes, and soon we're kissing, our lips moving in perfect unison. I drag my fingers lightly up and down his back and shoulders as the tip of his tongue touches mine. He cradles my face in one hand while the other caresses my waist, pulling me toward him so that every part of us is together. His mouth moves away from my lips and trails down my neck. I arch my back, take the bottom of his T-shirt, and begin to pull it up.

"Wait," he says, grabbing my hands. "I don't want you to do anything you'll regret."

"I might not even be alive tomorrow," I say.

He runs his hand down my cheek. "And if you are?"

"Will *you* regret it?" I ask.

"No," he says without hesitation.

"Neither will I."

I'm in the dark, my body curled up beside Josh, my head lying against his right shoulder. I crane my neck a little and glance around, as though I don't quite remember where I am. But faint memories from the last hour or two begin to come into focus, and soon my thoughts are completely filled with Josh's lingering kisses and his hands gripping my hips. I press my face on his bare chest. He stirs, bending his arm to hug me tighter.

I reach down and grab hold of the comforter, which is in a tangled clump near Josh's knees. I pull on the fabric until it reaches a few inches above his belly, and then I let my fingers delicately trace the area beneath his collarbone. I close my eyes, trying to remember every single place Josh touched me, and my leg mindlessly lifts and winds itself around his thighs, my foot tucking beneath the top of his calf. I hear him yawn and feel his muscles tighten beneath me in a long stretch. His eyes open into two weary slits and his lips graze my forehead.

"Did you sleep?" His voice is parched and sort of gravelly. I like the sound of it.

"I think so," I say, planting a kiss on his chin.

He smiles as his hand moves down to my stomach, his fingers massaging me in circles, sending a burst of electricity through me. "What time is it?" he asks.

I sit up a little to search for my tab, but my night vision hasn't quite kicked in yet. "Not sure."

Suddenly he takes hold of me in this swift wrestling move that makes me laugh and squeal. In less than a second he's on top of me. Our hands entwine as he pulls my arms over my head, leans over me, and kisses me, hard. The moment is sheer, absolute perfection, and after what we just shared, I never thought those heightened senses were something that could be duplicated. But then I think back to our first kiss—deep in the ice cave of the Mount Arvon Escape—and remember how euphoric I felt then, how I almost disappeared inside that cloak of happiness.

But still, I questioned it. When I returned, things between us felt uncomfortable and weird, as if we weren't sure if what had happened was the result of how we really felt or a product of artificially stimulated euphoria.

Josh shifts against me, and my bare legs swing around his lower back, pulling him closer. I know I should feel some sense of modesty, but I don't. With my hands still over my head, I lean forward to kiss him again, but the buzzing of one of our tabs interrupts us.

It's like both of us have been doused with freezing cold water. That sound is a signal that either Patrick is on his way or Zoe and Avery found something in the Oak Sector or there's news about Nora. Whatever it is, it means the hideaway we built together in this room is gone.

Josh lifts himself off me and then rolls off the bed, searching around the room for his tab. He finds it on a dresser, checks it, and says, "Not mine."

I wrap the sheet around me and crawl off the mattress; my feet pad across the floor to where my jeans ended up. Before I dig into my front pockets, I can feel the vibration of my tab through the fabric. When I finally have it in my hands, I notice the time—8:26 p.m.—and see a new message from Patrick.

Five mins away. Be ready 2 go.

At first I feel a rush of excitement. Patrick must have figured out a way to create those ping tunnels connecting the core Escapes, and with just enough time to beat the inoculation process that Bryce started. But then I click on my inbox and see that I have two additional messages from Zoe and Avery, which I must have missed while Josh and I were sleeping or . . . busy. Both are from about an hour and a half ago.

Two malls down. Nothing so far.

Nada at the next strip. Moving on to #4.

My stomach drops, and I sit down on the edge of the bed while Josh starts putting his clothes back on.

They haven't found anything.

"Regan? What's going on?" he asks.

"Pat's on his way," I say, trying not to let anything detract from the last bits of resolve I have left. "We should get downstairs; he'll be here any minute."

Josh begins collecting my clothes and handing them to me piece by piece, including my father's watch, which I'd set on the nightstand. I put them on as fast as I can and duck into the bathroom, hoping there's something in the medicine cabinet—a fragrance spritz, cologne stick, anything that will freshen me up a little. Unfortunately, the only thing in here is an air deodorizing dispenser built into the wall, so I press the button and wave my hands in front of the mist, spreading it over my neck and hands. I feel ridiculous, but I don't want Patrick to have any idea what Josh and I were up to.

Even though he might have already guessed it before he left the apartment hours ago.

I feel my tab vibrating again, and I take it out of my jeans.

At the door, let me in?

It's Patrick. He probably didn't want to request access, because it would be on the log.

"He's here," I say, walking back into the bedroom to find Josh straightening up like a good houseguest.

"Okay, let's go," Josh says, leading me out into the hall, his hand perched on the lower part of my back.

When we arrive in the dining room, the lights automatically come on at the lowest setting, and we open the door for Patrick. He comes in carrying three Equip visors, earbuds, and wristbands, and places them on the table. Then he just stands there, staring at nothing in particular, looking fried and wired. It seems like he's aged five years in the hours he's been away. His hair is disheveled and his eyes are wide open, like he's ingested fifty pod coffees.

"Are you all right?" Josh asks him.

I pull out a chair from the table. "Maybe you should sit down for a second."

"No, we have to move. Right now," says Patrick, picking up his tab and immediately activating the imaging plate.

"So were you able to do it?" I ask. "Link up the ping tunnels between the remaining Escapes?"

"Yes and no," he says, scratching the side of his ear.

"What does that mean?" Josh asks.

This time Patrick doesn't ask anyone to hit the lights. I guess there's no time for that. A hologram image appears, not unlike the one we saw before, but this time we can see that there are only two red globes left. I can't imagine why Patrick isn't more excited—the team inside Etherworld has managed to knock out three more Escapes, even with the antiviral running through the program.

"There are only two more Escapes left? That's incredible," Josh says, the thrill in his voice matching the hope that's rising within me.

"You don't understand," Patrick snaps, gesturing at a grouping of thin yellow lines sticking out of the red globes and intersecting with outer circles. I don't remember seeing those lines when he showed us the diagram before.

He points to the yellow lines and says, "These are tunnels I created to connect the Escapes together, but Elusion kept erasing them, one by one. It was like building a bridge and having a typhoon come by and wipe it all out the second I was done. And every time I started over, it was harder to build it."

He presses his tab, and the hologram switches over to an image that illustrates Patrick's point. Black lines extend and wrap around the globes, as if on their way to tie themselves together in the center to form a link, but the moment the lines touch, they turn a faint yellow.

"So what are our options?" I ask.

"Well, I was able to do something else." The hologram dissipates and another image appears. The two globes, which were previously lined up side by side, shift and move until they appear stacked one on top of the other, connected by some kind of strange-looking chimney-like structure.

"Holy shit," Josh mutters. "Did you create a trapdoor within the Escapes?"

"Sure as hell did," Patrick says, with a bit of a self-satisfied grin.

"So we can drop from one Escape down to the other," Josh says.

"I hope so. It will be impossible to know for sure until we're actually there. And I had to make it adaptive, so it blends into the landscape. Otherwise Elusion will be able to detect it."

"But how do we know it won't get erased like your ping tunnels?" I ask.

Patrick presses a button on his tab and the hologram disappears. "That's why we have to go right now. We have no idea how long those doors are going to be operational."

"Okay, let's do this," Josh says, clapping his hands and rushing to the table to sort out Equip components.

Patrick grabs me by my arms and locks eyes with me. "Listen, Ree, I have to tell you what the trapdoor looks like, just in case anything should happen to me—"

"Nothing will happen to you," I say quickly.

"I'm not a high responder. Everyone else in your dad's domain is. There's a chance I might not make it in."

I turn away, not wanting to think about what could happen, even though I know we should prepare for the worst-case scenario. "What are we looking for?" I ask.

"A mirage in the Silver Desert Escape," Patrick says.

"You can't be more specific than that?"

"I'm sorry," he says. "I had to be vague with the code—to make it look like I was improving the Escape somehow."

"Were you able to find out anything about the inoculation?" Josh asks as he hands Patrick and me wristbands.

"No, Elusion has totally blocked me from certain aspects of the program," Patrick says.

Josh hands me my visor, and suddenly there's this pull inside me, not unlike the one I felt when I was in the master program with Patrick. I take a deep breath, like I've been swimming for miles and am coming up for air.

"We should text Zoe and Avery," I blurt out. "Tell them to come back here and make sure we get out before our hour is up."

Josh glances at Patrick and something passes between them, because Josh takes his tab and sends out two messages.

"They're on the way back," Josh says, seconds later. "Should be here in about fifteen minutes."

Patrick extends his hand toward the sunken den. "Okay. But we should get started."

After we hook up our Equips, we all sprawl out on the floor, with me lying in between Patrick and Josh. My mouth is sticky and dry from all the anxiety, but when Josh notices Patrick typing on his tab, he leans over and quickly gives me a kiss. I touch my lips and smile just a little when he lies back down and whispers, "See you soon."

I hope he's right, and wherever my father is, I hope he can wait for us a little while longer.

"I'm sending you the new link now," Patrick says. "I have a destination code for Etherworld to use in place of an Escape code. This should get us right into the main base at Etherworld."

"Seriously? You found a way into Etherworld directly?" Josh says, totally amazed.

Patrick shrugs like it's not a big deal, but Josh shakes his head.

"David was right. There really is no one like you, man," he says.

I make sure the tips of my wristband are aligned with the pressure points on my wrist, the key pad facing up. The emergency warning flashes on the screen:

If your wristband alarm sounds and you have difficulty reawakening, please leave Elusion immediately. Staying in Elusion longer than recommended may result in brain injury.

I turn toward Patrick. He has been my best friend since I was a kid. I can't imagine my life without him, and even though this last week has been hell for us, he's proved himself to be the person I always knew he was. I reach for Patrick's hand and give it a squeeze.

"Okay," he says. "Your user invite number is 00-01-99-0001."

"That's the code? It's so long," I say, surprised.

"We're hacking into your father's system. Like I said, this isn't an Escape code," Patrick says.

"Right," I say, distracted. I have the sudden instinct to say something, maybe tell Patrick and Josh how much I care about them. But I'm not in the mood for sentimentality. I feel numb and resigned. Determined.

I type in the number, my breath shallow.

A second later a message flashes on the screen of my tab: *User 00-01-99-0001 has accepted invitation request. Please insert earbuds.*

"Ready?" Patrick asks.

I place the tiny earbuds in my ears.

Please engage video visor.

I slip the visor down over my eyes. Blind and deaf, I reach beside me, searching for Josh's hand. When I find it, he softly runs his thumb over mine.

An inner strength begins to charge through me, electric and defiant, as the calm female voice begins the countdown.

Five.

Four.

Three.

Two.

One . . .

SIXTEEN

A WHISPER LURES ME AWAY FROM SLEEP.

"Regan? You okay?"

I lift my chin and look up at Josh, his colorless eyes searching mine. We're both lying on the dusty ground in our real-world clothes, my head resting on his shoulder as he gently runs his fingers through my hair.

"Yeah, I think so."

I pull myself up to a sitting position; a hint of light is visible in the coal-gray sky. The honeycomb-shaped building that the Elusion survivors have been calling home is about a hundred feet away, the fire pit so close I can reach out and touch it.

We made it. We're in Etherworld. Right in the center of the Great Space.

A flicker of hope forms inside me, but it disappears when I realize how quiet and still it is right now. I can't help but feel like something is terribly wrong—a feeling that intensifies when Josh stands up and grips my wrists, yanking me to my feet.

"I think Patrick's hurt," he says.

A couple of yards away, Patrick is lying on the ground, his legs splayed out at strange angles, his translucent eyes open wide. He lets out a groan, and we race over to him and kneel down on either side of his body.

"Regan?" Patrick says, his voice hoarse. "Regan!" He suddenly springs up, his arms thrashing. I duck to avoid a blow as Josh tries to hold Patrick back.

"Take it easy, Pat," he says, restraining him. "We've got you."

"I can't see!" Patrick yells. "I can't see *anything*!"

I'm right beside him, but instead of looking at me, he's staring at a vague point in the distance. "Just give yourself a minute," I say. I squeeze his hand, hoping the pressure will calm him down. "Maybe your senses need some time to adjust."

"Are we there?" he asks. "Did we make it into Etherworld?"

"Yep," I say. "You did it."

Patrick lets out a deep breath, like he's incredibly relieved, but his eyes are still staring straight ahead. "Did this happen to you? Were you blind the first time you came here?"

"No, but I passed out," I say, remembering my brain's strong reaction to the increase in delta waves. "Josh and my dad had to carry me from the firewall all the way to the base."

"Now that you mention it, where is your dad?" Josh asks, looking around.

I stand up and face the building. "Hello!" I call out. "Anyone here?"

When there's no answer, I walk toward the cavern to get a better look. As I get closer, I see that the structure has crumbled: the solid rock that once made up its top floors is lying in chunks on the ground. The arched doorways are dark; the outdoor set of stairs and platforms has collapsed. What was once a tidy set of halls and rooms is now in ruins.

A cool, ashy wind blows through the Great Space, and I look over my shoulder at Josh, who is helping move Patrick to one of the stone benches near the fire pit. Once he gets Patrick set, Josh and I lock eyes. I can tell we're thinking the same thing.

Is there anyone left?

"I'm going to search the building," I say, as I head toward the cavern.

"Wait!" Josh shouts.

But I don't stop. I run as fast as I can, my jaw clenched as I pump my arms hard. I make my way around the clumps of rock, approaching the archway of my dad's room. I climb over a couple of huge pieces of stone to get to the door, and I slip my body under the caved-in archway. Running through the hall, I'm ducking down to avoid debris and jagged rock as I head toward his room.

The first thing I see is my father's workbench. It's smashed in half, crushed. The air is dusty, the room filled with rubble.

"Regan?"

I spin around toward the opposite side of the room. It's him. He's here, and he's trying to get up—pushing himself off a broken cot, legs shaking as he rises to his feet. I throw my arms around his neck, nearly knocking us both to the floor. He's lost so much weight since I was last here, I can practically feel his bones poking out through his shirt.

But it doesn't matter. I still feel like rejoicing. Even though I kept trying to convince myself that he was still alive and hooked up to Elusion somewhere, I couldn't deny the nagging fear that something much worse had happened.

"You shouldn't have come back here," he whispers.

"We had to," I say. "We knew you were in trouble. Elusion was starting to close off all the ping tunnels."

He takes a step back. "You know that Elusion is sentient?"

"Yes," I say, and he casts his gaze at the ground.

"I understand why you couldn't say anything," I add. "You were just trying to protect us. And that's why we're here now—to protect you."

"What do you mean, 'we'?"

"Josh and Patrick are here too."

"Where are they?" His voice is calm, but I can still hear concern weighting every word.

"In the Great Space," I say. "Patrick was able to find a direct path to Etherworld, so we didn't have to go through Elusion."

"Are you all okay?"

"Josh and I are fine, but Patrick's not doing so well," I say, as my father stifles a cough.

"Is he conscious?" he asks.

"Yes, but . . . he's lost his eyesight. I told him it was temporary, because of the lack of stimuli, but he's pretty panicked."

My dad limps toward the door, tripping as he reaches the broken archway. I grab his arm to steady him, and he pulls away from me, ducking under the fallen stone and moving as quickly as he can out of the cavern. I follow behind him, carefully tracking his every move in case he falters again, but he's found his strength. When he spots Patrick convulsing on the ground, his limping gait turns into an awkward trot.

"I think Patrick's going into shock!" Josh shouts, doing his best to hold Patrick still.

My dad kneels on the ground and takes Patrick's head firmly in his hands, holding it steady. "Regan, take his arms. Josh, get his legs. Don't pin him down, though; just try to keep him from moving around too much."

I position myself above Patrick and grab hold of his wrists, gently guiding his arms above his head. Josh places his hands on Patrick's ankles to stop his legs from flailing.

My dad presses his fingers against Patrick's temples really firmly—hard enough that I see the skin tighten around Patrick's eyes.

"Pat," my dad says, "you're fighting too hard to maintain your grip on reality."

At the sound of my father's voice, Patrick's eyes dart around in every direction, as if searching for a face that he hasn't seen in months.

"David?" he says.

"Yes, I'm here, Patrick. I'm right here with you."

Patrick closes his eyes, like he's trying to focus and control the tremors, but soon his breathing becomes shallow. I'm scared he's going to hyperventilate.

"She lied to me," Patrick says. "She told me you were dead, and I believed her."

We all know who he's referring to. Even as I sit here with her sick son, I still can't believe how much pain Cathryn has inflicted on the people she was supposed to love.

"We can talk about that later. Right now I just need you to breathe," my dad says to him. "Nice and easy, okay?"

"I'm trying," Patrick says. "I don't have . . . any control."

"I know. That's why you have to let go," my dad says, shifting his hands so that his fingers are positioned on different parts of Patrick's skull. "You need to clear your mind."

"What are you trying to do?" I whisper to my father as Patrick's hands tremble within my grasp.

"I'm putting pressure on the nerve clusters that control blood circulation to the brain," he says. "It should help prevent his reaction from worsening."

Patrick keeps his eyes closed, his chest rising and falling as if his lungs are slowly filling with air. The jerky movements in his arms and legs are becoming less frequent.

My father's right. It's working.

Patrick takes a couple more deep breaths and says, "I never thought I'd hear your voice again. When Regan told me she had seen you, when she tried to tell me that you were still alive, it seemed impossible. I thought she had nanopsychosis."

"It's okay," my dad says. "I'm here." He releases his hands and motions for Josh and me to do the same. Patrick lies still for a second, before pushing himself up into a sitting position. "I should've shared my suspicions about Elusion from the beginning, but I didn't. I'm the one who owes you the apology."

"Where's everyone?" Josh asks, interrupting. Now that Patrick's condition seems to be stabilizing, Josh is focusing on other things, like his sister. He crosses his arms over his chest as he stares at the destroyed honeycomb-shaped cavern, his brow furrowed with concern.

"Nora's still here," my dad reassures him. "But there's only a handful of us left. They're out searching the firewall for a working ping tunnel."

Josh closes his eyes and lets out a huge sigh of relief, but it only lasts for a moment. "What happened here?"

"The environment in Etherworld is weakening because the Escapes are being eliminated," my father says. "I'd anticipated that, but I wasn't sure how bad the collateral damage would be."

"It looks pretty bad to me," I say, my eyes taking in the virtual squalor around us.

"We won't be here for long," Patrick says, pushing himself off the ground with determination. When he stands, he wobbles a bit and stretches his arms out in front of him, signaling that his sight still hasn't returned. I get up and hover next to him, while Josh helps my father to his feet.

"I don't know. Even if Nora and the others can find an open tunnel, they may all be closed by the time we're finished bombing the next Escape," my dad says. "My autotimer isn't functioning anymore either, so none of us will be able to find a way back to Etherworld."

"That's okay. I was able to open up a trapdoor in between the last two Escapes, so we won't have to come back," Patrick says.

"How did you do that?" my dad asks.

As Patrick explains what he did and how he did it, I feel as if we're all sitting around the dinner table again, the two of them caught up in a conversation I can't understand. But instead of feeling jealous over the reminder that Patrick and my dad have something in common that I'll never share—an emotion I might have felt long before all of this happened— I'm thankful. There's someone who cares enough about my dad that he's willing to risk his own life to save him.

"What I don't understand," my dad says, "is how you even found out about what Elusion was doing to the ping tunnels. I mean, without being here to see it for yourself."

Josh and I tell him what happened at Bryce's house, about all the information he gave us—the truth about Elusion, the optical imaging plate, and other things that allowed us to overcome the huge obstacles that had been in our way. My dad is stunned by what we've gone through to get back here and help him. So much of what he's hearing, though, is simply validation—especially when it comes to Cathryn's powerful antiviral, which Patrick jumps in and explains in detail.

"The past few times we've entered an Escape, we've been under attack from almost the first minute we arrived," my father says, acknowledging what we feared to be true. "But why would Bryce tell you any of this? Hasn't he been in on this whole thing from the beginning?"

When I give him the rundown on Bryce's firing and his change of heart, I leave out the part about Bryce discovering that my dad was moved from Orexis, at least for now. I don't want to worry him. Then again, he must suspect that something didn't go right with our plan to break into room 5020. Otherwise, why would any of us be here?

"So he got you involved rather than go to the police and risk his own neck?" My dad clenches his fists tight, like he wishes he could wake up from this nightmare and slug Bryce himself.

That's when I know I have to tell him what I still can't bear to admit.

"Bryce was pretty drunk," I say, hoping to buy myself just a little more time. "The cops never would've believed anything he was saying, even if he did have some tangible proof."

My father stares at me, his eyes narrowing with skepticism. But before he can call me on my dismissiveness, a familiar voice echoes through the air.

"Josh?"

I turn and see Nora standing in front of the ruins of the cavern, her clothes torn to shreds and her face and arms covered in dirt. Behind her are Malik, Wyatt, and Zared, who look just as weary and spent as she does.

"That's the rest of our crew," my dad says as Josh runs over to his sister, enveloping her in the same kind of desperate hug my father and I shared in his room moments ago. I'm grateful for the reunion until something clicks inside my mind: out of the dozen or more survivors that were here a day ago, only five remain?

We still have two Escapes left to destroy, which will be much more difficult to do now that the inoculation is working against us. With fewer of us here to go on the offensive, what are our odds of winning this war?

The group approaches us, with Wyatt in the lead, his hands on his hips. Josh has his arms around Nora, whose body is limp with exhaustion and skin damp with sweat.

"Were you able to find an open tunnel?" I ask them. Even though it's only been a day in real-world time, the survivors have spent what probably feels like weeks working toward this moment.

There's no need for hellos. Not anymore.

"Just one. Along the southern border of the firewall," Wyatt says, glancing at my father.

"Then we have to get going," Patrick says, turning toward me.

"How can you go back into Elusion if you're—"

"Don't even think about leaving me behind," he cuts me off. "My sight is starting to come back. Everything is still hazy, but I'm beginning to make out some shapes."

My gaze shifts back toward my dad, his arms crossed in

front of him as if he's weighing his options. But I think we all know that there's only one thing left to do.

"Let's finish this," he says.

The walk toward the southern part of the firewall feels more like a funeral march than a quest. As we trudge through clouds of ash and mounds of soot, our torches held high above our heads, no one utters a sound. We stop off at the mine to pick up the bombs, and I'm surprised to see that the once-giant piles are almost completely depleted, used up on missions. Since we won't be able to restock in between the remaining Escapes, we each take as many as we can. I shove mine into the pockets of Zoe's sweater.

I wish we were trying to focus on our sense of direction, but without a visible moon or sun to guide our way, it's difficult. No one is speaking; the survivors are reeling from what Josh just told them: that we found Nora's body in the Island Sector, and she's now lying in a hospital bed, still hooked up to her Equip and completely unconscious, unable to be revived.

Withholding the truth, like we did before with Anthony, wasn't something we could do anymore. Not under these dire circumstances.

Even though everyone took the news hard, especially Nora, Josh did the right thing by telling them the truth. I feel guilty for not doing the same with my dad and explaining why his health is failing him like this, and why he's limping at least twenty paces behind everyone else. I'm so concerned that my dad's weakened state will make it difficult for him to reach the ping tunnel.

But not quite guilty enough to come clean.

"Why don't you catch up with the others?" my father says, lowering his torch a bit so the white light dances in front of his sallow face.

"I'm good right here," I say.

"I'm slowing you down. Really. Go ahead, I'll be fine."

"You're not. It's these stupid shoes."

That's partly true. The heels of Zoe's designer boots are continually getting stuck in the soil.

My dad stops in his tracks and blocks my path. "You don't have to do this, sweetheart," he says.

"Do what?"

"Remember what I said? It's my job to take care of you, not the other way around."

"Dad," I protest.

"Something is bothering you," he says. "What is it?"

"Josh already told the group everything they needed to know," I say defensively.

"Okay, but he didn't say what happened to the plan, Regan," my dad says, coughing into his free hand. "To go to the media and expose Orexis."

And find his body inside room 5020.

"It's a long story," I say, stalling.

"I'll bet we have enough time for the highlights, don't you think?"

Josh, Patrick, and the rest of the crew stalk ahead. "We should hurry," I say. "We're falling behind."

"We'll catch up in a minute."

"Please," I murmur, my head bowing down.

"The plan, Regan. What happened?" he asks, stopping.

I take a deep breath and look up at him. "I did everything you asked me to do, Dad. I made it inside Orexis. I got into that room. And you weren't there."

He reaches out to me with a trembling hand, and when I take it in mine, something plummets inside of me.

"I'm not surprised," he says. "Cathryn knew you were onto her, and she had to get rid of the most damning evidence."

"I don't know where she took you," I say. "But Bryce gave us a lead and my friends are looking for you right now."

"Good thinking," my dad says, winking. "I'm pretty lucky to have such a smart daughter."

I roll my eyes at him, my fingers slipping from his. "Don't patronize me, okay?"

"I'm not."

"I had one mission on the outside, and it totally failed."

As I turn away from my father, I tell him about my stay in the hospital, and the drama with Patrick and Cathryn—how she's trying to make it seem like he's mentally ill as well. "No one believed me. No one believed Patrick. Now everyone thinks we're suffering from nanopsychosis."

"None of that means you failed. It actually means that you're brave," I hear him say. "You kept going, kept pushing, no matter what got in your way. You never gave up. Not for a second."

"Yeah, well. I guess it's in my genes."

I feel his hand on my shoulder, and it's ice-cold. I spin around to look at him, and there are deep cracks forming on his lips, like he hasn't had anything to drink in days.

"What if we get through this—the inoculation, the destruction of Elusion, everything—but we can't find you when we get home?" I ask him, my throat tightening. "What if, after all this, I can't save you?"

"Listen to me, okay? What we're doing isn't about saving one person. It's about saving millions of people," he says. "Deep down, you already know that, or else you wouldn't have come back to help us, right?"

Before I can answer, Josh's voice roars through a cluster of leafless trees and slams into the stone fortress of the firewall.

"Regan! David! Come quick!"

Without another word, my father and I begin running along the rocky path, dust and dirt kicking up behind us. I don't even look back when I realize he's lagging behind. I just can't get the sound of Josh's urgent call out of my head.

A million horrific scenarios flood my thoughts, all of them ending with one of my friends either injured or dead. Then the worst thing of all occurs to me: right now, we're in worm country.

"Hurry, Dad!" I shout, picking up the pace, pushing my legs to move as fast as they can. I skip over the remains of a burned-out tree, not waiting to hear a response from my father. I slow down to a light jog when I see the backs of Josh, Nora, and Wyatt huddled around a giant mound of sizzling flesh.

What the hell?

As soon as my father catches up to me, totally out of breath and almost wheezing, Patrick and Malik appear from the other side of this disgusting carcass, holding their shirts over their noses. The skin of this beast looks likes it was burned and charred, so the awful smell is carrying on the wind, and there's no way to escape it.

"This is the worm, isn't it?" Malik asks, grabbing for Nora's hand.

Josh walks up to what used to be the head of the hideous slug, and examines the remains of its all-too-familiar jagged teeth. "Looks like it."

"I wonder what killed it," Nora says.

"We were here a little while ago, so this must have just happened," Wyatt adds.

Patrick squints at the decaying creature, looking frustrated that his eyesight hasn't returned to normal. "So there was a living organism in here?"

"Yeah," Zared says. "That thing was scary as hell."

"Amazing," Patrick says. "We tried to develop living organisms for Elusion, but it was too hard. I finally managed to create a butterfly in a Phase Two Escape, but it wasn't easy. I worked on that thing for months."

It's only been one night since Josh and I saw Patrick's

butterfly, one night since we made our way through the firewall and were reunited with my dad. It feels like weeks.

"Except I never developed this thing," my dad says. "That happened all on its own."

"It's a by-product of Elusion becoming a sentient organism, isn't it?" Patrick asks.

"I think so," my dad says. "My guess is the worm was a result of Elusion's self-defense mechanism. The mines with the bombs weren't too far away. If Elusion is sentient, perhaps the worm was its way of trying to keep us away from our stockpile."

"That still doesn't explain how this guy got fried," Zared says, bending down to get a closer look.

"Maybe it has something to do with the adaptive bombs," Josh suggests. "Maybe Elusion is growing weaker."

"You could be right," my dad says enthusiastically. "If you think of Elusion like a biological system, the bombs we've been setting off have been infecting it with a deadly disease. We're destroying it little by little, hoping for some residual damage." My dad is getting more excited with each word. "I think this," he says, motioning toward the dead worm, "is a sign that we're making some headway."

"But what about the antiviral?" Patrick asks.

"Maybe it's not working as well as your mother hoped," my dad offers.

"So destroying the Escapes has had a positive effect?" I ask. "We're getting somewhere?" I repeat, just to make sure I've heard him correctly.

"Yes," he says without hesitating.

For the first time since we've come back here, I feel a surge of hope. Maybe things are not as futile as they seem.

"We can do this," my dad says. "We're going to defeat Elusion, and then we're going home, do you hear me?"

We all raise our torches in the air, cheering. It seems as if a huge weight has been lifted off all our shoulders, a sign that we can truly make it out of here. All of us.

Alive.

Josh walks over to me and, with a smile, grabs my hand and gives it a squeeze. After all the disappointments and bad news we've received over the past day, it feels amazing to know that we might have a fighting chance.

We follow as my dad, suddenly energized, leads the way toward the ping tunnel.

SEVENTEEN

I'M STANDING IN THE SILVER DESERT Escape. A violet moon and pink stars glitter in the night sky. Mounds of sterling dunes unfold as far as the eye can see, shimmering so brightly I'm almost blinded. I know it should scare me, going into combat against a system with the ability to kill me in self-defense. But trypnosis is good that way, filling me with excitement and confidence instead of fear and uncertainty. I catch up to the others, keeping my thoughts in check and consciously pushing away any knowledge that could give Elusion a leg up on me—just like my father instructed us to do before we reentered the Escape.

"Regan, over here!"

I turn to the voice and see Zared and Patrick running toward me, their feet sinking into the hot sand with every step they take. They're wearing long cloaks and lace-up boots that reach their knees, and I'm dressed the same way. In the pockets of my cloak are the adaptive bombs that I'd shoved into Zoe's sweater earlier.

"Your dad found some ATVs," Zared says, his face lit up. He gestures over his shoulder, and we follow him past a dried-up ravine and through a small set of dunes, where we see three black all-terrain vehicles with enormous deep-tread tires and cherry red-flagged antennas attached to the backs.

"Are you guys ready for a wild ride?" Patrick asks as he climbs inside. His eyes are blue again and, for the first time in days, completely free of worry.

"How should we split up?" Nora asks, the rising current of the wind ruffling her short hair.

"You and Malik go with Zared," my dad says. "Patrick and Wyatt can go in the other one. I'll be with Regan and Josh."

I have to admit, I'm encouraged by his appearance. He looks healthier than he did in Etherworld. His eyes are almost sparkling, and his skin has regained some of its luster. Josh smiles, and a ribbon of peace winds its way around me. The trypnosis must be intensifying, because I'm feeling so content about everything I'm almost giddy.

There's no doubt in my mind we'll succeed.

"I'll drive," I offer, even though I've never operated an ATV before.

"I have a lot of hours clocked with four-wheelers at the academy," Josh says, jumping in front of me.

"And I own, like, ten of these," Patrick jokes to Wyatt as he climbs into the ATV alongside him.

"Hop on," Zared says, motioning for Nora and Malik to join him.

"Why are the guys driving?" Nora yells at me. "We should know better than that!"

I laugh as I jump in the front, taking a seat next to Josh. He steps on the gas pedal, propelling us forward at a high speed, leaving a mini sandstorm in our wake. As the cloud of silver dust dissipates, I look back up at the violet moon. It's a beacon, leading us across the ripple of silver dunes, and we drive under its light for what seems like a couple of miles, the roar of the engine still loud in our ears.

"Are you sure this is the right way?" Josh yells to my dad, who is holding on to the rim of the seat with both hands.

"Yes!" my father shouts back.

"Do the others know what we're looking for?" I say loudly.

"The trigger was designed to resemble plant life, so look for something like that," my dad says.

"Like a tree," I ask, "or a cactus?"

"Yes, that's what I told the others," he replies.

"Hold on!" I hear Josh yell.

Our ATV swerves hard to the left as I grab on to the hand strap, almost falling out of my seat. Josh steers us toward a steep incline, the base of one of the silver dunes. The tires grind in the sand as Josh slams on the brakes. Zared's ATV is scuttling along on the right side, as Patrick's veers to the left.

As we continue to climb up the dune, I twist around, searching for anything tall with branches or leaves. But there's nothing like that in these dunes. I don't spot anything in the ravines, either.

Zared's ATV careens to a stop beside us.

"Where are Patrick and Wyatt?" I ask.

"It looked like they were heading up the other side of the dune," my dad says.

Josh hits the accelerator and we zoom down the incline, my lungs filling with air and my heart leaping into my throat. I watch Josh's lips turn into a wide, ecstatic smile. It's almost as if we're back home, driving his motorcycle through the open streets of the Heights Sector, the scenery whipping into a hazy blur around us.

As we close in on level ground, my gaze shifts from Josh's happy face to something in the distance. I can't quite make it out, but from here it looks like a giant man with his arms sticking up, surrounded by smaller men in the same position. I tug hard on Josh's shirt, hoping he'll want to investigate.

"I think I see something. Over there," I say, pointing to the left.

Josh squints, looking in that direction. "Yeah, I see it too. Let's check it out."

The ATV charges ahead about 150 yards before it hits a divot in the sand and begins to spin out of control, but Josh keeps his cool and recovers quickly. Within a few seconds, we reach a large field of cacti, staggered in about five or six rows. Most of them are about fifteen to twenty feet high, their spines slightly curved, sharp needles covering thick branches. But toward the end of the field is one cactus that towers above them all, with huge, crooked branches spurting from the base all the way up to the top. It looks like some kind of monster, ready to bend over and crush us all.

"That has to be the trigger, right, Dad?"

"There's only one way to find out," he says.

We cruise around the field for another minute or two before we spot Patrick's ATV barreling toward us off the other side of the dune. Josh slows down a little as the three ATVs line up, all circling the giant plants. As Zared navigates his ATV, Nora stands up, holding on to the hand strap with one arm, the other poised over her head with her bomb in hand, ready to launch it at the largest cactus. I reach into my pocket and grip a bomb in my hand, preparing to shoot if she misses.

Just then, the sky blazes with light, as a barrage of stars begins to fall toward the earth, like a meteor shower. They crash into the ground, sending dust everywhere and shaking the earth below us.

Zared screams, "Look!" and all the euphoria I felt the second I stepped foot into this silver desert drains from my body, like all the oxygen is being sucked out of my blood.

Some of the cacti burst into inferno-like flames, the fire quickly spreading, leaping from one to the other and heading toward the trigger at a rapid pace.

This has to be the antiviral program at work. These stars

are weapons that are trying to exterminate the triggers and prevent us from destroying this Escape. There are too many enemies: the cacti, the stars. It's like the whole world is out to get us.

"Now, Nora! Now!" my dad shouts, as another flurry of stars begins to rain down upon us.

My jaw clenches as Nora leans back and gets in position. But Zared swerves to avoid being hit by the cascading stars, so when Nora finally launches the sphere, it goes wide and misses.

"Shit!" she yells out. "Sorry!"

How can we possibly get at the trigger through this mess of destruction?

Josh keeps driving, doing another lap around the field, but visibility is now becoming a real problem. The burning cacti have created a thick plume of black smoke encircling the entire area. It's almost impossible to see.

"Get us a little closer if you can!" my dad shouts at Josh, as the ATV narrowly misses a crater left behind by a star bomb.

We speed through the smoke, all of us choking. I can't see the others. Where are they? Are they okay?

Josh steers the ATV around raging plant fires and toward the enormous cactus. Another ripple of exploding stars streaks toward us, pummeling the two cacti next to the target and nearly hitting the trigger.

My father stands up and holds on to the hand strap of the ATV. He pulls out two of his bombs and heaves them at the cactus. One of them misses the stem by a foot or two, and the other skims one of the lower branches. A flurry of bombs fly toward the cactus, but the smoke makes it impossible to see who threw them or if they made contact. I join in the barrage, throwing bombs into the billowing almost-black clouds.

"Hold your fire! We have to conserve ammo for the last Escape!" my dad shouts.

Josh diverts the ATV away from the cactus field as a seismic tremor tears through the ground, and it once again sounds like the sky is about to split in half. The gigantic cactus explodes, signaling that one of the bombs struck it. Now everyone is driving as fast as they can, trying to avoid the sharp fragments of plant tumbling down around us.

We're not going to make it if we don't find the mirage and only Patrick knows where it is.

"Pat!" I scream.

An ATV comes roaring out of the dust. Patrick pulls up beside us just as we hear another loud rumbling and the sand turns from silver to a dark, putrid green. "Follow me—I don't think the mirage is far."

But before he can lead the way, more debris from the cactus pelts the ground around us, and I hear Wyatt shrieking. A huge cactus needle has impaled his thigh, and magenta-colored ooze is gushing down his leg. He falls out of the side of the ATV, and Patrick slams on the brakes and scrambles to help him.

Both Josh and Zared circle back toward them, but by the

time we reach them, we're already too late. Wyatt's leg has disappeared into the same yellow light that consumed Claire in the rapids.

Patrick is holding on to Wyatt tightly, trying to ease his suffering, but we all know there's nothing we can do to save him. I'm just about to get out and help him when another strike is unleashed from the sky.

"Take cover!" my dad shouts.

But there's nowhere to go, at least not for Zared and his crew. The star strikes his ATV, and it explodes on impact, creating a fireball so huge it takes Patrick's ATV with it.

Josh throws his body on top of me as a star explodes in front of us. There's the sound of twisting metal, and when we look beside us, we can make out the smoldering ruins of an ATV. Patrick is running toward it, weaving through the clouds of billowing smoke.

Josh navigates our ATV toward the wreck, but we're too late. All that's left is a huge, gaping hole in the olive-colored sand.

No, no, no . . .

Nora, Zared, and Malik are gone.

We stop, staring at the spot where Nora's vehicle was hit. Giant cracks begin to form in the ground, and sand spills down into the crevices, as if falling into an old hourglass timer.

Patrick jogs over to our ATV, streaks of soot all over his face. "The mirage! I think it's just over the next dune!"

"Get in the back!" my dad says.

He hops in next to my dad, his body shaking. Josh's eyes are still fixated on the spot where Nora's ATV was blown up, paralyzed with shock.

"We have to hurry," I say. "We have to get to the next Escape before the trapdoor closes."

No reaction at all. And the cracks in the sand are becoming bigger, the particles quickly drifting into them.

"If we finish this, she'll be okay," Patrick reassures him. "Please, Josh."

Stars explode around us—one comes so close it almost grazes the front fender, shaking the front of the vehicle really hard. It's enough to break Josh out of his trance, and he throws the ATV into gear.

"Where to?" he asks Patrick, his voice weak.

"The second dune to your right," Patrick replies, "I think."

The Escape seems to be worsening with each quarter mile we travel—the sky bleached of all its color, the stars spiraling down in corkscrew-shaped motions, gusts of wind nearly blowing our vehicle over, the sand collapsing and forming massive sinkholes.

But we reach the top somehow, and Josh stops the ATV. We wait a moment, looking around, and it's not long before the entire back side of the dune begins to sink behind us. Below are the remnants of a large lake, the muddy water that's left draining rapidly.

"That's it," Patrick says. "The trapdoor!"

"What do we do now?" I ask.

No one says anything, but it doesn't matter. I know what's about to happen.

Josh hits the accelerator and drives straight off the top of the dune. As the ATV flies into the air, he lets go of the controls and I grab his hand, holding on tightly as the vehicle arcs and then plummets into a shallow pool of darkness.

But it isn't over yet.

We've made it to the last core Escape, our bodies materializing on top of a hill as if by magic. We're high above a thick rain forest, surrounded by a canopy of leafy green flora brimming with bright, vivid colors. Patches of light mist form below us, and although the air should be pretty thin at this altitude, oxygen pours into my lungs with each inhalation.

I feel amazing—as if losing Nora and everyone else were just a bad dream. I'm buzzing with positive energy. I know I'll see them all again back home, as soon as we're finished.

My dad is outfitted the same way as the rest of us, with a cargo vest that has metal latches attached to it and a pair of gray cross-trainers. And there's Josh, who no longer seems upset, his amber eyes as dazzling as ever. He looks back at me and I grin, sure we're unstoppable.

"Wow," Josh says, leaning over the ledge a little. "It's a long way down."

Unlike the previous Escape, here it's daytime, and even though the rain forest is overcast, a shadowed sun illuminates our view. "It's all relative," I say with a laugh. The height doesn't scare me. Why would it? We just drove into an abyss and here we are, totally fine.

"This Escape was one of the most difficult to design," my dad says.

"And the most difficult to change," Patrick says. "I tried to alter some of the colors, but they kept self-correcting. It took forever to fix."

"Are there any gliders or bikes we can use?" I ask.

"No, the only thing here is a zip line," my dad answers.

"A state-of-the-art system, naturally," Patrick chimes in.

"How much ammo do you guys have?" Josh asks after checking the pockets of his vest. "I'm down to three."

We all stop and take stock. I reach into my vest pockets and hold up two bombs, all too aware that this is our last hope for survival.

"Here's what I have left," I say.

"I've got a couple more, too," Patrick chimes in.

"So do I. Now let's look for the cable and harnesses," my dad says. "They have to be around here somewhere."

A low rumbling noise thunders, the sound of an oncoming storm. As one of the puffy gold clouds turns black, Patrick and my dad exchange a look. I'm sure they're wondering if these clouds could be signs of the inoculation at work, and since there aren't any other Escapes left, I don't see how it could be anything else.

"We need to hurry," my dad says calmly.

We back away from the ledge and branch off in different directions, ducking behind candy-colored trees and stepping over fluorescent buttress roots. I look up to see if there's any kind of wiring popping out above us, and notice the dark clouds multiplying on the horizon.

"See anything?" Patrick calls out from a few yards away.

"No, nothing," Josh calls back.

"Found them!" my dad bellows, and we all scramble toward the sound of his voice. With each step my mood darkens, the elation of trypnosis wearing off. Images of stars blasting through the atmosphere flash through my mind: Wyatt, Nora, Zared, and Malik—all of them taken down by Elusion.

"You okay?" Josh is beside me, reaching out to hold my hand.

"Fine," I say. He still seems high on trypnosis, a hopeful smile on his face. It's as if he doesn't have any recollection of what happened in the desert, or concerns about the antiviral threat or an attack that might occur any moment. I look around for anything unusual. But I've never been in this Escape before and everything seems different and weird: the flora, the clouds, even the zip-line equipment.

When we find my dad, he's standing at the base of the tree, in front of a ladder that leads up to what looks like a man-made wooden platform. Directly above him are two parallel cables that stretch out for what seems like the length of four football fields, dangling over the rain forest beneath us, hundreds of feet aboveground. My stomach tightens—and I lunge toward the pile of harnesses at the bottom of the enormous tree connected to the launch deck.

"Everybody suit up, quickly," my dad orders, with an eye on the sky.

Josh helps me with my equipment and I help him, while Patrick and my father assist each other. Once we have all our gear in place, we scale the ladder that leads up to the wooden platform, where we'll jump off and careen down with the help of a pulley.

"Looks like we'll have to go in pairs," Patrick says. "Regan and Josh, you go first. David and I will launch as soon as you get to the next platform."

"What are we looking for?" I ask my dad.

"A rare plant. It's called a corpse flower," my dad says. "It's blood red, and one of the world's largest. The bloom can reach a total width of almost four feet."

A corpse flower? My father's design can't get any more literal than that.

I think about the beautiful flowers in the Thai Beach Escape—each one the size of a human head. To think I considered those big.

"Should be easy to see from the zip line," adds Josh.

"And to hit from the air," I say.

"The problem is going to be the speed," Patrick explains, as the thunder grows louder. "If we're tearing through the rain forest on the cable, it will be hard to brake."

The wind picks up, as warm drops of water begin to fall. They sizzle a little bit as they touch the ground.

"We need to go!" my dad says.

"Josh and Regan first," Patrick adds.

I take a deep breath and jump off the platform. As my

body begins to soar, I instinctively work the brake, balancing my weight in the harness. The pulley rattles down the cable at what seems like a hundred miles an hour. Everything is a blur of color, like I'm sliding through a rainbow. I'm whipping past gigantic dew-covered leaves, trying to keep my eyes focused and my hand ready to grab a bomb from the pouch on my vest. The cable drops precipitously as branches slap at my legs. I look toward Josh, whose cable is starting to drift away from me.

"Slow down!" he yells, his voice echoing above all the trees. The rain is picking up now, and I wipe the wetness away from my eyes as I pump the brakes.

And then I see it.

In the middle of a cluster of blue flowers is a giant red blossom.

Josh pulls up alongside me, with a bomb in hand and his eyes focused on the flower. He raises his arm, taking aim, but before he can shoot, a ray of light zings around the forest, setting fire to everything in its path.

Josh drops the bomb, then grabs his shoulder. "Damn it!" he yells in pain.

His arm is bright yellow, fading away. He's being sent back.

"You can do this!" he shouts. "I have faith in you!"

"Hang on," I say as my harness swings back and forth, ricocheting from the aftershocks. I have to help him.

I let go of my brake and zip down, crashing into the platform. Stumbling to my feet, I unhitch myself and turn around as another harness crashes into the platform. It's empty. I grab hold of it, searching the horizon for Josh. Where is he?

"Josh!" I scream.

No answer.

I lean over, bracing my hands on my knees. I feel sick.

Patrick lands beside me. "Where's Josh?" he asks, his voice heavy with worry. I shake my head.

"Shit," Patrick murmurs.

"Where's my dad?" I ask.

"That laser beam hit the platform and he was knocked off. It all happened so fast," he replies. "I'm sorry."

Josh is gone.

And so is my father.

The rain is starting to pour from the sky, yet the fire shows no sign of slowing. The leaves around us are beginning to burn, the fire spreading. I can't let myself think that things are hopeless, not now when we're so close.

"Did Josh hit the flower?" Patrick asks.

"No," I say. "He didn't have a chance to throw any bombs. I think those laser beams were from the antiviral."

"Do you think we're too late?" Patrick asks.

I point toward the area where I saw the flower and say, in a shaky voice, "It's over there."

Patrick tosses his harness on the platform and steps onto the ladder. He's halfway down when a massive vine erupts from the earth and wraps itself around the base of the ladder, growing with astounding speed as it snakes its way toward Patrick. He attempts to escape, hurrying back up, but just as he steps onto the platform, the vine clamps around his ankle.

"Watch out!" I yell, slipping on the wet platform and falling face-first. The vine yanks Patrick down across from me, dragging him toward the edge.

"Patrick!" I scream, scrambling after him. I grab onto his arm, trying to wrench him away from the vine. A surge of wind whoops up through the forest as another enormous flame hits the base of the ladder. The vine has caught fire; the blaze quickly spreading up its thick stem.

"Get out of here, Ree!" Patrick shouts, still trying to kick free.

"No," I say, hanging on to his shirt as I pull him toward me. "I'm not leaving you."

But he tries to push me away. "You have to destroy that flower!"

Suddenly a huge gust of heat and flames shoots upward and I fall back against the platform, letting go of Patrick. The fire engulfs him almost instantly and heads toward me. I scramble to the pulley and jump, racing down the wet cable like it's coated in oil. As I soar through the burning trees, I glance over my shoulder as the platform explodes in a burst of light.

I close my eyes, the horrific image searing into my brain.

The rope releases at the end of the line, and I tumble to the ground, hitting a part of the mossy jungle floor yet untouched by fire. I pick myself up, and step over the thick mass of vines and shrubs as I make my way back toward the platform where we launched. I trek through the underbrush, the wind blowing so hard it's like walking through a hurricane. The temperature has risen at least twenty degrees since we arrived.

The closer I get to where I spotted the flower, the more intense the storm becomes. I reach inside my pocket, my fingers grasping the smooth bomb. A horrible pain pierces the base of my skull. My legs are beginning to feel numb. I look down at my arms and legs, positive that I'm beginning to disintegrate. But I'm not. I'm still in one piece.

Keep moving, Regan.

Fight the wind!

I grab onto the vines and use them to pull me toward my destination.

I'm going to make it.

I'm going to make it.

I'm chanting in my head, my vision growing blurry as the pain intensifies. I see a glimpse of bright red in the distance. It's the flower.

I'm almost there.

The ground beneath me shakes; another earthquake. There's a crashing noise as the trees begin to fall, the jungle destroying itself. The rain is coming down hard, and the drops are practically scalding me.

With the flower in sight, I grab a bomb and aim. I stop, my arm dropping back to my side, bomb in hand. Where there was once one red flower, there are now four, all clustered together.

Which one is the target?

"Regan!"

My dad. My dad is still alive.

I follow the sound of his voice and find him lying on the ground.

"My harness unhitched and I ran here as fast as I could," he says.

"I found the flower," I say. "But there's more than one."

"It's adapting. Elusion knows what we're after. It's trying to protect itself."

"Do you have any more bombs?" I ask.

He shakes his head. "I fired my last ones at the flower before I realized there were decoys."

He hit the wrong one. And if my dad couldn't tell them apart, how can I?

I have the bomb in my hand and another in my vest pocket. I only have a fifty-fifty chance.

The ground shakes again, the undergrowth breaking apart as crevices form around us. My dad winces, glancing toward his feet. They're no longer there. He's disappearing, about to be sent back into the world.

"There's still a way," he whispers. "Believe . . ."

He tries to say more, but now he's just making choking noises. He motions in the direction of the flowers, and I know I have to go, despite my gut telling me not to leave him.

But if I don't, there'll be nothing left for us.

There's a crash in the distance, most likely the sound of the platform toppling into a smoky pile of rubble.

Believe. Or as Josh would say: *You can do this.*

If I don't, Elusion will win.

I turn toward the cluster of giant buds, still pristine in spite of the acid-like rain. My eyes drift over the flowers, my gaze settling on the one on the end. I raise a bomb over my head and throw.

The petals splinter as I take out the other bomb. I aim at another flower, the one at the very top, and fling it with all my might.

I hit the target, and for a split second, everything stops. No rain, lightning, or earthquake. Then the earth begins to tremble. The giant blossom explodes, and before I can turn to say good-bye to my dad, I'm thrown backward, caught in a gust of hot wind.

I reach out to latch on to anything I can find, but when I look at my hands, all the skin is gone. As the world around me erupts into a noxious hellfire, I am staring at my bones.

And then I'm nothing but dust.

EIGHTEEN

"REGAN?"

Josh is whispering to me. I blink, my mind trying to cling to the sound, but my eyes won't stay open.

"She's coming back!" another voice calls out. A girl's voice. Tart yet raspy.

"Give her some room, Avery," Josh says.

I sense him beside me, his fingers gently caressing my forehead as he brushes my hair away from my eyes. "Just breathe. I'm here. I need you to come back to me."

Josh made it.

"You're going to be okay," he says confidently. My eyes are closed, yet I see my dad lying in the burning rain forest. He knew that even if he made it back, he might never be the same.

Believe, he said. *Believe.*

And so I believed, certain that I could destroy Elusion at its own game. But did I?

How could anyone destroy something so powerful?

"Ree? Are you okay?"

"Pat?" I cough. My tongue feels thick and heavy as I do my best to talk to my friend.

"I'm right here," Patrick says, and I feel his reassuring grip on my hand.

"You were on fire . . . ," I begin.

"Yeah. On fire. In hell. No big surprise, right?" he says, attempting a smile.

Josh and Patrick, both back, both safe. My body begins to relax, the adrenaline fading.

"Here's some water," Avery says.

My head is being propped up. I open my eyes but I can't focus; Josh's face is floating in and out of frame. I want to touch him, but I can't move my arms. A glass is pressed against my lips, and a tiny bit of cool liquid trickles down my throat. I swallow, and Josh gently places my head back down.

I blink again, and slowly the world around me begins to spin into focus. I'm still in the sunken den, but I've been moved from the floor to the couch. My wristband and earbuds are gone, no doubt pulled off by my friends, who are now standing over me, their brows furrowed with worry. Panic rises in my throat. What if I didn't destroy the corpse flower?

"Did we do it?" I breathe.

"*You* did it," Josh says proudly.

Patrick grins as he shoves his tab in front of me. "It's gone."

I blink as my eyes focus on the screen.

"The deletion code is all that shows up when you start the app," Patrick says. "Elusion has been wiped from the system."

My shoulders relax as I clutch Josh's hand; a small happy sound escapes my lips. But any joy is short-lived as I remember what Bryce told us. Cathryn was only keeping my dad alive until she no longer needed him. If she planned on getting rid of him after Elusion's independence, why would she keep him alive after its destruction?

I push myself up. My dad is in danger, now more than ever.

"Whoa," Josh says. "Slow down."

As I press my feet against the plush carpet, trying to get my balance, I notice that I'm still wearing Zoe's clothes, her hooded knit sweater and pants. I touch my finger to the soft sleeve. Even though I realize everything that happened in Elusion took place in a virtual reality, it felt so real. The outfit I wore in Elusion was destroyed by the fire, and here I am perfectly untouched.

"Where's Zoe?" I ask Avery. My voice is getting stronger, almost back to normal. "Did you guys find out where Cathryn is holding my dad?" Avery shakes her head no.

"Then why aren't you out there helping her?" I say, attempting to stand.

"Because we decided one of us should stay behind and watch over you, just in case," Avery says. "Since I know more about Elusion than Zoe, she went back to check out the last couple of leads."

"She can't do it all by herself," I say to Josh. "We need to help her."

The floor rotates beneath my feet, a wave of dizziness hitting me. Josh grabs my waist, steering me back down onto the couch and wrapping me in his arms. "We'll go, as soon as you're stable. Zoe left about forty-five minutes ago. I'm sure she'll check in any minute."

"Forty-five minutes?" I ask. We were only in Elusion for about an hour? My head twists toward the closed blinds, as if to confirm. I can't tell if it's night or day.

Everything is slowly coming back into focus: the escape from the hospital, running into Cathryn at Orexis, waking up Josh, finding Nora, Bryce . . .

I inhale sharply as I remember the watch he gave me.

My dad's watch.

I run my finger over the mother-of-pearl face as my breath grows tight. In all the Etherworld chaos, he never even noticed I was wearing it.

"You okay?" Josh says, watching me carefully.

"My mind feels fuzzy," I say.

"It's the cortisol levels. It takes a while to come down from that."

"It didn't seem to have much of an impact on either of you," I say.

"You were in for a good fifteen minutes longer than us,"

Patrick says. "It makes a difference, especially when the levels are so high."

"Yeah," Josh says. "I was pissed when I realized I was getting sent back and leaving you in there alone. But you seemed to manage just fine." He grins, lacing his fingers with mine.

"Have you heard anything about Nora and the others?" I ask.

"Nothing yet. But the program hasn't been disabled for that long," Josh says.

The oversize InstaComm on the wall opposite us switches on automatically as it receives a call, and we all jump.

Zoe Morgan awaiting connection. Accept or deny?

Patrick hits accept, and an AutoComm image of Zoe's face fills the screen. She looks almost luminescent, lit only by the light on the car's mini-camera and the skyline of the city in the car's window.

"Hola!" Zoe says enthusiastically, glancing toward the camera. She turns her attention back to the road and slams on her horn. We all jump at the sudden noise. "How'd it go?" she asks, this time keeping her eyes on the road.

"We did it," Patrick says.

Zoe pumps a fist in the air.

"What about you?" I ask, hopeful. "Any news on my dad?"

"I think I tracked down his location—or at least I figured out where the movers went after leaving Orexis. I'm sending you the link now," she says, her finger pressing a button on the AutoComm.

A huge, old multistory brown building with a glass-domed top fills the screen. It looks familiar, and I know I've seen it before.

"The old Menlop Hills Mall," Zoe says. My heart sinks. The Menlop Hills Mall was gigantic. I went there once with my mom when I was a kid and still remember sitting with her next to the ten-story fountain in the center atrium, staring at the rows and rows of stores. Most malls had closed a long time before then, people having lost the inclination to leave their homes to shop, but Menlop Hills held out, shutting down just last year.

"Orexis bought it a year ago," Patrick says. "We're going— we *were* going—to turn it into a distribution center for Elusion."

"I should be there in five," Zoe says, the AutoComm focused back on her. Through the window behind her I see glimpses of the towering condominiums that crowd the Oak Sector, where the Menlop Hills Mall is located. "Want me to call the police?"

"No," I say. "I doubt they'd believe us, and worse, they'd probably want me to go back to the hospital."

"And then they'd make sure we didn't break into the mall," Josh says.

"Okay, okay," Zoe says. "No police. So what should I do when I get there?"

"Wait for us," Patrick says, grabbing his coat.

"Will do," Zoe says, signing off.

Patrick is about to turn off the InstaComm when a news ticker flashes across the bottom of the screen: *Bryce Williams,*

VP Production Services of Orexis, found dead of apparent suicide at age 43. . . . Elusion is experiencing technical difficulties that may impact release. A small image of Cathryn appears on the ribbon; she's dressed in a light blue suit and standing behind a podium in the Orexis auditorium. It's the same place where Patrick gave his presentation on Elusion, but unlike then, the reporters are standing up, crowding around the stage.

"Oh my God," I breathe.

Bryce is dead.

"Turn it up," Josh says quietly.

Patrick clicks on the ribbon and her image fills the screen.

"As I said, a complete shock. I knew about Bryce's impending divorce, of course, but none of us had any idea . . ."

"Do you think it had anything to do with us?" I ask. "With our visit?"

"No," Josh says firmly, wrapping his arm more tightly around my shoulders. But I can see by his anguished face that he's every bit as upset as I am. And so is Patrick. He looks stunned.

"It seems like everyone who has anything to do with Elusion either ends up dead or close to it," a reporter points out. "David Welch, Bryce Williams—even your own son, Patrick Simmons—"

"No," Cathryn interjects, flustered. The crowd yells out so many questions at the same time that it's hard to tell who's saying what.

Finally, a reporter asks: "Is Bryce Williams's death connected to the problems Elusion is currently experiencing?"

"I don't see how. I told you already, our engineers are working on it as I speak. We hope to have it up and running in no time."

Up and running again?

Elusion is gone. We destroyed it.

"What about reports of the CIT pulling approval of Elusion?" another reporter asks.

"Unfounded," she says quickly. "Now, if you'll excuse me." She spins away from the camera, heading back into Orexis. Patrick turns off the InstaComm.

No one speaks. I can't get Bryce's face out of my head, nor the images from the photos in his house—his sons playing basketball, he and his wife dancing and in love, a family Thanksgiving. Did our confrontation somehow push him over the edge?

"I told him I felt sorry for his sons," I say. "That they were going to be ashamed."

"Regan," Josh says forcefully. "You had every right to speak out. Bryce Williams kidnapped your father."

"No," Patrick says, practically shaking as he takes the seat across from us. He's wringing his hands; his neck has turned bright red. "My mother kidnapped David. Bryce is just her most recent victim."

"I don't know what happened with Bryce," Avery says. "But I can tell you this for a fact: none of you are responsible. That man was seriously messed up. Kids are dead because of his actions. And he knew it."

I think it's the first time I've heard Avery attempt to comfort anyone. And her timing couldn't be better.

"Thanks, Avery," I say, picking my Equip up off the coffee table. "Why is Cathryn acting like there's just a problem with the signal or something?" I ask. "She's got to realize by now that her plan to vaccinate Elusion didn't work."

"She's probably just trying to defuse the situation and calm down the nervous investors until she can cover her tracks," Patrick says bitterly, as if the mere mention of his mother makes him sick.

My eyes drift toward the blank InstaComm screen as I visualize the look on Bryce's face as we left. The sadness. The shame. The fear. I wish I had known how desperate he was. I might've handled it differently.

One thing is certain. There has been enough death.

"We need to find my dad," I say. "Now."

"Don't worry," Avery says, adjusting her glasses. "We will. And then we'll bring that bitch and her entire evil empire *down*."

Avery, Patrick, Zoe, Josh, and I stand in the middle of the old Menlop Hills Mall, the only light coming from our tabs. Entering was easier than I had thought it would be. Giblin's passcard once again came in handy, allowing us to disable the security sensors and use the delivery entrance of an old department store.

"How are we going to find him?" I ask Patrick as I shine my tab toward a wall of shuttered stores. We're in the grand lobby of the old mall, surrounded by hundreds of dark, empty stores and former restaurants.

I turn back toward the oversize circular staircase and follow it up to the top floor, craning my neck backward to look at the soaring glass atrium ceiling. Thick Florapetro clouds are blocking the moon, but a few of the night stars are still visible, casting the inside of the mall in an eerie yellow glow.

This place is huge. And everything looks so pristine, as if the occupants just moved out yesterday. The giant artificial palm trees still look brand-new. The fountain isn't turned on, but the water is a crystal blue.

"So how are we going to find him?" I ask, trying to keep my voice steady.

"We could split up and go store to store," Josh suggests.

"Wherever he is, he's probably still attached to an Equip and tab. The news conference we saw was live, and Orexis is a good fifteen minutes away. I doubt my mom would have had time to get here yet," Patrick says.

"You think it's still emitting a signal?" Avery asks him.

"Maybe. We all need to turn off our tabs and I'll see if I can pick it up."

We shut down our tabs, with the exception of Patrick, who is typing something on his screen. He finishes and we wait, all staring at him.

"I'm picking up four signals," he says. "Two on the sixth floor, one in the northeast corner, and one opposite."

Avery scoots behind him, looking over his shoulder. "One

on the fifth floor—looks like it's directly north," she says. She scours the tab with her eyes. "Oh," she says, pointing toward the touch screen. "And one on the second floor, southwest."

"Good catch," Patrick says.

"Can we turn our tabs back on now?" Zoe asks. "If I'm going to decipher these directions, I'll need a compass. I'm completely turned around in here."

"Yeah, turn them back on," Patrick says. "I've sent you all the coordinates. Use your GPS—it'll get you to the general area. Beyond that, we'll just have to search the stores."

Josh lets go of my hand as we reach for our tabs. "We'll split up in pairs," he says. "And I'll go alone."

"No," Patrick says. "I'm going alone. My mom is the bad guy, remember? I'm probably the only one here who's safe."

"Pat . . . ," I begin, ready to protest his decision.

"Ree," he interrupts, raising his hand to silence me. "Don't."

"And when we find him?" Zoe whispers as we begin to move.

"The plan stays the same," I say. "Get video evidence."

"Too bad some asshole had my site disabled," Avery says, referring to what Patrick did to her vlog earlier this week when she was talking about the rumors regarding the dangers of Elusion. I know he regrets it, especially since she turned out to be right.

"Well, you have my permission to get this on any other site you wish. I have confidence in your ability to work around it."

Avery gives him a snide grin. "Come on, Zoe," she says.

"We'll take the second floor and work our way up."

"Josh and I will take the sixth floor," I say. If Patrick's going to be alone, I'd rather not have him taking the floor with two possible leads.

"Got your OC spray?" Zoe asks, nudging me in the arm as we head toward the steps.

I open my hand, revealing the small canister. "Out and ready to use as needed," I say.

Zoe winks, unfolding her fist and showing me hers as well.

"Patrick, you should take mine," Avery offers. "Each team should have one."

"No," he says. "I told you, she's not going to hurt me—"

"Pat," I say. "Please."

"I'm good," he insists, heading toward the steps and leading the charge.

Zoe's eyes catch mine, and for a minute I see the truth behind her eternal optimism. It's an act. She's just as worried about Patrick confronting his mom as I am.

Zoe and Avery head to the second floor, Zoe staring at the compass on her tab as they veer off from the group. "Hey," Patrick says, looking at Zoe. "Contact me the minute you see anything suspicious. Don't confront my mom yourself, okay?"

"Sure," Zoe says, giving him a little smile before hurrying to catch up with Avery.

As Josh, Patrick, and I watch them leave, I know we're all worried about the same thing. None of us want to separate.

But we have little choice if we're to find my dad, and so we continue on, making our way up flight after flight. As we hit the fifth floor, Josh grabs Patrick's arm. "Be careful," he warns. "Desperation can do strange things to people. Even those we love."

Patrick hesitates before shrugging off Josh's hand. "You guys be careful too."

I take Josh's hand and we climb the remaining flight, stopping at the top of the stairs to take a close listen. It's completely silent.

Glancing at the compass, I motion to my left. Josh turns his tab on the dimmest light possible as we begin to walk the rows of empty storefronts, most with their security grilles in place. As we get to the end, we spot a store with the grille half open. Josh slips under the partition. I turn down the dimmer on my tab and follow him in.

The long and narrow store is clogged with broken shelving and naked mannequins, some still draped in the odd piece of clothing. I look for Josh, but he's disappeared, so I tiptoe down an aisle, heading toward the back of the store. There's an InstaComm on the counter. It's still transmitting images, its volume muted.

Great. This must be the signal Patrick found coming from the sixth floor. I turn off the InstaComm and head back toward the front of the store. I meet Josh halfway and we shake our heads at each other. Both of us have come up empty.

We make our way back toward the front, but just as we're

about to crawl under the partition, there's a glimmer of light.

Someone's here.

Even though I tell myself it's probably just one of the gang, I grab on to Josh's shirt and tug him back toward me. We lean up against the wall as the light grows brighter, followed by the click of heels.

We see a flash of white-blond hair, a bright red coat, and a black, rectangular bag.

Cathryn.

"Alert the others," Josh whispers. And before I can protest, he's gone, slipping into the darkness under the door.

I send a quick group message, tucking my tab in my pocket before following. When I get back into the hall, it takes my eyes a second to adjust to the dim yellow light.

Somewhere down the hall, a door creaks.

I take out my tab and shine the light toward the noise. An old-fashioned metal emergency exit door at the end of the hall is swinging shut. I run and grab the old steel handles before it locks. It squeaks as I yank it open.

I'm in the fire stairwell. To my right is a partially open door, a side entrance to a store. I open the door and walk in, shining my tab around the room. I stop when I see the gurney in the corner. A pale, withered figure lies on top, his face barely visible, his eyes covered by a visor, his body under a blanket.

My dad.

As I hurry toward him, I forget all about Cathryn and the danger. But as I get closer, my stomach twists into a knot. My dad's completely still, his complexion pallid and waxy.

I get to his side and place my hand on his cold forehead. There's no sign of life. I yank off his visor. His eyes are open, and even though the natural brown color has returned, they're staring lifelessly at the ceiling.

"I've never watched anyone die before," a voice says, breaking through the darkness. Cathryn. I twist around, shining my tab toward her voice. She's standing opposite me, in the far corner of the room.

"Is he . . . ?" I ask. "Is he . . . ?"

Dead.

I can't even bring myself to say the word.

"Not yet," she says.

I take off his wristband and feel for a pulse, my hands trembling with rage. He's still alive. Barely. "How could you do this?" I breathe.

She ignores my question and yanks something out of the case on the floor, a tiny telescope-shaped tube attached to a black leather sling.

"You were like a second mother to me. You were part of our family."

She continues setting up the machine, ignoring me.

"I cared about you," I continue. "I even compared my own mother to you, wishing she could be more like you, more assertive and smart." It makes me sick to remember, but it's true.

"You spoke at my dad's funeral," I say, practically spitting the words. "You let us believe he was dead. And the whole time you were keeping him locked inside Elusion, destroying his life. Destroying my mother. How could you watch us suffer like that?"

"It wasn't personal," she says, her voice sounding surprisingly sad. "Your father didn't give me any alternative."

"He knew that Elusion was dangerous," I say, my fists at my side. "He wanted you to pull Elusion—"

"I couldn't do that," she says simply.

"Why not?" I ask. "Look what's happened. People are dying." An image of Claire flashes through my mind. "Kids who had their whole lives ahead of them!"

"You're not a scientist, Regan. I don't expect you to understand."

"What about me, Mom?" Patrick is standing in the doorway, glaring at his mother. "Do you think I'll understand? Because I don't."

"Stay where you are," Cathryn tells Patrick, her voice shaking as she slips the sling to the machine over her arm.

"Or what?" he asks. "You're going to vaporize me with one of our new military rifles? You don't even know how to shoot a gun!"

She raises the rifle in his direction as she primes what looks a lot like a trigger.

"You underestimate me," she says quietly.

"I get it," Patrick says. "You can shoot a gun. Is this how you took down the HyperSoar that David was supposedly killed in?"

The HyperSoar. My dad's plane. Josh and I both knew it could be autocontrolled.

"I'm not a monster!" Cathryn says, still pointing the rifle at Patrick. "I did what I had to do. I never wanted to hurt anyone. Especially David. He was my friend." She sounds almost choked up, like all these deaths are beginning to bother her. "But what David created was bigger than both of us. He may not have realized it, but the world needed—*needs*—Elusion. And unfortunately, sometimes people give their lives for the advancement of technology. For science."

"You're not doing it for the science," Patrick says, walking toward his mom once again. "You're doing it for the power. It was always about the power."

Cathryn swings the rifle back toward my dad and me. "Patrick, I swear—if you take another step, I'll kill them both."

Patrick stops. From the way Cathryn's hand is shaking and the fact that she's already primed the rifle, there's a possibility of that happening anyway.

I back up, my hips hitting the gurney, my arms outstretched.

"If you're going to kill them, then you might as well kill me too," Patrick breathes. "Because I will make sure the truth comes out."

"No one will believe you," she says, keeping her finger on the trigger. "Everyone knows you're an E-fiend. You were forced to leave your job because of it. Didn't you see the press release?"

"You can't convince people I'm sick," Patrick says.

"Oh, really?" his mom asks. "I bet Regan would beg to differ."

She's right. Even my own mother thought I was going crazy.

"Killing them isn't going to solve anything," Patrick says, trying a different tack. "Elusion is over and Orexis is ruined."

"I'll rebuild," she says. "Orexis is a strong company. We'll settle the lawsuits and come back stronger than before."

Her cold blue eyes lock on mine. "Regan, get out of the way," she says. *"Now."*

"No," I say, sounding a lot braver than I actually feel.

"You can't save him," she insists. "It's too late. The father you knew will never return, even if his body survives." She closes her eyes for a second and then opens them, ready to shoot. "Your dad wouldn't want you to sacrifice yourself. And neither would your mom. She barely survived the loss of your father. How will she continue without you?"

The door squeaks open and Josh appears. Not seeing Cathryn, he steps into the room, his eyes focused on me before flicking toward my dad.

Cathryn points the rifle at Josh, her finger on the trigger.

She's going to kill him.

I race across the room and charge her, slamming us both against the wall.

Patrick lunges for the rifle as Josh grabs Cathryn, yanking her away. I push myself up as Josh restrains Cathryn's arms behind her back.

Avery and Zoe burst into the room. As we all catch our breath, they survey the scene, astounded. "Now can I call the police?" Zoe murmurs.

"Yeah," I say. "Now would be good."

"Patrick," Cathryn pleads. "Please. Don't do this. You can

still save me. You can still save us."

"You getting this?" Patrick asks Avery.

"Oh yeah," she says, her tab pointing in Cathryn's direction. "*AveryTruStory* exclusive."

"You're welcome," Patrick says to Avery, knowing full well that she didn't thank him. His eyes shift in my father's direction, and his face fills with concern.

I turn back toward my dad. His eyes are still unresponsive, his gaze fixed on the ceiling. I grab his wrist, once again checking his pulse.

Nothing.

I move the placement of my thumb as my own breath seems to get caught in my throat.

There is no pulse.

My dad is no longer breathing.

Before I can say anything, Patrick is there, gently pushing me out of the way and pressing his hands on my dad's frail chest as he begins CPR. I'm aware of voices around me, people shouting out commands and calls for help. Zoe's hands on my shoulders, her voice telling me everything is going to be okay, as I stare at the man on the gurney.

Breathe.

Please just breathe.

I touch my father's watch, my fingers wrapping around the cool steel as if clinging to a lifeline.

Finally, a sputter, then a cough, as my dad starts gasping for air. Patrick yanks the O2 shield off his belt and places it over my dad's face.

"You're going to be okay," I murmur, placing my hand on top of my dad's.

And then I feel it, his thumb lifting over mine.

He's coming back.

NINETEEN

Six months later

If Avery doesn't stop bossing me around, I think I'm going to scream. But then again, what did I expect? I knew this was a bad idea the moment Nora suggested it. The constant bickering between Avery and me over the summer had really begun to annoy her and Josh, so Nora decided a little alone time would help the two of us get along. But what I agreed to was clearly a huge mistake.

Avery. Me. A kitchen. A cake. And now a knife.

"What are you doing? Give that to me!" she says, wresting the knife out of my hands and nearly taking off my finger. She pulls the spatula out of the bowl and smooths the frosting across the cake gently. "This," she says, pausing for effect, "is how it's done."

"You win," I say, raising my hands in surrender. "You're much better at frosting a cake than me. Happy?"

"Delighted," Avery gloats, smiling.

Nora enters the kitchen, rolling her eyes and smirking. "It's so nice to see you two getting along. I think Josh is going to be very pleased with this development."

Avery and I both force a smile.

Nora walks around the kitchen island and over to Avery, doing her best to hide the limp in her left leg. In the last few months, she has made amazing progress. She woke up within hours of Elusion's destruction and regained her mental faculties almost immediately. Her physical ones, however, have proved more of a challenge; originally, her doctors were worried she might never walk again. Josh and Avery became Nora's own private physical therapists, determined she would get back on her feet before Josh left for college. About a month ago, she took her first step.

Avery wraps her arm around Nora's waist and smiles, pulling her in for a kiss. Their tenderness makes me blush a little. The truth of the matter is, I don't dislike Avery. In fact, I respect her and will be forever grateful to her for alerting everyone to the danger of Elusion. I'm glad that she and Nora got their happy ending.

A lot of us weren't as lucky. In the days after Elusion's demise and Cathryn's arrest, the terror we'd dealt with in the virtual world spilled over into the real world. Some of the missing kids who had helped us in our fight were finally found, but they never woke up; their bodies and minds were too damaged. There were funerals and memorial services, grieving and tears. And though today is cause for celebration, there's no denying the shadow of pain that surrounds us.

But right now, I'm going to focus on the beauty of life, not the darkness—which is why I dip my pinkie in the frosting bowl and give it a lick.

"So I got a text from Josh. He picked up Piper about a half an hour ago, and they should be here any minute." Nora says this to me, although she can't seem to take her eyes off a smitten, grinning Avery. "Have you heard from your mom yet?"

"My dad just got discharged, so they're on their way," I say.

After two months in the hospital and four months of Well-Care, it's about time he came home to us. I'm hoping he isn't too overwhelmed by the small party my friends and I are throwing for him. My mom wasn't too thrilled with the idea at first, but she warmed up once I showed her all the concerned texts they'd sent me over the summer. After seeing those, she couldn't say no to having them here to welcome him.

"I guess I should change," I say, wiping my flour-covered palms on my pants.

"For Josh?" Nora laughs. "He doesn't care how you look."

"Yeah, but I do," I say, brushing a stray, frizzy hair from my face.

Josh left Detroit to start his freshman year at the University of Michigan a month ago. Although we're texting and

InstaComming as much as we can, it's still not the same as being together every day, like we were the whole summer. He's been home almost every weekend since he left, but I still miss him—and I'd really, really like to look decent when he arrives. Or at least not have flour all over my body.

Avery gives me a thorough once-over. "Yeah, well, I'd recommend a full-blast decontamination shower. Just to cover your bases."

"Ave," Nora says, giving her a stern but affectionate stare. "Apologize."

"No, she's right; I'm a mess," I say with a grin. "Can you guys keep an eye on things while I go upstairs?"

"Sure, no problem," Nora replies.

I walk out of the kitchen, pausing to turn on the lemon-scented candles clustered together on the table in the hall. My dad used to love their smell, and my mom would always make sure they were lit every night when he came home from work. After his disappearance, she kept up the ritual, almost as if it was a vigil—hoping he would return from the dead.

Now her wish is coming true.

As I walk toward the steps, I hear Avery calling out to me from the kitchen. "Your InstaComm just turned on! Zared's here!"

Before I can tell her to accept his visitor request, the door opens and Zared peeks his head in. He looks completely different than he did in Elusion, sporting a button-down shirt and a short new haircut.

"Zared, you can't disable someone's security system like that. It's kind of creepy," I say, shaking my head.

"I tell him that all the time," says a sweet, high-pitched voice.

I recognize it immediately and smile. Ayesha.

Zared walks inside and Ayesha trails behind him, holding his hand. The jet-black hair that was always braided in Etherworld is hanging loose around her shoulders. Her almond-shaped eyes are a deep blue, accented with a dash of purple eyeliner. She's wearing jeans and a sexy sweater that falls off her shoulder.

"Hey, lady," I say, throwing my arms around her and bringing her into a warm hug. "Good to see you. How's group been?"

"Boring as hell, now that you've left," she says, squeezing me back. "I was beginning to think you forgot about us."

I pull away and lock eyes with her. "That's never going to happen."

After we had destroyed Elusion, Avery organized an official support group to help us Etherworld survivors get over the trauma. Since we are spread out all over the country, and a few are still in the hospital, we meet mostly on InstaComm and support one another however we can. But lately I've been really busy helping my mom prepare the house for my dad, so I've had to skip a bunch of sessions.

"I'm teasing. We've just missed you, that's all. Especially this guy," she says, as Malik sneaks in through the front door, his brown eyes shining. He looks almost like I remember him in Etherworld and Elusion, all lanky arms and legs.

"I'm so glad you could come, Malik," I say, grinning at him. "It's going to mean so much to my dad. And me."

He grins back and follows Zared into the kitchen, where I hear Nora offering the frosting bowl to both of them. Ayesha gives me a helpless shrug.

"He's still a little self-conscious about talking," she says. "The speech therapist said he's doing really well, though. He just needs some more time."

In Etherworld, Ayesha had promised Malik that she would find him and take care of him after they returned to reality, and when they did, she kept her promise. Malik was a foster kid in California, so Ayesha's parents have paid for his care; and when he was well enough, they flew him back to Miami, where he's been living with them ever since. Ayesha's parents have begun formal adoption proceedings.

"He's starting school next week," Ayesha says.

"Eighth grade?" I ask, even though I already know about it. Josh and I have been spending some time with Zared lately, and he talks about Ayesha and Malik nonstop.

"That's right," Ayesha says. "I'm a little nervous for him. Kids can be cruel, you know."

"He'll be fine. I've taught him all my self-defense tricks," Zared says, popping back into the foyer and looping an arm around Ayesha's shoulders. "It's nice to have her here in Detroit, isn't it?" he says to me. "Help me try to convince her to go to college here next year."

Ayesha shakes her head and laughs. "I'm not ready to think about that yet. I've been through enough change already."

I know exactly how she feels. The thought of college feels unsettling, especially with my dad coming home after all this time. I can't help wondering what life is going to be like, now that most of the hardships are behind us.

"Make yourselves at home," I say. "I'm just going to take a quick shower."

Although my mom and I stayed up late last night cleaning the house, I haven't had a chance to straighten my room. My mom likes it neat, so I've done my best, but between school, visiting my dad in the hospital, and homework, bedroom maintenance has been last on my list. I pause at the top of the stairs, weighing my options. Picking hygiene first, I hop into the bathroom, take a quick shower, and dry off.

Back in my room, I gather up the clothes that are tossed on the floor and stuff them all into the overflowing hamper in my closet. I throw on a red sweater and a black skirt. I catch my reflection in the mirror, and I step toward it, wetting my finger and rubbing off the mascara smeared under my eyes.

As I walk over to my closet, I hear someone say, "Hi, beautiful."

Josh is leaning in the doorway, wearing a leather jacket and jeans, his hands tucked casually in his pockets. His military crew cut long gone, his shining amber eyes hide behind shaggy brown hair.

"How long have you been standing there?" I say, smiling.

"A fraction of a second, I think," he says.

I walk over to him, and his hands snake out of his pockets to pull me toward him.

"I've been counting the seconds a lot lately," he breathes into my ear. "I wonder why."

I run my hands underneath his jacket and up his back. "Because you're a physics major?"

"Good guess, but wrong," he says, bending down to press his lips against my right cheek on the way to grazing my mouth.

I kiss him back as his fingers slip down my hips, gripping them tightly. I hate pulling away. "My parents will be home any minute," I tell him. He gives me a soft peck on the forehead.

"We better get back down there, then," he says, putting his arm around me as we head toward the stairs. "How are you doing? Nervous?"

"A little. More excited than anything else. I'm glad we don't have to go back to that WellCare place anymore."

"No, you don't. Your whole family can be here, together," he says. "Life is going to feel normal again."

Normal—I've forgotten what that is. For months, Mom and I have been commuting every day, first to the hospital and then to the therapy center, to see Dad. At first it was horrible. He was completely incapacitated for eight weeks, and that entire time, we felt like we could barely breathe. Things got better when he was finally able to speak again, but it's been a long road to recovery. As he gradually regained his strength, my mom and I developed our own routine and rhythm too. We even made friends with some of the staff members.

All of it—the hospital, the therapy, everything—would have been much more stressful if we'd had to worry about the medical expenses, but *someone* paid for every cent of my father's treatment, and will go on paying until he gets back on his feet.

By the time Josh and I get downstairs, that someone has made his way into the kitchen with the rest of our friends, and he's smiling with his best girl right beside him.

Patrick and Zoe.

"Hey, Ree," he says, giving me a hug the moment he sees me. Wearing old jeans and a big wool sweater, he barely resembles his old corporate-drone self. Instead, he looks like he used to, before he was president of Orexis—mussed hair, bright hopeful eyes, and a smile that lights up the room.

"Yay! We're all here!" Zoe squeals, jumping onto the hug pile, squeezing Patrick and me hard. I haven't seen her since she left for college in upstate New York, but she's as gorgeous as ever. Her sleek hair is held back with a white headband, and she's wearing a cute little jacket that shows off her curves.

"Okay, Zoe, you're crushing us," Patrick says, chuckling.

"Deal with it, babe," she says.

Zoe and Patrick spent quite a bit of time together this past summer, and although for months neither of them admitted that they were a couple, it was obvious to everyone that it was just a matter of time. But it took Zoe leaving Detroit for Patrick to realize what he had. This is the first weekend she's been home since she left, and I know how happy he is to have her back.

When she unleashes us from the Hug of Death, Zoe steps back and straightens out my sweater for me. "Patrick was just telling me about the observatory. Sounds like it's going to be so cool."

Now that the Orexis trial is wrapping up, Patrick is finally able to start focusing on his own life again. He's founding a massive conservation effort in the area, and in the process of building a state-of-the-art planetarium that will take the place of the old Detroit Observatory, which is now more or less a museum. I'm proud of Patrick. He's so smart he could've done anything, but he's committed himself to preserving whatever natural beauty is left in our world.

"Did he tell you he's hired Zared as program director?" Ayesha says.

"No," Zoe says, impressed. "He just showed me the architectural drawings for the building."

"We're hoping to have the planetarium open by January," Patrick says.

"I can't wait," I say.

"People are going to love it," Josh adds.

All the excitement is interrupted by the sound of a car pulling up into the driveway. I hurry over to the kitchen window and see my mom behind the wheel of our car. She waves at me cheerfully and I wave back, my heart fluttering. My dad is in the backseat, and I can see him looking around the neighborhood, his face totally in awe. He hasn't seen this place in almost a year.

I'm about to go to the door when Malik sidles up next to me. Now he sees my father getting out of the car too. And I hear him say my dad's name, slowly and quietly.

"David."

So I take Malik's hand and smile at him. "He's finally home."

"The cake looked beautiful," my dad says, his voice not quite rising above a whisper.

My father is seated next to me in his automated wheelchair, his hands cupped around a mug of tea. His antique watch is back on his wrist, the dial once again set to the correct time. Everyone else is milling around and chatting while my parents' collection of jazz standards streams through the InstaComm speakers.

"Thanks," I say.

"Did you make it all by yourself?"

I glance toward Avery, who is lost in conversation with Nora and Josh, and holding a plate full of cake.

"I had a little help," I admit.

"Why don't you go and talk to your friends?" he says. "Everyone came such a long way."

"To see *you*," I say, placing my hand on his. "That's why they're here."

"It's good to be with everyone again, especially my daughter."

He grins at me, but when he casts his eyes around the room, his smile fades and I know he's thinking about all the ones who aren't here. The ones who didn't make it.

"It is," I say. "Can I get you any more hot water?"

"No, thanks, I'm fine," he says, his gaze landing on Patrick and Zoe, who are perched on the upholstered bench right near the window. "Has Patrick told you anything more? About the trial?"

"Not too much, no," I say, which is the truth. Patrick is pretty guarded when it comes to conversations about Cathryn. I think he's been to visit her in jail once, but even then he came back tight-lipped and very quiet.

Actually, I've been tight-lipped about it too. While my dad is interested in the news story of the century for obvious reasons, I've only recently become open about it. At first, I refused to discuss the trial with anyone, even Josh. I couldn't deal with the media anymore.

When word got out that my dad was alive, journalists were all over my mom and me, harassing us for comments and sound bites. But we weren't alone. Every other family whose child wound up in Etherworld was also hounded by the media.

Patrick had it the worst. In fact, he actually had to leave Detroit and stay with his dad until things settled down. He's immune from prosecution now, but after the truth about Elusion came out, everyone who had worked at Orexis was scrutinized, including my dad. It seemed impossible for people to believe that a system like Elusion could've become sentient by accident—and even harder to believe that Bryce and Cathryn were the only ones behind the deceit.

"I hear the recordings that Patrick and Avery made were ruled admissible," my dad says. "Prosecutors think that Cathryn is going to be put away for life."

"Orexis officially filed for bankruptcy too," I say.

"This is a party, you two," my mom says, wandering over to hand me a plate loaded with a gigantic corner piece of cake. "No more talk about the trial, okay?"

"You, my dear, have amazing hearing," my dad says, looking up at her with adoring eyes.

She gazes back at him. The glow that had disappeared from my mom's face has returned, radiating from every part of her. "Really? Well, I also have amazing taste in husbands. What do you think of that?"

"I think you're right," he says, laughing a little.

I feel silly for thinking this, and maybe I'm just feeling a wave of sentimentality, but I hope that years from now Josh and I will be joking with each other the same way.

"Are you really going to eat all of that cake, Ree?"

Patrick is standing next to the sofa with his hands perched on his hips. I pat the seat cushion next to me and he sits down, leaning forward a bit so he can smile at my dad.

"This is just five hundred of the millions of calories I plan on ingesting before the night is over, so watch out," I say, shoving a big forkful into my mouth.

"So Patrick, tell me more about your planetarium," my dad

says, his voice perking up a little.

"It's going to be great," Patrick says, rubbing his hands together. "There's going to be an indoor-outdoor amphitheater and a room for celestial navigation. The main focus is to teach people about the earth and the natural world around us. I was kind of hoping it might be a sort of homage to . . ."

"Thoreau?" my dad asks.

Patrick grins. "Exactly. I'm thinking of naming it after him. What do you think?"

My dad beams at him, like a proud father would. "That's a great idea."

"I'm showing Zoe where we're building it tonight," he says. "She has to leave tomorrow morning and wants to see it before she goes."

"Sounds romantic," I say with a nudge.

"Actually, she wants everyone to come. Kind of like an after-party," he explains. "Are you in?"

"You guys can go ahead. I'm going to stay here with my dad."

"You sure? It won't be the same without you," he says.

"You can InstaComm me or something. It'll be like I'm there."

"Hold on," my father interjects, looking at me. "Patrick, could you give us a minute?"

"Yeah, of course," Patrick says, revealing a heartfelt smile. "Welcome home, David."

Once Patrick is gone, my dad sets his cup down on the side

table and takes my plate, setting it next to his mug. Then he puts his hand on top of mine and looks at me with concern. His face has changed a lot since the last time we sat in this room together. There are more deep lines traveling across his skin, and since he's still not eating solid foods, his cheeks are much sharper. His once salt-and-pepper hair is now completely gray.

But his eyes are the same kind, thoughtful, and energetic eyes I looked into the day he was taken from me. I'm so grateful to have him back, but I'm still secretly terrified that if I blink he might disappear from my life again.

"Are you okay?" he says.

"Shouldn't I be asking you that?"

"You do, all the time," he says. "That's why I'm worried about you."

"I'm fine, Dad. You don't have to worry."

"Regan, listen to me. I know I tell you this a lot, but it's true: I'm the one who's supposed to worry. I'm your father, and you're my daughter, and that's how it works. Parents worry about their kids, even when they turn into adults."

There's an awkward moment of silence. My dad looks down at his lap and lets out a big sigh, and then focuses back on me again.

"It's not supposed to be the other way around," he murmurs. "But for the past year, you've either been worried about me, missing me, or searching for me."

"Dad, wait—"

"No, let me finish," he says, and I stay quiet as his hand

trembles a bit. "I couldn't ask for a more devoted and brave daughter. It's because of you that I'm here, Regan. It's because of you that I made it. That we all made it."

I'm not sure that's entirely true—everyone in this room played a significant role in taking down Elusion, and we couldn't really have done any of it without one another. But I know my dad is trying to thank me, so instead of arguing with him, I just smile.

"But now that I'm home, I don't want you to worry anymore," he continues. "Actually, I want you to get that time back. I want you to live your life, and go out with your friends, and plan for college, and . . ." He takes a moment to look over at Josh, who is now talking with Piper and Malik, making some strange gestures like he's telling them military-school stories. "And take off with your boyfriend on his motorcycle."

I let out a loud laugh, which attracts everyone's attention. "Yeah, right!"

"Okay, that last part was hard for me to say," he says, chuckling. "But I mean it. You know how I feel about him."

Dad adores Josh, and rightly so. He's not only taken care of Nora, but has bent over backward to help with my father as well.

"I know," I say.

"Then why don't you go with him to Patrick's planetarium tonight?" he says. "You've been helping your mom take care of me, and we both appreciate it. But we want you to have this time, sweetheart. You're never going to get it back."

"But you just got here."

"And I'm not going anyplace," he says, tapping me on the nose. He hasn't done that to me since I was six, and when he does it now, it almost breaks my heart. "I promise. When you get back, I'll be here. And so will your mom."

I know my father is still pretty fragile, but I lunge over the arm of the couch and hug him as tight as I can.

"I love you, Regan," my dad says.

"I love you too," I say.

It's funny. I was worried that things wouldn't be the same between us when this was all over—that he'd have gone through too much to be the person he was before, and maybe I would have too—and I was right: things aren't the same.

They're actually better.

We're alive, our family reunited. And we all know how lucky we are.

When we pull back from the hug, Josh approaches us carefully, lingering next to me like he doesn't want to intrude.

I reach out and take his hand. "Hey, you."

"Hey. How are things over here?" he asks, grinning at me.

"Great," I say.

"Regan was just telling me how excited she was about going to the planetarium tonight," my dad tells him.

"Really? Patrick said you weren't coming," Josh says, a bit confused.

"I changed my mind," I say, giving my dad a little smile.

"Good. Everyone is about to leave, though," Josh says.

"Go ahead; have fun," my dad says.

Josh takes my other hand and pulls me off the couch. And just as we're about to step away, my dad adds, "And be careful, okay?"

Josh tips his head at him respectfully. "We will."

After a few last minutes of good-byes, everyone is filing out of the house, thanking my mom for having them over. I thank her too, and give her a kiss on the cheek, but when I linger a bit, she nearly pushes me out the door. Now Josh and I are right behind Patrick and Zoe, whose fingers are intertwined as they head for his car at the end of the driveway.

It's dusk, and the sky is full of pinkish hues from the setting sun. The O2 levels are so good, there's no need for shields. I'm standing on the sidewalk where Josh's bike is parked, watching all my friends gather along the curb and talk about the quickest way to get to the sector where the observatory is located. I know the best way to get there, of course, but I keep quiet. I like listening to them bicker and tease one another, like family members do.

"Ready to have some fun?" Josh says finally, as he hands me a helmet.

I smile, glancing back toward the light coming through the window of the house.

"Yeah, I think I am."

ACKNOWLEDGMENTS

WE'VE RACKED UP A LOT OF IOUs IN THE nearly four years we've worked on *Elusion* and *Etherworld*, and we want to thank everyone who helped us on our journey. We couldn't have done it without each and every one of you.

A huge thank-you to our families, particularly our husbands, Brian Klam and Ben Lindvall, without whom we never would've made it past the finish line; our ultrafabulous daughters, Lily and Sadie Klam; and our parents, Yvonne C. Gabel, Paul C. Gabel, Randy Guttridge, and Barbara Robinson—your encouragement meant the world to us.

Thanks to Julie Anbender for all your time and effort. And to Ryan Guttridge, who answered phone calls and emails with an amount of patience that went far beyond the duty of blood relatives; we will forever be indebted to you for your overwhelming knowledge of science and technology. Thank you!

As for our agents, Christy Fletcher, Josie Friedman, and Esther Newberg—you were the first people we picked for our team for a reason: you're the best. Thank you!

Thanks to our amazing and fabulous editor, Jill Davis, who bravely plunged into *Etherworld*, skillfully nursing us through Aftershock, and to Sarah Shumway, for helping to bring this duology to life. To the incredibly talented Erin Fitzsimmons and Tatiana Plahkova, who designed the book covers, thank you for creating such incredible art.

We owe a great bit of debt to the rest of the Harper team: Susan Katz, Kate Jackson, Rosanne Romanello, Rhalee Hughes, Samantha Dell'Olio, Lauren Flower, Onalee Smith, Amy Ryan, Karen Sherman, Kathryn Silsand, and Laurel Symonds.

And finally, thanks to our awesome publisher, Katherine Tegen. It's been an amazing ride!

ESCAPE TO A WORLD FILLED WITH BEAUTY . . .

AND LIES.

"A tense read full of twists, mystery, and romance. Be ready for a mind trip!"

–Sophie Jordan, *New York Times* bestselling author